DAYS OF DANGER

THE DEPARTMENT Z SERIES

DAYS OF DANGER

DEPARTMENT Z

JOHN CREASEY

INTEGRATED MEDIA

NEW YORK

ISBN: 978-1-5040-9184-8

This edition published in 2024 by Open Road Integrated Media, Inc.
180 Maiden Lane
New York, NY 10038
www.openroadmedia.com

To
MY BROTHERS AND SISTERS,
by marriage or otherwise,
and, of course, their children

DAYS OF DANGER

1

MR. MORT IS FRIGHTENED

I beg your pardon," said the small man at the wheel of the Frazer Nash. "I'm afraid I didn't quite catch—"

The stolid, ruddy-faced policeman who found the misdoings of that Somerset village enough to keep him fully occupied during his working hours scowled, wished the little man to Jericho, drew a deep breath and started again.

"Fust left—second right—fust left, second left, and then right up the hill." He was very careful with his aitches, was that country policeman, whose early days had certainly been spent within reasonable distance of the Bow Bells. "You can't miss it, sir. Good morning, sir."

"But look here," protested the little absurdly ugly man, "I'm really in a hurry, and I always go dithery on directions and what-not. I suppose you wouldn't care to take me there?"

The policeman, now two yards away, turned half about and stiffened.

"*Take* you there?" he echoed. "*Take* you—it never struck you I'd want to get back, did it?"

"But," protested the little man with the ugly face, "I thought all country people liked walking. Wrong again, eh? Oh, don't go. If I can't take a passenger, let me write it down for the love of Mike. I tell you I must get there in the next half-hour, and if I turn right instead of left the Lord knows when I'll arrive. Now, you said 'first right'—or didn't you?"

He had a pencil out of his pocket and an old envelope resting precariously on the steering-wheel. A piercing wind, unusual for that September, was making him shiver and wonder what the house would be like when he reached it. Would they have a fire? Or would they be superstitious and wait until September was out?

"I said," said the constable grimly, "fust left—"

"Got it."

"Second right—"

"That's the second on the right after I've taken the first left, isn't it? I want to get it clear, old son, and I know you folk have the devil of a lot of patience." The little man beamed and looked as though he meant what he said; and the policeman told himself he'd like to wring his neck. The policeman was cold as well as busy, and his patience deserved a medal.

"That's right, sir. Second to the left after the fust on the right, and then—then—have you got that?—fust left again—"

"After I've taken the second on the right and the first on the left, I take the first left? I know I seem dense, but—"

The policeman's patience and his aitches disappeared at the identical moment.

"'Ere," he said downrightly, "lemme write it down fer yer."

"Oh, stout fellow!" said the little ugly man, and he relinquished the paper and pencil with every evidence of relief.

As the policeman wrote laboriously, and even made a brave attempt at a sketch which would tell the little man just where he turned left and where right before he reached the house which was known as The Maples, and the village called by the fastidious Tarrington and the locals 'Tanton,' the little man—whose name was Tobias Arran—eyed not the stalwart of the law, but the saviour of the brewers; in short, a hostelry of Michford. Michford was a small market town some seven miles from Tavistock; it boasted three inns, the largest of which was called the *'George.'* A pleasing, comfortable country sound had the name of the best pub in Michford. Also it had— or so Tobias Arran had been led to believe— an astonishing list of regular visitors even for the star turn-out of the little town.

"And now," said the policeman, recovering his poise and his aitches, "you can't go wrong, sir. *Here* you are."

He passed over the envelope, the scrawled instructions and the map, touched his forehead and turned, obviously anxious to get away before the little man could ask for explanations. Explanations were in fact called for, but Mr. Tobias Arran puzzled them out, took a last glance at the 'George,' started the engine and was away. He went strictly according to instructions, and when he took the last right turn he found himself amid desolate moors and, as far as he could see, many weary miles from civilization and Tarrington.

"Blast," said Toby Arran with emphasis. "I wonder where the blazes I went wrong? Only thing for it, I suppose, is to turn back and look up every lane I passed. Why in the name of the raging furies did Craigie tell me to find my own route? Oh, well."

He turned the car and started back, more slowly and with bitterness in his soul. For he was hungry as well as cold, tired as well as impatient, and Gordon Craigie—at the moment in a small office in Whitehall and talking to the Prime Minister— had told him he must be at The Maples, Tarrington, by five o'clock. It was now four-forty-five, and the chances seemed negligible; but Toby Arran was nothing if not a trier.

* * *

About the time that Toby Arran, who was known by many folk as a man-about-town, wealthy beyond avarice, energetic beyond all reason, and by a few as a member of that peculiar Department called Z—or by the pedantic the British Intelligence—was searching, three men were in a room on the first floor of the 'George,' at Michford.

Two were ordinary men to look at; they might have been met and passed without a second thought in any crowded High Street; they looked as though they owned first-class season-tickets from the outer suburbs to the centre of London, and used them regularly. One, indeed, was so sleek, fat and prosperous-looking, that he might even have travelled from the country day by day.

His name was Mort.

He was fat enough to have a ponderous paunch, nicely covered with blue serge, two chins and flesh that almost hid his eyes. His flesh was smooth and dimply. His hands were very white, almost those of a surgeon or a woman, and on the little finger of his left hand gleamed a diamond ring. The only other point of note was that he wore patent-leather shoes: to the right man that said a great deal.

Mr. Mort—Julius Mort—was ample of flesh and economic in surname syllables. Mr. Augustus Mannopoli was the reverse. He was abnormally thin; too thin; and somehow unpleasantly thin. Perhaps his eyes, aslant, small and always narrowed, created the atmosphere of unpleasantness. He was dressed in dark brown; his knuckles were sticking out like knots on his bare fingers; his clean-shaven face was hollow at the cheeks and yellowish skin stretched across a square jaw so tightly that it looked painful. Mr. Mort was an Englishman; Mr. Mannopoli, as his name suggested, had connections not far removed from Greece; and others, if his eyes were any criterion, with China; the yellowish tinge of his skin bore out the latter suggestion.

There was another difference between Mr. Mort and Mr. Mannopoli. Mort talked a great deal, and his voice was deep and unctuous—a true board-meeting boom. Mannopoli talked rarely, and then in a harsh, dry voice and clipped sentences which suggested that he wished he'd been born dumb.

There remained Mr. Mulling.

Mr. Frederick Mulling was the happy medium. He was neither fat nor thin, but well covered. He looked prepared neither to be oozing benevolence nor creating unpleasantness. He seemed normal. His hair was mousy, his face nothing special and not even redeemed by his eyes, which were indeterminate blue-grey. He was comfortably dressed in a herring-bone tweed suit of plus fours, and looked as though he lived in it. He talked enough but not too much; sometimes he talked as though he was a little nervous of expressing himself, but he felt it his duty.

Thus Mr. Mort and Mr. Mannopoli and Mr. Mulling.

As it happened, Mort lived in London, Mannopoli in Bournemouth, and Mr. Mulling in Michford. He was the owner of the 'George' and had turned a white elephant—as he was fond of saying—into a flourishing country hotel, and no one could deny that was a remarkable accomplishment, especially for a so indeterminate-looking man.

Mr. Mort was talking—unctuously, as could be expected.

"It's like this, my dear fellows," he boomed, "we *must* bring Fallow in with us. We must, I'm convinced. Confound it, Polly, it'll make all the difference between success and this annoying, humdrum, neither-one-way-nor-the-other situation which is— I'm not joking, I assure you—getting very worrying." Mr.

Mort smiled tremulously, as though he was less confident than he sounded. "We *must* enlist Fallow."

"You're talking," said Mr. Mannopoli, "out of the back of your neck."

Just that and no more; he took no notice of the flush that mantled Mort's podgy cheeks, or the frown that crossed Mulling's face. He said what he had to say and nothing else.

Mort frowned.

"Of course, if that's your attitude—"

"Now look here, Mort," said Mr. Mulling, "don't start that damned board-meeting attitude again; we can't stand it. I agree with you that we need Fallow, and I'd like Mannopoli to tell us why he's so much against it. Well, Polly?"

"Fallow's got too many friends," said Mannopoli brusquely; "besides"—he smiled, stretching his skin still more, until it seemed that it must give way somewhere—"he's honest. Ever think of that, Mort?"

"Don't be absurd," said Mr. Mort. "We can offer him a quarter profits in a million pounds, and—"

"Money and Fallow don't mix. Man's honest, I tell you."

"Oh, nonsense! No one could resist money like that; easy money. Why, he'd be infernally grateful to us for giving him the opportunity. I'm convinced of it. As for his having friends —well, look at me!"

Mr. Mannopoli obliged, and charitably kept his thoughts to himself; he disliked Mr. Mort.

"Look at *me*," continued the fat gentleman. "I've hosts of friends. My house is never empty of them. I—"

"Hangers-on — sycophants — borrowers — gigolos — business men who've got to be pleasant. You haven't a friend in the world, Mort, and you know it."

Mr. Julius Mort's flabby body went rigid; for a moment there was hatred in his glance, a hatred engendered through past brushes with Augustus Mannopoli and a knowledge that the other man spoke the truth. Mr. Mort was rich, which explained the first three and the last of his 'friends' according to Mannopoli; Mr. Mort's wife was pretty, tinsel-pretty, and neglected by her husband, which accounted for the gigolos. But of friends for friendship's sake there was none.

"Now look here," said Mulling agitatedly, "you two must stop arguing. Hang it, all our time goes in arguments. What do you mean by saying Fallow has too many friends, Polly?"

"What I say."

"But what friends in particular?"

"Among others, a man named Craigie."

"Who's Craigie?"

"A Government official."

"What department?"

"Mystery."

"Damn it all!" exclaimed Mr. Mulling, his patience at an end, "be explicit, man. We haven't time to go on like this; there's business to attend to."

Mr. Mannopoli grinned; and the result was not pleasant.

"All right. Craigie—Gordon Craigie—is known as the Chief of Department Z—British Intelligence. He works a lot with Sir William Fellowes, the Commissioner of Police at Scotland Yard, and with Superintendent Miller. Miller once got on your tail, Mort, and you managed to get rid of him more by luck than judgment. Now, Fallow is a good friend of Craigie's. Craigie doesn't have friends of men who'll touch our stuff. Take my advice and think of someone other than Fallow."

Mr. Julius Mort had listened to this, one of the longest consecutive utterances Mannopoli had ever made, with increasing perturbation. Mannopoli saw the fat man's right index-finger was playing about his right cheek, a habit of

Mort's when he was worried. He didn't say what his worry was, but as soon as the thin man finished he burst out:

"It's nonsense! Fallow can have all the friends he likes—money'll talk louder. Look here, I'm putting it to the meeting. I want Fallow invited. Mulling does all the staff work—keeps all the records. I look after the finances. You, Mannopoli, make a splendid job of the—er—"

"Dirty work, but I don't mind. Go on."

"And we need—we *must* have—a chemist. Just to help us with the dyes and the inks and the metals. Since Marshall died last year the quality of the stuff has been going down and down, and we'll be in trouble if we don't replace him. Fallow's here, living near headquarters, unsuspected—he's just the man. Now, Mulling, you know the poor results we've had lately. Am I right?"

"Ye-es," Mulling seemed doubtful.

"Of course I'm right. Now—I say, get Fallow. Mannopoli is against it. You've the deciding vote. What is it?"

There was silence in the room for sixty seconds.

Mort was eying Mulling tensely; Mannopoli was eying him sardonically. Mulling wanted Fallow, and yet trusted Mannopoli's judgment where men were concerned. On the other hand, the syndicate badly needed the expert, as Mort had pointed out. In fact, if a man wasn't forthcoming soon there'd be trouble. Mr. Mulling drew a deep breath and spoke at last.

"I think we ought to try Fallow," he said. "Mort knows him well, and he looks in here at least once a week. If he's approached carefully, I don't think we need fear that he'll say anything to anyone who's dangerous, even if he doesn't accept the suggestion. Eh, Mannopoli? That's reasonable, isn't it?"

"It's reasonable," said Mr. Mannopoli, and seemed to lose interest in the subject. "Fallow's approached. All right."

Mulling breathed more freely, for he had been afraid of more obstinate opposition. Mort breathed with relief, and touched his vest pocket. Earlier in the day he had proposed showing the others a copy of a letter which he had sent to John Fallow, who lived at The Maples, Tarrington. Now he decided it would be wiser for them to think Fallow had been approached after the meeting, not before.

Nothing more to worry about, anyhow, although he'd remember the way Mannopoli talked. Mannopoli would go too far one of these days. But for the moment—business. Crooked business, to be sure, but as it happened not quite so crooked as Mr. Mort and Mr. Mulling thought.

For Mr. Mannopoli was a man of many parts.

For the next hour he appeared to give full attention to the many points that were raised and, after a little discussion, settled. The activities of the syndicate, whose operations were not honest, spread a long way from England and naturally took a great deal of preparation. But they were finished at last, and although it was barely six o'clock they went into Mulling's dining-room—he was a bachelor—and dined. The 'George's' chef was a good one, and the monthly meeting of the syndicate always ended in that fashion. Mulling believed and hoped it helped them all to be friendly.

But conversation lagged that night.

Mort was still worried; from time to time he would shoot a venomous glance towards Mannopoli that might have been simply hatred and just as likely mixed with fear. Mannopoli, never talkative, was dumb. Mulling did his best to revive the dying spirits, but he failed. He told himself he would be glad when this was over.

It ended soon after seven. Mort and Mannopoli were travelling together as far as Salisbury, and Mulling wondered what kind of a journey it would be. He shook hands, watched them disappear together in Mort's Daimler, and frowned. But there was work to do for the pub as well as for the syndicate, and he couldn't waste time thinking of the happiness of his two partners. Mort was an unctuous old fool, but at times Mannopoli's manner was enough to break down the patience of a job.

Mr. Mulling was thinking on those lines when Mannopoli, sitting in the rear of the car with Mort—the Daimler, of course, was chauffeur-driven—broke a strained silence that had lasted for five minutes. Mort was smoking a cigar, and puffing at it with every evidence of nervous tension; Mannopoli guessed why, and acted on it.

"When did you write to Fallow, Julius?"

Mort stopped the movement of the cigar from his fingers to his lips. He looked like a punctured balloon.

"I—I—look here, Mannopoli—"

"You were born a fool," said Mr. Mannopoli dispassionately, "and you'll never be anything else. You've written to him, haven't you?"

His words were softly spoken, with just sufficient emphasis to worry Mort and make him talk. The fat man sighed, and avoided his colleague's eyes.

"Well—well, yes. To tell you the truth, Polly old man, I was so sure you'd both be behind me that I *did* post the letter last night, instead of waiting until to-day. But it doesn't matter, does it? We'd have written in any case."

"Let's see the copy," said Mr. Mannopoli.

It was on the tip of Mort's tongue to protest against the other's attitude, when he remembered that he had broken a rule of the syndicate. There were few rules, but those which had been established were rigidly upheld, and one of them was that no single member should take any action without consulting the others unless an emergency arose to make it imperative.

Mort licked his lips.

"I—er—you're a deuced smart fellow, Polly; *I'd* never have guessed anything about it. Here's the note—just a brief one, you see, nothing to worry about. Nothing at all."

Mr. Mannopoli took the note and read it; his yellow face was expressionless, and his bony hands did not tremble.

My dear Fallow,

I have an idea that you could help me in a little matter I have in hand. Plenty of money in it, you'll be glad to know! As a matter of fact I and some friends need the specialized assistance that you would be able to give us, and we'd all be happy if you could join us.

May I say this is a matter of considerable importance and that we are keeping it very 'dark.' Not a word, in short, to anyone. But if you'd care to join us, slip down one night and have a chat with Mulling—ah, that's a surprise !—at the 'George', in Michford. Mulling knows a little—not all—about it.

All good wishes, my dear fellow. I'll look forward to hearing from you soon.

> *Yours ever,*
> *Julius Mort.*

Mr. Augustus Mannopoli finished reading, and then, holding the letter in his right hand, regarded Mr. Mort contemplatively. His lips were curling, and his narrowed eyes were somehow more frightening than usual. Mort felt his lips were very dry.

"You see, Polly, nothing that—"

"You ruddy fool!" snapped Mr. Mannopoli. "You must be insane. To send a letter like this—like this!"

"But—it says nothing, it says nothing!"

"It says that you and Mulling are connected, and if Craigie

or any of the others at Whitehall learn that I wouldn't like to be in your shoes. Listen, Mort—"

There was such concentrated venom in his voice that Mr. Mort could not have done otherwise. He stared, his lips parted a little, his plump hands trembling.

"Don't ever—ever, do you understand?—send letters or talk to anyone at all without telling me first. If you do you'll get a lot worse than this."

Mr. Mannopoli, every word at the same low level, suddenly stopped talking and on the 'this' brought his open palm across Mort's face. The fat man half screamed, and then seemed to shrink into his corner, stung by the blow but terrified by the expression in Mannopoli's eyes.

"I—I—"

"Shut up," snapped Mannopoli, and glanced out of the window. He knew the district well, and he knew that a village—by name Granning—was some mile and a half ahead. "I'm leaving you at Granning. Get straight back to London, and take your wife out. That," added Mr. Mannopoli unpleasantly, "will shock her nearly as much as I've shocked you. And—keep quiet."

Mr. Mort could do many things, but keeping quiet wasn't one of them.

"Listen—Mannopoli! I can't understand you. Where—where are you going?"

"I'm going to try and get the letter back."

"The letter back!" Mort had forgotten the blow, forgotten everything but those last words. "Why—he'll have read it, I tell you, he'll have read it!"

"Maybe he has. I hope not. In any case we've got to get it back. Now stop yapping, will you?"

Mr. Mort tried but failed.

"Supposing—supposing you can't get it?" he muttered. "Is it—is it important? What will you do?"

But Mr. Augustus Mannopoli didn't answer; he still hadn't answered when they reached the village of Granning. Mr. Mort saw Mannopoli get out, and he shivered, for there had been something worse than he had ever seen before in Mannopoli's eyes and his expression. He dreaded Mannopoli; and he dreaded still more the results of what Mannopoli might do.

2

MR. ARRAN ARRIVES

C ome on, Lucy dear, just a little more—just a little more
—*blast* you! You obstinate son of a what's it, you! I—"

Mr. Tobias Arran, completely at a loss for words, licked his finger and then looked about him.

Desolation.

Not a sign of anything that didn't grow from the earth for miles around. No cottage, no farm; hang it, not even a horse. Not that a horse would have helped him much, apart from giving him a little encouragement.

The bonnet of the Frazer Nash was lifted; the works looked lovely and yet they wouldn't go. There were limits to most things, and Toby Arran considered he'd reached the bright peak of this day's adventures. No punctual visit for Mr. John Fallow; no Tarrington; no means of transhipping himself, and no one in sight.

Unfortunately he knew little about the insides of car engines, and in the past two hours he had touched everything that was movable and much that was not in an effort to give a spark of life to the Frazer Nash. He had failed. The method of his progress had, in fact, deserved success, but it hadn't worked. He'd made an adjustment—blindly, it was true—with each and every part that moved and then hopped round to the driving-seat and pressed the self-starter. A whirring screech had resulted, but not once had he won a gentle purr from the engine, while in the processes of getting into and out of the driving-seat he had contrived to damage himself or his clothes thus:

Item: a torn right trouser permanent turn-up. Item: a smear of oil on an otherwise silver-grey suit. Item: a two-much scratch on the toe of a dusty tony-brown shoe. Item: a scratched finger. Item: a torn nail. Item: a now badly trodden trilby; and, of course, major and minor etceteras.

He had, moreover, shown himself of an inventive turn of mind. The Frazer Nash, until that day on those desolate Somerset moors, with an unseasonal wind whistling across and seeming to blow from the four corners of the earth towards it, had been christened. First Peter; then Liza; then Lucy; and alternatively darker things, for Toby Arran knew his vernacular.

But it had all been of no avail. He was still standing isolated, solitary, scowling and worried. He was colder than ever, and Barton, his man, had forgotten to pack his whisky-flask. He was hungrier than he had been for weeks, and the only thing he had to eat was his wallet; he didn't fancy it.

Of all the things that concerned him, however, anxiety was the greatest. He made no comment on it even to himself, but he was getting damnably worried, and not without good reason.

Toby Arran had worked for many years for Gordon Craigie, whom a certain Mr. Mannopoli knew as the leader of the little-known Department called Z. Toby was, in fact, the oldest agent in years of service on the Department's unwritten ledgers. Gordon Craigie had sent him down to Devon, or, to be precise, The Maples, in—or on the outskirts of—the village of Tarrington.

Craigie did nothing, Arran knew, without a purpose. Therefore it was important from the Department point of view that he should see Mr. John Fallow. It had been equally important that he should see the man at five o'clock; but he'd failed. It was now seven, and already the first dark streaks of dusk were dulling the blue of the otherwise clear sky.

Toby finished an experiment with the dynamo-brush, and then sat wearily on the running-board. He lit a cigarette, although he was dry and his lips were sore. Smoking was the only comfort left to him.

And then, looking towards the left, he saw something.

On three hundred and sixty-four days of a year, Toby would not have worried about that. It was, after all, no matter of vital moment to see things; Toby had been known to see things that didn't exist. But here, the first moving object apart from the birds since four-forty-five, was a miracle, a god-sent object, a positive phenomenon. And what was more, the thing moved on wheels and was propelled by an engine. It was, in fact, an overloaded and precariously lurching farmer's lorry, and it was coming towards the Frazer Nash.

Toby went hurriedly to meet it; there were things his patience couldn't manage, and to wait until the thing lumbered up was one of them. The driver, who was alone, was a befurred and bewhiskered man of past middle age, with ruddy red cheeks and clear blue eyes and a slouch cap. He pulled up as Toby ran towards him, and cut off his engine; a gentleman of economical turn of mind, Toby thought, or else hard of hearing.

No, surely not that; anything but that. An argument with a

man who was deaf would be so far past his limit that Toby was scared of his own reactions.

But the farmer wasn't deaf.

"Good evening to you, zur. Can I be helping?"

"That's awfully good of you," said Toby. He looked blue and cold, and the farmer felt sorry for him. "I'm stuck, and I must get to Tarrington as quickly as possible. I wonder if you could give me a lift? I'd be infernally grateful."

"Ay," said the bewhiskered one. "But what about your car, zur?"

"I can send someone from the garage for that. There is a garage at Tarrington?"

"Oh yes, there be. Owd Tom'll send for it or do zummat. But ye be going the wrong way for Tarrington, zur."

The Frazer Nash, its nose pointing towards the stationary lorry, seemed to reproach its owner. Toby, climbing into the seat next to the man of the soil, drew a deep breath. For if the car was now pointing in the wrong direction before he had turned round he had once been going in the right one.

"Then where"—he managed to speak firmly—"is Tarrington?"

"Two miles farther on," said the farmer, "up the hill."

"But I couldn't find a hill."

"Maybe that," said the farmer, "was because you didn't go down t' other hill first, zur. But ye be in a hurry and we mustn't be talking."

He pressed the self-starter and the lorry rattled off. For the duration of the short trip the farmer said—very grimly—nothing. Toby Arran said—very quietly—all manner of things. For had he gone two hundred yards farther on than the point where he had first turned the Frazer Nash he would have seen the dip in the road, and realized where the hill—which the policeman had indicated with a laborious 'h'—was situated. In fact, he would have reached Tarrington before the trouble had developed with the Frazer Nash, and he would now have been safe and comfortable with Mr. John Fallow; even probably about to start dinner, and an excellent dinner. Toby's hopes of The Maples cuisine had risen as his depression had deepened and hunger increased.

They reached Tarrington at last.

It was not a large village, but it possessed a pub, a garage and two churches. Most of the roofs were thatched, most of the windows oak-beamed. It looked quiet and restful, a dream village in a place of delight. Even at the end of a hot, dry summer the village green was smiling in the last rays of the evening sun. The whole contrived to quieten Toby's frayed but turbulent spirit; he thanked the driver of the lorry profusely, and yet knew enough not to offer the man money. He did learn, however, that Whiskers would be at Tarrington pub during the evening; Toby promised himself a visit before setting off, dusty and on foot, for the house called The Maples. A word to the 'owd Tom' of the garage—a tin shed stocked with some second-hand tyres and two petrol-pumps—had obtained a promise to go and look at the Frazer Nash and if necessary tow it in.

Now—The Maples.

It was a pleasant house, four hundred yards from the village, built on the side of a hollow that hid Tarrington from sight of its windows. The grounds were not large, but they were well cared for. In the dusky light there was that same evidence of peacefulness and quiet that Toby had seen in the village.

He saw this as he approached, for from the village he had to walk downhill most of the way. He saw the open windows, and caught sight of a flutter of something white inside. For a moment a girl's face appeared at a window; a slim girl, a presentable girl, although perhaps the dusk made her seem even more desirable than she would have done during the day. Toby didn't know; Toby didn't care. All that worried him was that no suggestion of bother or trouble surrounded The Maples, and the girl looked lovely.

And then, when he was less than twenty yards from the gates, the car passed him.

It was an old, battered Morris, driven by a man whom Toby glimpsed in profile as the car passed him. There was one remarkable thing about the profile that struck some hidden chord of memory in his mind. It was very sharp—the word that sprang to Toby's mind was 'vulture', although he told himself he was being melodramatic—and the skin was yellowish. A saturnine countenance, and by no means a pleasant one.

"Now, where," asked Toby, "have I seen such a man before, or heard of such a man before, or— *Damn* it!"

For the Morris turned in at the gates of The Maples and went rapidly along the short drive. Already a small Singer Sports car was standing outside the house.

Before Toby had reached the gates the man was standing on the porch of the house and knocking at the door. A visitor, obviously, for Craigie's Mr. Fallow.

And then the visitor did a queer thing.

He took a handkerchief from his pocket, a large one that he waved as though in a great show of delight. Then—Toby whistled—then he wrapped it round his face. The lower half of his face.

Toby Arran stopped thinking.

There were times for thinking and times for acting, and this was definitely one of the latter. He didn't act normally. He stepped away from, not towards, the gates, and looked hurriedly for a gap in the hedge. One appeared, providentially, and Toby, being a small man, was able to squeeze himself through without any trouble.

The scream came from the house at the same moment.

It was short and sharp, a high-pitched cry that was broken off abruptly. Toby Arran, staring towards the now open door of the house, saw a splash of white move downwards; sag towards the floor, in fact. And the man who had driven past in the Morris stepped into the house and over the outstretched body of a girl.

Toby Arran gritted his teeth; and then he swore.

Craigie'd mentioned that man! A sharp-featured fellow, with a yellowish skin. A sharp-featured fellow—

Craigie'd mentioned him as connected with Fallow; and here was Fallow being visited by the gentleman, who had either used a gun or a cosh to strike the girl down. Toby Arran, his eyes very narrow and his lips set, streaked across the soft grass of the lawn.

He hardly knew what to expect; he guessed there would be trouble and nasty trouble, and he didn't know how to stop it.

The door had closed with a bang; there'd be no admittance that way, and if Toby was any judge admittance in double-quick time was essential. He was thinking as he ran, and at the same time fidgeting with his hip pocket.

He drew the gun out as he reached the edge of the lawn.

He'd approached the house corner-wise, and he could now approach either the front door or the french windows at the side of the house, which he could just see. He wasn't sure which to take when the man's voice came; it was not raised, and yet was very hard.

"What's the meaning of this, sir?"

Fallow—Fallow for a pension! And from the room with the french windows. Toby had all he wanted for the moment, and he moved, slowly now, for he was walking on gravel, towards the sound of the voices. He was terribly afraid that he might be too late to prevent the damage that was certainly coming, but if he made a row he'd lose every chance he had.

The voice that followed was distinctive; a hard, metallic voice, with all the words clipped and uttered very distinctly.

"You had a letter, Fallow, from a man named Mort?"

"Supposing I did?" Fallow's voice was still low-pitched, a pleasant one, yet that of a man who knew how to tackle even an awkward situation. "And may I suggest you put that gun away?"

The man with the metallic voice and the sharp features laughed; Toby Arran had heard most degrees of laughter, but few of them had been as bad as that.

"Don't be a fool—and keep your hands in sight. I want that letter."

"You're being absurd," said Mr. Fallow.

"You're being damned silly," said the other, and the menace in his voice was more pronounced now. "The letter—or a bullet. Have which you like."

The words came clearly, spoken dispassionately and yet ominous, and more than ominous. Toby Arran, within a couple of yards of the french windows now, could just see into the room, and saw that its walls were lined with books.

"I'm afraid—" began John Fallow; but the man whom Mort and Mr. Mulling knew as Mannopoli broke across his words.

He didn't do it with his voice—he did it with a shot from his gun. Arran was near enough to hear the *zutt* as the bullet came from the silenced automatic. Never in his life had Toby been so tempted to rush like a bull at a gate; he stopped himself, for he knew that if the bullet had taken a fatal effect, rushing tactics would be useless. If it had been meant as a warning, rushing tactics would be fatal.

A warning, thank God!

"You see," said Mr. Mannopoli, "I mean what I say. Now that letter, Fallow. The next one will be more painful."

Fallow didn't speak; Mannopoli waited for a few seconds; and Toby Arran crept sideways towards the french windows, able to see most of the room now—and Fallow! Fallow sitting at a desk and the other man standing with his back towards the window. Toby began to smile, for this was what the doctor ordered. But where had Fallow been shot?

In the ear; so much was soon obvious. Blood was streaming down, but the wound was probably more messy than painful. Fallow had a strong face—a face of the type so popularly called leonine because of its strength and the thick head of tawny hair—and he was staring at the man with the gun, the man whose sharp features were covered by the white handkerchief.

Fallow spoke at last.

"That letter, my man"—how Toby loved the 'my man'!—"is being looked after. If you've come for it, you're unlucky. If you're wise you'll get away quickly. Because—"

Mannopoli's oath came first; his second shot came afterwards. It was directed to Fallow's heart, but fortunately for John Fallow something else came between the oath and the shot. A bullet, in fact, from Toby's gun, that smashed through the glass of the french window, sending the pane shivering and the pieces flying, and struck into Mannopoli's forearm. Mannopoli's gun was wrenched out of his grasp, and as the bullet left its muzzle it bit into the carpet. Mannopoli swung round, and if ever eyes blazed, his did then.

But Toby Arran, looking very perky and confident, still held his gun. He was visible through the windows, and he pushed his left hand through the broken glass and turned the handle. The window opened towards him and he stepped into the room.

Neither of the others had moved; they'd had time to, but they were paralysed, or so it seemed, and Toby didn't mind.

"What-ho," he said, and he said it cheerfully. "Fireworks at the party and we won't be home to-night. Good evening, Mr. Fallow. Sorry I broke your window."

"I—" began Mr. Fallow, and then stopped; it was understandable, for less than sixty seconds before he had seen death; and at close quarters death looked ugly—even more ugly than the face of Tobias Arran as he looked at the lean man and ripped the handkerchief off.

"The better to see you with," Toby said gently.

The man seemed struck dumb; but Toby didn't like his expression. That face with its sharp outlines and its taut skin, its narrowed eyes and its yellow tinge, was definitely outside the list of Toby's favourite types.

"Who the hell," said Mannopoli, "are you?"

"Name's Smith," said Toby cheerfully. "I use a gun for pleasure and I'm Mr. Fallow's bodyguard, and he'll bear me out, I'm sure. We can't," added Toby Arran, standing on his dignity, "have people coming here and trying to pinch Mr. Fallow's valuable formulae without some rudiments of protection. Er —and you?"

The thin lips of the man whose name was Mannopoli according to some people tightened: the lips of a man who could play poker and withstand third degree. Toby knew the signs.

"It's a pity," he said. "We'd have been so comfortable sitting together, and now you've got to go away. It's most unfortunate, but I distinctly promised the police that if ever I saw a man with a yellow face and thin lips I would send for them immediately. Any servants, Mr. Fallow? Handy, I mean."

"You don't need any servants," said the lean man. "Who the devil are you?"

"Don't be funny. I am ever-present, omniscient, over-whelming, and Mr. Fallow's lifelong protector. Mister —move."

Arran's gun jerked; the man whose forearm was streaming blood obeyed. He didn't seem to realize he had been hit, but he did understand the threat of that automatic.

"That's right—in the corner—away from the door. Doors are always opening and shutting, aren't they? Er—oh, *damn!*" exclaimed Toby. "I forgot her!"

His attitude changed subtly. He had been fooling, but now he was serious; even Mannopoli realized it.

"What did you do to her?" Toby demanded.

Before Mannopoli could reply, Fallow was out of his chair, his eyes blazing.

"What's that? You didn't touch Ellen? Ellen opened the door, and—"

Mr. Mannopoli curled his lips.

"I hit her over the head," he said; "she'll be all right."

"When I hit you over the head," said Toby Arran, "you won't be all right. Mr. Fallow, if you'll make sure El—she—is all right, and then come back to the telephone, I'd be obliged. I want this cove in gaol."

"You won't get it," sneered Mannopoli.

"A fiver to a pint. Is it on?"

"Are you," inquired Mr. Mannopoli unpleasantly, "quite mad? Who—"

"The devil are you? I've heard it before, and I told you my name's Smith. Now—"

While Toby talked Fallow hurried out of the room, and had probably reached the hall. Toby Arran was trying to decide whether the lean man would make an effort to beat him off when the telephone bell rang.

It rang very stridently, from a corner of the room opposite

Mannopoli. Toby's eyes twitched, but he hesitated. One job at a time was all he could conveniently tackle, and he wanted to make sure the fellow stayed in the corner. Judging from the cut of the man's jib and the rate of his actions, he was a specialist in trouble and he didn't mind much what damage he caused. The telephone could wait.

Burr—Burr—Burr! It was strident and incessant, and, like all telephone bells, it sounded urgent. Toby wished Fallow would hurry up. He edged towards the 'phone, keeping his gun trained on the man in the corner all the time. He didn't like the way the other took this thing, although he told himself the fellow was probably bluffing. No one with a face like that could fail to be the perfect bluffer, and certainly he looked confident and unafraid. Almost as if he knew that his present spot wouldn't last much longer.

Toby reached the telephone and the man in the corner moved his left arm.

He moved it with incredible speed, the hand towards the armpit. Toby saw what was coming and fired, but the man with the yellow face ducked and the bullet hummed over his head. The gun from the other's shoulder-holster leapt into sight and the flame stabbed out. Toby saw something light blue flutter to the floor, but he also heard the unpleasant *plump* of the bullet in the wall behind him, and dropped on his knees behind the desk, firing as he went.

The man with the yellow face didn't hesitate either to move or to take chances.

He blazed away at the desk, and Arran heard the bullets biting and saw the wood flying. Flashes of flame came too, and he knew the fellow was moving towards the open french windows. He fired twice, but didn't stop his man; Mannopoli reached the french windows, and then was suddenly outside.

There was a hush in the room.

27

And then the telephone again, burring insistently. A shout from somewhere inside the house. Thudding of footsteps on the gravel, and then silence. Toby swore at the telephone and reached the window in four strides. As he did so a bullet, fired from a spot near the battered Morris, crashed through another pane of glass, and the splinters showered Toby's head and shoulders unpleasantly. The man was in the Morris now, and the cunning devil had its nose pointing towards the gates!

And then, out of the blue, the blow came.

Toby hadn't heard the slightest sound, but the man came from behind him. There was just the dull, sickening thud as the sandbag struck him; the whirring of his head and the roaring in his ears and then—silence.

Broken, although Toby Arran didn't hear it, by the roar of the Morris engine and the scrunching of tyres on the gravel drive, a sudden bellow from John Fallow, outlined against the french window and the tap—tap—tap of shots from the gun in Fallow's hand.

3

THE FIRST COLOURS

Tobias Arran had lived for thirty-five years, and in the course of them he claimed he had been knocked out on seventeen occasions, exclusive of minor injuries on the fields of cricket, rugger or point-to-point. The occasion of the visit of Augustus Mannopoli to the home of Mr. John Fallow was, therefore, the eighteenth knock-out; but if it was the last it was by no means the worst. In something under five minutes Toby, a little dazed, more than a little angry and with a pain at the back of his neck, opened his eyes and blinked at Fallow.

"So you're still here," he said, after a pause and a spot of whisky which Fallow had ready.

"Thanks to you," Fallow said.

"We'll agree to differ," murmured Toby, struggling to a sitting position and gazing thoughtfully round the room. His head had cleared sufficiently for him to see the chaos, and he didn't like it. He was sitting on broken glass; there was so much broken glass that it would have been hard to avoid it. Plaster had sprayed the walls, the wall-paper was peppered with little buff blotches, the desk was chipped in half a dozen places, and splinters of wood mingled with the rest of the débris. But as Timothy struggled to his feet with Fallow's help he nodded.

"It might have been a lot worse," he said. "No, *I* didn't stop that gentleman's bullet from biting you, Mr. Fallow. I was the instrument of a high command, and a damned bad one at that. I refer," said Toby, who was speaking much more slowly than usual—he had a staccato manner of uttering words, and a machine-gun-like rapidity when he was feeling himself—"to the instrument and not the command. How's your daughter?"

No one could blame John Fallow for looking surprised; men recently recovered from unconsciousness rarely, if ever, behaved in quite the way Toby was doing. Fallow looked as if he wasn't certain whether to laugh or take a firm hand and send for a doctor. He took the middle course and answered the question.

"I haven't a daughter," he said.

"What, no *daughter*?"

"No—you'll forgive me," added Fallow hurriedly, realizing that he had been very close to bandying words, "if I say you're not quite fit, won't you? I'm immensely grateful for what you did, but—but—"

"You're puzzled," said Toby, with triumph and getting to his feet, without Fallow's aid this time.

"I am," said John Fallow without hesitation. "May I ask who you are?" He chuckled, and Toby warmed to the man. "Unless you prefer to stick to the name Smith, of course."

"Please yourself," said Toby, reaching for the decanter of whisky. "Have a spot? No, all right." He helped himself. "I could have put my last dollar on Ellen—forgive the familiarity—being your daughter. But let's leave the subject. My name's Arran, Mr. Fallow. A friend of yours asked me to call, but I arrived rather behind time. Craigie—"

"Craigie!" exclaimed Fallow, and he looked as if a great load had been lifted from his mind. "Well, that explains a great deal, Mr. Arran. I'm really sorry you had such a warm welcome."

"If the welcome hadn't been in the offing I probably wouldn't have arrived at all," admitted Toby frankly. "It's a damned nuisance that fellow got away, though. Know him?"

"I've never set eyes on him before in my life." Mr. Fallow was a man who believed in making himself clearly understood.

"Some people," Toby said, eying Fallow's damaged ear, "have odd ideas about courtesy. Have you ever shot a piece out of a man's ear the first time you've seen him? All right, I know you haven't. He wanted a letter, didn't he?"

Fallow nodded grimly; the gleam in his eyes was very hard.

"Yes. A letter I'd received from a man named Mort. I had sent it on to Craigie."

Toby Arran for once seemed bereft of words. He stood a couple of yards away from Fallow and eyed him; his smile had gone from his lips, but in his eyes there was a glint of admiration.

"Well, well, well! So Craigie had the letter. You must have hurried to send it along."

"I did, but"—Fallow looked awkward—"I promised Craigie I'd talk to no one about it. Of course you've come from him, but—"

"Discretion forever, eh? And quite right too," said Toby. He drew a deep breath, took a cigarette-case from his pocket, lit one after Fallow had refused, and then nodded slowly. He seemed a different, somehow more capable, man now.

"Everything else aside," he said, "this fellow with the yellow face wanted the letter you'd had from the Mort monster. He wasn't going to hesitate much about the way he obtained it. It suggests, anyhow, that Mort's connected with our visitor, and

31

it's a greater pity than ever that the man got away. You tried to stop him, of course?"

"I used all the ammunition in your gun," Fallow said.

"That's a good recommendation, anyhow. The chances of catching him are negligible, of course. I'd better 'phone Craigie. And—what's that?"

For Mr. John Fallow looked startled; worse than startled, he looked thunderstruck.

"We—we haven't sent for the police! Confound it, how the deuce did I come to—to *forget* that? Call them first, Mr. Arran, and then—"

"And then what? Didn't Craigie also warn you not to tell the locals anything about this?" asked Toby. "We never call them unless it's imperative, and I can't see that it is this time. We'll make sure and ask Craigie. By the way, what about your—er—Ellen? Is she all right?"

"Yes, quite all right. She was hit over the head, and there's no serious damage, I'm glad to say. A maid is with her."

"Maid to the fore, eh? Where was the maid when the fellow knocked at the door?"

"Up in her room at the top of the house. She came downstairs as I hurried out into the hall while you had that fellow with his hands up," Fallow said. "I saw Ellen was all right, and then I heard the firing in here."

"It must," said Toby ruminatively, "have sounded lousy. Yellow Mug lost the silencer on his automatic, and that's a bad habit. Anyhow," he added, going to the telephone and lifting the receiver, "as Ellen's all right, and there's no more damage than the bit out of your ear, I suppose we mustn't grumble. I wonder who was telephoning? Hallo? Oh, thanks, Whitehall 81212. Yes, 81212...."

"Gordon," added Toby Arran, "will be peeved about this. I

shall get my knuckles rapped, and—*whist!* Car coming up the drive. Take a gun, Fallow, in case of accidents."

John Fallow had seen a great number of men in the course of his life, but he had never met anyone who reacted as quickly as this ugly little man named Arran. Arran talked most of the time like a fool, but occasionally he was impressive; and when he moved or suggested a course of action there was something—was 'dynamic' the word?—about him.

Fallow let that thought flash through his mind, while Arran slipped a small spare automatic into his hand. Arran was looking through the broken french windows, and the lights from a car—it was almost dark now—were waving to and fro, like ghosts against the trees.

"Do you think it's—it's him back?" Fallow was nervous although he was doing his best not to let it seem so.

"No. But it might be a friend of his. Here, you hang on to this and ask for Craigie, and I'll tackle the gent. It might," added Toby with a sudden beam, "be a man trying to sell you a vacuum cleaner. Unless you've got a vacuum cleaner, when it will probably be a new car."

He talked as he pushed the telephone into Fallow's not unwilling hands, retrieved the automatic, and stepped towards the door. By the time he had reached it the car had stopped outside, and the darkness seemed more impenetrable as the headlights were switched off. He was within sight of Fallow when the knock came.

Even to Fallow it was a curious knock.

Short and sharp; long and lingering. Short-long, short-long. A positive tattoo of a knock. Fallow frowned; but Toby Arran let out a roar that seemed too vast for his small body.

"Friends!" he cried. "That's friends!" He was out of sight now, but still talking. Fallow heard him fiddling with the catch

on the door as he added: "Hang Craigie on, will you? Ah—I—
Hallo! Craigie in person!"

"So you got here, then?" asked Mr. Gordon Craigie, as he
entered the hall. "I wondered if you would. Trouble?"

"Trouble," said Tony Arran in tones of disgust. "Trouble!
You sent me down here by myself when it needed half a dozen
men. But come in, Gordon, and tell the exchange that you're
down here, will you? Now listen—"

Gordon Craigie listened.

He was in the library, three of whose chairs were still
usable; Toby sat opposite him, and Fallow by the ruined desk.

Craigie was a man of medium height, thin, gaunt-faced—
almost as gaunt, in fact, as Mr. Mannopoli—with a long,
pointed jaw and lips that drooped at the corners and yet did
not seem bad-tempered or sour. His eyes were grey, keen and
piercing. He was dressed neatly in grey, and, to complete the
colouring, his hair, once fair, was iron-tinged. It was also thin.
Craigie was a man who knew what worry was, and that was
understandable, for the leader of the Department called Z
knew most things about anxiety.

Not personal anxiety: Craigie was a bachelor, and had no
ties. But in his Whitehall office he held his fingers on the pulse
of the nation; in fact, all the nations of the world. During his
life he had several times seen the tragedy of war; on a dozen
more occasions had he prevented an even worse catastrophe.
He was the recipient of more secrets than any other man in
England not excluding the Prime Minister. He had agents in
every corner of the world, even those corners that were so
lousy that the black man called them hot. From these agents
trickled a continual stream of rumours and facts, some impor-

tant, most unimportant, many redundant. But from time to time there would come an item of news that stood out from the rest; and then another item, apparently disconnected and yet, to Craigie, closely allied. And then he would concentrate his best men on the points where the news was leaking, and he would get an even greater flow of coded communications, most of them unpleasant.

For the news that worried Craigie and interested Craigie was always bad.

Good news could be published; the world could know it. Bad news had to be repressed; bad news meant ugly developments that had to be stopped if it was humanly possible. Bad news, in fact, was Craigie's lot from morning to night. He should have been a confirmed pessimist, but a glance at his gleaming eyes proved that he was anything but that.

And as he listened first to Toby Arran's flippant recital of events and then to Fallow's more mellowed comments, he was thinking of disquieting items of news that had been leaking from various quarters in the past few weeks.

Some of them concerned a man named Mort.

As Mannopoli had told that fat gentleman, he had once been under the eyes of the police. He had also been under the eyes of Gordon Craigie, for the Yard and Department Z worked well together. As a direct result of this information concerning Julius Mort, Craigie had made certain inquiries among Mort's acquaintances; he was as well aware as Mannopoli that Mort had no friends.

He had contacted with Fallow for a very good reason.

Fallow had worked for many years in the Government Gas Research factories near Penzance. He had been retired. But he was, as near as a man could be, a close friend of Mort's; and Craigie had asked him to report anything unusual about that gentleman. Craigie felt safe in making the request;

once in the past Fallow had been concerned in some of the Department's investigations and had kept in touch with Craigie ever since; Fallow was, after all, an expert in gas of the lethal kind.

An odd chance, some might have thought; but Craigie never worked by chance unless the situation was desperate.

He knew that until a year before, Mort had worked a great deal with a chemist, by name Marshall. He knew Marshall had died. He wondered if Mort would need have contact with a second chemist and imagined Fallow most likely to be favoured with the financier's attentions. And, as he had heard by letter that morning, his long shot had come off.

He had half expected trouble; for that he had no very good reason, only that trouble had so often followed Julius Mort. He had therefore sent Arran down to John Fallow's house, and only Providence—Craigie was a devout man—had saved the chemist from an unpleasant end.

Craigie was glad Fallow was safe; but he was even more glad that the attempt had been made on his life. It proved as nothing else could have done that where Mort went real trouble followed. It suggested other things to Craigie, but he didn't voice them that evening. It wasn't wise. The reasonable thing to do was to let Fallow think as much as he liked, leave Arran at the house for the time being and go back to London and get even more closely on Mort's tail.

Craigie was worried by Julius Mort and the man with the vulture face and the yellow skin. He had heard so many rumours, all of them unpalatable, and this affair seemed to have lifted them from rumours into facts.

* * *

"And so," said Toby Arran, "the swab got away. And if I may say so, I need a wash-and-brush-up and a good meal. That's if Mr. Fallow can go to it, of course."

Fallow smiled.

He was an urbane man, a contented-looking man, who was not immensely worried by what had happened. One didn't worry if one was of John Fallow's temperament; one just went on doing what one wanted to do, and took what chance sent along without raising more than a speculative eyebrow.

He was a bigger man than Toby had first thought, a little on the fleshy side, although that wasn't surprising with a man who had turned sixty. His leonine face was kindly; his reddish countenance bespoke the out of doors whenever he could get there; his blue eyes emphasized that impression of kindliness.

"Of course," he said. "The evening meal is ready—or it will be very soon. We don't dine here"—he looked apologetic—"but I can promise you something substantial."

"That'll do me fine," said Toby. "Can I have a wash?"

"I'll take you to the bathroom," promised Fallow. "Would you care to have a look round here, Craigie?"

Craigie said that he would, and Toby Arran followed his host upstairs. Fallow was a likable man, and the less likely to panic than anyone Toby could think of casually. He still chuckled when he thought of the man's handling of Sharp Face.

A quick wash refreshed the little man immensely. He was curious about several things, and dwelt on them as he splashed. Yes; quite a lot of developments, in fact, that were more or less inexplicable. This, in short, looked liked a kettle of fish. Craigie was a quiet old cuss, but he did find trouble.

The points, Toby thought, were chiefly:

1. Who was the man who had raided The Maples?

2. What was his connection with Mr. Mort?
3. What and who was Mort, anyway?
4. Who had cracked Toby over the head while Fallow had been making sure what had happened to his d— Ellen?
5. Where had that second man gone to? (He must remember to ask Fallow whether he could help there.)
6. Was Ellen as lovely close to as she had seemed in the twilight?
7. Who was Ellen?
8. How long would Craigie expect him to stay down here?
9. Would he—Arran—get on with Ellen if he did?

Toby Arran put the finishing touches to his sleek, dark hair, eyed his ugly face reflectively, sighed, put on his coat, opened the bathroom door and emerged quickly—and cannoned into Ellen. It was the kind of thing that Toby Arran could be relied on to do nine times out of ten.

There was no gentle hint about that collision. He banged heavily into the girl, sent her staggering against the opposite wall, lost his balance and sat down. The sitting down hurt, but he controlled his expression and stared up at the girl.

She wasn't more than a girl. Twenty, Toby thought. And, b' God, she was a lot better in the electric light than she had been in the dusk. A positive picture.

"Hallo," he said encouragingly.

She wasn't smiling; she looked—now she had recovered from the shock of the collision—surprisingly demure and a little—just a little—on the prim side. Her skirt and blouse were severe; her hair—long, luxuriant hair—was done in plaits, and coiled about her head; one pink lobe peeped out, the other was lost.

"Hallo," she said.

"I'm dreadfully sorry," Toby apologized, scrambling to his feet and feeling, somehow, that he had been put in his place. "Darned clumsy of me to rush out like that. I really am full of apologies, and I hope you didn't hurt yourself."

"Not at all, thanks," said Ellen. She hesitated for a moment, as though trying to remember what she could say next, and then added calmly: "Did you?"

"Oh, not a bit!"

"You went down with a dreadful bump."

"I'm used to bumps, I assure you. Full of them. A tumbling-champion, in fact."

"I see." She appeared to consider whether the man was sane, whether any further remark was necessary, or whether she could safely leave him. Toby hoped she'd stay. She said: "You mean all-in wrestling, do you?"

Toby lowered his right brow a shade, and began to wonder just what Ellen meant, just what Ellen was thinking, and whether she was really dumb.

"In a—er—manner of speaking," he said.

"I thought perhaps you did." Her face was beautiful but quite blank. "Shall I have the pleasure of seeing you at supper?"

"I'm hoping so," said Toby Arran, getting more than a little hot under the collar. "I—"

He stopped, for she had turned away from him; she was turning when he saw the gleam in her eyes, a gleam that transformed that odd beauty of hers into something vital, something alive. He saw the way her lips were quivering too, and he said very plainly: "You little devil!"

Miss Ellen—he could not yet fit in the remainder of her name—continued along the short passage to a room at the far end. She walked quickly, and he fancied he heard her laughter escape as she opened the door and disappeared into the room. He scratched his chin, grinned, told himself that Ellen was more than twenty by several years, and then turned towards the stairs.

A little green card lying by the wainscoting of the passage attracted his eye. It was distinctive, for the woodwork was brown and the walls buff; the little patch of green stood out. He was sure it hadn't been there when he had entered the bathroom; he was as sure that she'd dropped it when he had cannoned into her. He smiled, picked it up, glanced at it curiously—it was diamond-shaped, perhaps two inches on every side, and a plain, pale green—and slipped it into his pocket. He'd have an opportunity of returning it to its owner in the near future. She was—

"What's the matter with you?" asked Gordon Craigie.

That thin man was standing at the foot of the stairs, his drooping lips somehow accusing. Toby Arran frowned; his expression had obviously been a key to his thoughts, which were pleasant.

"Dreams," he said.

"You won't have much time for dreams," said Craigie soberly, "if this game is anything like I expect it to be. Ever seen one of these before?"

Craigie held out his hand; Toby Arran saw what was in it and stared. A shock—physical as well as mental—seemed to paralyse him, and for a moment he didn't speak.

"Have you?" asked Craigie again, and laid the thing on the flat of his palm. It was a diamond-shaped piece of pasteboard, a replica of the card Toby had found upstairs, excepting that it was blue where the other had been green. Toby Arran hardly knew why it had been such a shock; green and blue were likely

enough colours for the girl. And yet—there had been something in the way Craigie had spoken that had hinted at dark
things.

"Yes," Toby said. "Where'd you find it?"

"I'll show you," said Craigie.

He led the way into the library—which had not yet been
tidied or touched—and pointed to the corner farther from the
french windows.

"On the floor over there," he said. "Why?"

But Toby Arran didn't answer immediately; the words
wouldn't come. It was absurd, it was fantastic; and yet—

The man with the sharp features and the yellow face had
been standing in that corner when he had snatched at the gun
from his shoulder-holster. The card had dropped from his
pocket; Toby remembered that fluttering thing of blue.

And this was practically a replica of the card the girl had
dropped.

4

BOB KERR GETS BUSY

L et's know all you know," said Gordon Craigie easily.

He broke the silence that had lasted several seconds and yet had seemed to drag out much longer. Toby drew a deep breath before he obliged.

"I found this"—he took the green card from his pocket slowly—"upstairs. The girl—Fallow's whatever-she-is—dropped it. At least, I think she did."

"And the man with the gun dropped the blue one?"

"That's my reasoning," admitted Toby.

"Although you don't like to say so." Craigie smiled fleetingly, and slipped the two cards into his vest pocket. Arran saw the opportunity of returning it to the girl disappear, and mentally shrugged his shoulders. He was getting his second wind now, and he was also beginning to believe that he was thinking and behaving like a madman. He said so, to Craigie.

"I can't *swear* the girl dropped the green one," he said. "I can't be *sure* the blue one wasn't in the corner before the attack. Call it unread, Craigie. Probably they're scented cards

—the lassies do have such things, I'm told—or they may be, damn it, anything."

Craigie's smile was thoughtful.

"They may mean anything," he admitted. "The thing is to find out just what. A green card and a blue card, each shaped like a diamond. They're interesting, if nothing else."

"Yes," said Toby Arran, and he felt strangely disconcerted. The cards might mean nothing; but his own spontaneous conclusion had been that they were somehow connected with the man who had attacked John Fallow. Yet if the girl had had one of them, that seemed absurd to a point of fantasy.

Toby shook his head, and decided to forget it. Craigie encouraged him. It was easier said than done, but Toby managed it more or less.

The girl helped him.

Before the meal, which Toby needed sadly, Fallow told them who she was; a relative of the chemist's, several times removed, who did occasional secretarial work for him and made herself generally useful in the house. She was capable, Fallow told them, and reliable. Toby Arran imagined her at the Eclat or at other places and told himself it was a crime that she should be buried down here, even with such an excellent fellow as John Fallow.

She didn't seem to want pitying; she positively scintillated for the rest of the evening, and Toby—who had, or so it was said, certain prejudices against the fair sex—was caught. The girl fascinated him; she was fair and yet not too fair; beautiful and yet not pretty. She had a figure, too, and a grace that many might have envied; but if there was anything above all others it was the fact that she seemed natural. Natural, he decided, was just the word. No airs and graces, no pretences; she was Ellen Granting, dependent on a far-removed relative for a livelihood, happy and within reason content. A disturbing presence for Toby Arran, particularly after the funny business of the cards.

It was madness, of course, to think there was anything in that. The whole affair of the man with the yellow face had upset his calculations, sent him off his balance, and he'd made a fool of himself. What was more, he'd sown suspicions in the mind of Gordon Craigie. Toby Arran knew Craigie only too well. Once the man had an idea he would never leave it until he had proved that the subject was harmless, innocent; or, in brief, genuine.

Damn it, could that girl be anything else?

They were at biscuits and cheese when Toby asked himself the questions. But for the disturbing and absurd business of the card he would have been thoroughly happy. That she had pulled his leg beautifully after their abrupt encounter outside the bathroom was a fact; there was also another fact, and not so pleasant when he thought hard about it. She wasn't in any way perturbed by her own crack over the head, the attempt to shoot her uncle—Toby used the word for the sake of convenience—or the general upheaval. Almost—dared he even to think it?—as if she had been half prepared for trouble.

Another remarkable thing came suddenly to Tobias Arran's mind.

The affair of the earlier evening had beeen a long way from the normal; hang it, the ordinary household would have been worried more than they could say by what had happened. But here it was taken calmly, too calmly; there was no excitement, no recapitulation of the events, no expressions of fear of what might develop. It was true that Fallow was thoughtful and occasionally glanced at the girl in worried fashion. But she might have spent the afternoon playing tennis and the early evening knitting for all the appearance she gave of untoward events.

Of course Fallow was of the placid type—a man never disturbed by anything. She'd lived with him for years, it seemed, and naturally she had absorbed a great deal of his own temperament. And yet—

Toby Arran almost stopped breathing.

For Gordon Craigie, who had talked most of the time with Fallow and left Ellen Granting to Toby, took something from his pocket. A slip of pasteboard, in fact, coloured green.

He put it deliberately on the table in front of him.

The girl had been talking; what it was about Toby forgot. He watched her, and he saw her eyes widen, saw her lips part for a moment above those perfect teeth. She seemed motionless. All the vivacity, all the fire, was gone from her. Her cheeks—coloured by Nature, he had noticed earlier—paled. She stared at the card and her body was rigid.

Toby Arran drew a deep breath; Craigie saw it and yet affected to notice nothing.

"I'd almost forgotten this," he said casually. "I found it in the room, Fallow—where Toby held the gunman up. Ever seen anything like it?"

Fallow leaned forward and took the card. The girl was still staring. Fallow turned it over, frowned and shook his head.

"No. It's quite plain, is it?"

"Absolutely plain," nodded Craigie. "I thought perhaps it was something of"—he put the words quickly, and glanced across at the girl, smiling as he did so—"Miss Granting's. But obviously I'm wrong, and that suggests the visitor brought it. Interesting." He took the card back and slipped it into his pocket, and as he did so the girl's tension seemed to relax.

"Queer," Toby said, constrained to say something.

"Yes," said Fallow; and then Ellen Granting went on with what she had been saying; but now Toby knew her brightness was forced, and beneath the air of gaiety he could see, very

45

clearly—almost frighteningly—the anxiety under which she was labouring.

One thing was certain above all others: the card meant something, and she knew what it was.

Fallow, Craigie and Arran were in the library after the evening meal. The window had been boarded up, the room made habitable again. All three were smoking—with Fallow, as Toby could have expected, fingering a well-burned briar.

"Now, don't you think," Fallow said, "you could tell us a bit about it, Craigie? It's something of a mystery, you know."

"And you've hidden your curiosity well," Craigie said.

"Yes, I didn't want to worry Ellen."

Craigie, who must have noticed the girl's reaction to the card even if the uncle had failed to do so, nodded and yet made no comment. He looked sober.

"Briefly it's this," he said. "I've heard that Julius Mort is mixing himself up a great deal with foreigners; I don't necessarily mean foreign politics, I just mean foreigners. And he has a great number of connections abroad—agencies for his various financial syndicates. That's clear?"

Fallow nodded and waited. Toby Arran's thoughts were divided between the subject and the girl.

"Well," Craigie went on, "for a long time Mort was a friend of this man Marshall. The chemist."

"You've told me that."

"I wondered whether there was more in it than just friendliness. Few of Mort's friends are—friends. I knew you and he were acquainted and I asked you to let me know if he approached you at all."

"I had that letter last post yesterday, and you had it first thing this morning," said Fallow.

"I know, and I'm grateful. And—this may seem fantastic, but it's true—I was worried simply because something *might* develop unpleasantly. I told Toby to come down here and to keep an eye open for the 'George'—where that man Mulling lives, you told me."

"Mulling owns the place. He bought it a couple of years ago. Yes?"

"Toby came. You know what happened, and we've learned a great deal more. Mort wrote the letter; your visitor learned about it and yet didn't want it to be in circulation. The visitor—"

"Call him X," implored Toby.

"All right, X. X came after the letter, was prepared to do murder to get it. As he knew about it, it's reasonable to assume he's a friend or acquaintance of Mort's. It's reasonable to assume also, that he saw Mort to-day. I know that Mort left London this morning by road, heading southwest. So Mort was here, and the other man—"

"X," murmured Toby, forgetting the girl.

"X. And Mulling, who's in this thing somewhere, was the likely host for them. The 'George' their likely port of call. We'll first find," added Craigie, "whether there were two visitors at the 'George' this afternoon; and then we'll watch Mulling or ask him one or two questions."

"I've always found Mulling an excellent fellow," Fallow said slowly.

"Perhaps. But friends of Mort aren't necessarily all they seem to be. However—we'll see."

"I suppose you want to go to the 'George'," said Toby Arran, lighting another cigarette. "It's getting a bit late, old son.

Turned nine-thirty. What time do they close round here, Fallow?"

"Ten o'clock, I think," said Fallow; he seemed amused, and Toby wondered why. "Are you going to—er—try to learn something to-night, Craigie?"

Gordon Craigie gave one of his rare chuckles.

"I hope I've learned a lot," he said. "Kerr came down with me, Toby, as far as Michford. He's in the bar of the 'George' now, learning all he can. He'll either telephone me or come over very soon. I'm expecting word any moment."

Toby Arran stood up, and looked affronted.

"Damn it," he said, "you might have told me someone else was coming down. What am I here for? To draw the fire or just be the mug?"

Fallow was looking bewildered, and Craigie explained while soothing Toby.

"Kerr," he said, "is one of our agents, Fallow. I sent him down because I wanted two or three men in the neighbourhood. I sent you alone, Toby, because visitors in twos might have been suspected and there was just the possibility that the house—this place—was being watched. I don't think it's likely—"

"*Don't* you, by Jove!" exclaimed Toby Arran. "*Don't* you? Then explain away in a better way the man who coshed me."

Craigie pursed his lips.

"Of course. There was someone beside the—"

"X".

"Besides X."

"And probably," hurried Toby, now in full cry, "he'd been watching the place, saw what happened, came over and helped the—X—out of the spot, and then vanished."

"Or," murmured Craigie, "stayed near."

Fallow went rigid; for the first time that evening—saving,

of course, for the safety of Ellen—Toby saw him express something in the way of concern.

"You mean he might be watching still? That more trouble might come?"

Craigie shook his head very slowly.

"No. If anyone is watching now, it's for Toby and I. They were after you for the letter. They must guess by now that it's gone, that I've seen it. You'll not be troubled any more by them, Fallow, don't worry about that. What did you say, Toby?"

Actually Toby had saved himself from speaking in the nick of time, and he was glad he did. For it had burst on him, suddenly and with a glorious light, that Ellen had been knocked over the head—and no man who knew her (assuming there *was* a connection between those coloured cards) would have been likely to have knocked her out.

Toby grew grim again.

She hadn't been hurt; she hadn't been hit hard. She *might* even have feigned unconsciousness. And her reaction to the card had proved she had recognized it. 'Oh, damn!' thought Toby Arran.

And then he wondered whether Bob Kerr was having any fun at the 'George,' and wished the situation had been reversed. For Kerr was a hard-hearted devil, and a girl's pretty face wouldn't send him off his balance even temporarily.

"Beer," said Robert McMillan Kerr largely, "is best when it's brewed in the South, eh? I always think so."

Mr. Mulling, a rather pale and worried Mr. Mulling who looked even more self-effacing behind his bar than he had done at the meeting of the syndicate that afternoon, nodded.

"Indeed you're right, sir."

"I have heard," said Mr. Kerr, "of people coming all the way down here for a week-end simply to sample the beer."

"Have you indeed?"

'Indeed', thought Kerr, was one of Mr. Mulling's favourite words. Mr. Mulling looked the man who would use words some years after they had gone out of fashion. He seemed completely innocuous; and in Kerr's comparatively brief but hectic association with the Department called Z he had met many rogues, but none quite like this specimen.

"I have," said Kerr. "A man I know—named Mort—comes down here regularly I'm told. Bath, I believe, for the waters; or so *he* says. Beer, more likely. Much more likely!" Kerr was acting the fool beautifully.

"Ye-es," said Mr. Mulling, and Bob Kerr began to take more notice than he had for some hours past. For the name Mort brought memories to Mulling, and not all pleasant memories. Mulling looked like a cat on hot bricks.

"Do you have many visitors?" Kerr asked.

"Visitors—well, yes, occasionally. None lately, of course. A little bit late in the year. Occasional callers. We had two here this afternoon"—Kerr was just noticing Mulling's Adam's apple, which was beginning to work up and down at consider- able speed—"for a rest and a dinner. Had to get dinner early for them." As he finished Mulling had looked round, almost as if he was making sure that he was a liar, and that he had dined with the callers himself. To Robert Kerr he looked a rabbity and badly frightened man.

'So,' thought Kerr, and went to the telephone. But his call to The Maples remained unanswered, and he went back to the pub.

He was not a large man as men go; rather under than over medium height, he made himself impressive with a pair of shoulders that had to be seen to be believed. His chin was on the heavy side, and set slightly aslant, giving the curious impression that his face was askew all the time, and not set properly on his neck. He was a fresh-skinned man, with between-coloured hair and a pair of grey eyes that could be remarkably far-seeing.

Kerr looked a man of achievement; and no one would have denied that he looked what he was.

Until early that year he had been Bob Kerr, Britain's most popular and most successful flying-ace. By accident he had met Gordon Craigie, at a time, it so happened, when he had felt that he had run his luck in the air far enough. Craigie had introduced him to Department Z. Kerr had acquitted himself with more than the usual distinction; and Craigie looked on him—with relief—as his star agent.

There was something particularly ruthless about Bob Kerr. And with the Department, ruthlessness was so often the only way to success.

Craigie had dropped Kerr some two miles on the other side of Michford. Kerr had travelled into the village by bus, and therefore seemed not only to be a stranger but not connected with any of the others whom the keen eyes of the impatient and—he believed—overworked local policeman had seen that day.

Kerr's orders had been simple: Talk to Mulling; find if he'd had visitors; and find out what they'd been like.

Kerr had achieved the first part of his job, and he took his bitter to a corner table. Mulling looked relieved. Kerr saw him slip through a door at the rear of the bar, and then looked round for someone who might be talkative. He chose, as it happened, a potman who was under notice for the trivial offence of helping himself to beer. Damn it, what man could have resisted such a temptation?

Kerr reordered, and asked the potman to have one. The potman, who looked gloomy, accepted with a slight lightening of his countenance. Kerr kept the conversation going—the

'George' was now empty in that section but for himself and the potman—until he had learned that two gentlemen had been at the 'George' that day, a very fat one—Mort for a pound—and a very thin one. That they came once a month. That they were friends of Mulling, and that Mulling was a—

Kerr heard him out, and then slipped away from the 'George' and found a telephone. It was a kiosk on the village green, and suited him well. He spoke to Craigie, and told him what he had heard. Craigie, sitting in the library of The Maples, didn't lose much time, gave Kerr a succinct résumé of the events at Tarrington, and then said:

"Follow Mulling if he goes out. Book a room at the pub for the night, act as you think best, of course, if there's an emergency, and keep your eyes open. All right?"

"All right," said Kerr.

He replaced the receiver and stepped out of the kiosk; and as he did so he caught a glimpse of the man who had been hiding in the shadows of the trees lining the village green. He watched the man moving, his eyes narrowed; and then he saw the form of Mr. Mulling. Mr. Mulling had been watching him, and that knowledge made Kerr very thoughtful.

Mulling was in the private bar of the 'George' when the Department Z agent returned. He eyed Kerr strangely; and Kerr eyed him affably, booked a room and looked more than a little tipsy. He went to his room early, and then started a tour to find the bathroom.

The bathroom was likely to be useful, for the simple reason that in searching for it he could open every room door and, if he blundered, apologize profusely. He didn't blunder. The 'George' was free of visitors, but in one room, three doors removed from his own, Bob Kerr saw an interesting thing.

A suit-case was open on a bed; the case was half filled, and drawers in a dressing-chest were open. Someone was packing;

and as the initials on the case were 'F.M.' it was not hard to imagine that it might belong to Mr. Mulling.

"Beating it," murmured Kerr to himself. He saw all he wanted to see, and turned towards the door, hoping hard that his luck would last. It lasted; it lasted in a remarkable manner, although most people would have admitted that Kerr had more than a little to say about the issue.

For as he reached his door he saw that it was shut.

He had not closed it when he had left; he had deliberately left it ajar, in case of urgent need to get away. He eyed it thoughtfully. Someone had been in, and had been too careful about closing the door. That meant someone was either in there still, or had been searching, or had left something. Possibly a maid, of course, but Kerr wasn't happy.

In his brief talk with Craigie he had heard of the shooting and he knew that this was no child's play. He wondered whether Mulling was really suspicious of him, and knew, in his heart, that the man was. He wondered whether Mulling had tried any trick, and he told himself that it wasn't likely. Damn it—

Footsteps came slowly up the stairs at the end of the passage, and Kerr looked round. He half expected Mulling. With a sigh of relief he saw the gloomy-faced potman, hater of Mulling.

"'Night, sir." The potman was civil to the dispenser of free beer.

"Hallo," said Kerr, lying on the spur of the moment. "I say, I've shut my door and left my key inside. I wonder if—"

"*Soon* put that right, sir." The man took a ring of keys from his capacious pocket. "Master-key'll do it, sir. Won't keep you 'arf a mo."

It happened before Kerr could stop it, while Kerr was wondering whether he ought to let the man go in.

The potman turned the key in the lock and pushed the door open. The explosion that came was a deafening detonation. A flash of vicious white light that blinded Kerr; a red-and-yellow glare followed and then a gust of wind that sent Kerr flying against the wall, his head buried in his hands to save himself from flying débris; and from other, grimmer, flying things than débris.

5

MULLING BREAKS DOWN

K err didn't know how long he leaned against the wall, his head thudding, his eyes blinded. A minute at least, but probably more. He didn't hear the thudding of footsteps up the stairs, the raised voices of frightened maids, the clattering of the wood of the door and the plaster from the walls. He was stunned mentally if not physically, and for that few minutes the horror of it was the only thing that pierced his mind.

The man was dead, literally blown to pieces; and he'd sent him there.

Another man than Kerr might have had as his first reaction a relief at the escape from being blown into eternity; Kerr's first thought was the fact that he'd been responsible for the man being wiped out. God! It was ghastly.

And then someone was shaking his arm, someone else was slapping his cheeks. A man; a woman. Voices came vaguely through the droning haze of his mind.

"Are you all right, sir—are you all right?"

A man was speaking, but there was nothing about the voice

that was in any way familiar. Kerr blinked and stared at the fellow stupidly. A tall, pot-bellied man, with a red face that was now tinged with the pallor that had come from shock.

"Sir—*are* you all right?" The man was plaintive now as he appealed. And the woman—a neat little body who seemed very self-possessed—spoke fast on his words.

"I'll 'phone for the doctor, Ted."

It was the word 'doctor' that brought Kerr back to normal; and it was typical of the man that it happened quickly, as quickly almost as the shock which had stunned him. He drew a deep breath, looked about him, and then found a smile; it was a mockery of a smile, but it served its purpose.

"Yes, I'm all right," he said. "I could do with a drink."

"That ye could," said the woman, and she turned away quickly. Kerr saw that she shooed half a dozen scared maids away from the head of the stairs, and then he regarded the pot-bellied man, whose name was Ted and who was assistant manager of the George Hotel.

That gentleman was immensely relieved.

"I was afraid someone was hurt, sir. It was a dreadful noise —dreadful! What on earth—"

"Steady," said Kerr. "Someone was hurt."

He eyed the man keenly, and saw that the news was really unexpected. He felt sick again at the need for telling what had happened; but there it was, and he couldn't avoid it.

"The potman," he said.

"There's no sign of him," said the other.

"A bomb went off," said Kerr simply.

And then the thing happened that did more than anything else to bring Kerr round completely. For the man with the pronounced paunch and the red face simply stared; and then his eyes closed and he collapsed. Kerr could understand why. He steadied the other's fall, and then he lit a cigarette. He wanted to think. Think! He had to; he had to decide what next to do and how to do it. The obvious answer was—find Mulling, and by the time the woman was back with a tumbler of whisky he had reached the decision, although he had to postpone acting on it for a few minutes. For the trim little woman eyed the man on the floor in alarm.

"What's *he* bin doing?"

Kerr took a sip of the neat whisky and found it good, and then he eyed her steadily.

"Can you take bad news?" he asked.

"I can take good and bad, sir."

"Well, there was someone else here when the explosion happened. That's all."

"Someone else—" Her eyes widened, and for a moment she didn't understand what he meant. Then the realization flooded through her mind and what colour she had disappeared. But she kept her feet and her nerve, although she looked hard at the whisky; Kerr obliged her with a spot.

"Who was it?" she asked quietly.

"The potman."

"Oh. Jerry. Poor—devil."

Kerr eyed her shrewdly, nodded, and eased himself away from the wall.

"'Poor devil's right," he said. "Now I must see Mr. Mulling. Call a doctor, and then call the police. Do you know where Mulling is?"

"He was downstairs in the office a minute ago, sir."

"Didn't he hear the bang?"

The little woman, sharp-featured and self-possessed, seemed to hesitate. Then she shrugged her shoulders.

"He must have. But he didn't come out."

"Thought it was outside probably," said Kerr. "Downstairs and then turn right for the office, don't I?"

"Turn left, sir. The second door."

"Thanks," said Kerr, glad of the information.

He went down the stairs slowly. The group of scared and curious maids, not without one or two of the menservants at the 'George', were eying him with something more than interest. He didn't seem to notice them as he pushed his way through, turned towards the left and approached the second door.

Mulling's clothes were upstairs in his room, some of them packed. The man had been preparing for a flight, but Kerr was by no means sure that he'd gone. The thing was—what was he to do if he found Mulling in there? What was the best plan? Craigie had advised him to follow the rabbity owner of the pub, but Craigie hadn't contemplated immediate flight like this.

Kerr didn't take long to decide.

The explosion had been a deliberate attempt to kill him, of course. Mulling must have inspired it. True, Mulling had not created the impression that he was the type capable of setting a bomb that would do such devastating damage as the thing had, but there were others in this game besides Mulling. Kerr had never seen a man who was so decidedly a tool in stronger hands.

Who were the others?

Kerr knew that Julius Mort was connected with this affair somehow or other, but from his slight knowledge of Mort he judged that the financier was not a man with nerve enough for a job of that nature. Someone else, then. But who?

Mulling would know.

Mulling must talk, and the quicker the better.

Robert McMillan Kerr, with a memory of the murder he had just seen clear in his mind's eye, entered the office with a grim determination to get at the truth, or some of it. He didn't knock; the door wasn't locked, although he'd been half prepared for such a contingency, but as it happened Mulling had made a fatal mistake and forgotten to turn the key.

The pub owner was sitting at a large desk with a mass of papers spread about it. Another heap of papers was on the floor, and yet another, burning merrily, was in the open grate of the room.

Mulling swung round in his chair as the door opened; and when he saw Kerr he just stared. Kerr was getting used to people staring at him; but that horrible fixed glare in the man's eyes, a fear that almost seemed audible, was different from anything he had met before. Mulling didn't speak; his lips were open and he seemed transfixed. It was literally as though he was looking at a ghost.

Kerr's smile wasn't one of humour. He entered the room and closed the door very slowly.

"You didn't expect me, Mulling?"

There was no answer; that fixed stare didn't alter.

"Back from the dead, eh?" said Kerr, and he sat on the corner of the man's desk, less than two feet away from him. "I'm back, but someone else has gone. Murder, Mulling, is an offence punishable by death by hanging. Didn't you know that?"

The man was scared, of course, and Kerr wanted to break down whatever resistance remained. He wanted to reduce Mulling to a shrieking, frenzied creature who would talk—talk—*talk!* Who would tell everything he knew, and would help Kerr and the Department in a great many ways. But would the ruse work?

Mulling tried to speak. He couldn't. Kerr went on in his low, casual voice almost as though this was an ordinary conversation and he had known Mulling for years.

"Your potman—a man named Jerry, I'm told—caught it

instead of me. He's quite dead. It's a shame you'll have to hang for the wrong man, Mulling, but there it is."

"I—I didn't! I didn't!" The man's terror was nauseating, but it was what Kerr wanted just then, and he laughed. There was something jarring and unpleasant in the sound.

"Didn't you?" asked Kerr. "What didn't you?"

"I didn't do it—I didn't, I tell you!"

"No? Then who did?"

"I—I can't tell you. But it wasn't me; I tried to stop it! I swear I did, Kerr. I'll do anything, anything—"

"You'll hang by the neck," said Robert McMillan Kerr, "until you're dead. Didn't you think of that?"

"I tried to stop it, I tell you! They couldn't hang me for that! He forced me away from the passage—I couldn't stop him—"

"The 'he' being?"

Kerr hoped he'd won; but Mulling, scared out of his skin as he was, didn't answer immediately, and Kerr needed no telling that the man had an even greater fear of the 'he' than of Kerr and the police—at the moment.

"I mustn't tell you. I—*can't!*"

"Will you ask the Court to believe that?"

Mulling's terror increased, if that were possible. He shot his hands out imploringly, and Kerr was half afraid he would go down on his knees. Kerr's face was set, grim and relentless.

"The Court—needn't know," Mulling gasped. "Don't tell the police about this, Kerr! I swear I tried to stop it. I tell you—"

Kerr went on remorselessly, with the ruthlessness that made him the star agent of the Department that had started on the heels of a game which had already led to murder and attempted murder. His voice hadn't raised once above the low, almost monotonous level at which it had started. His eyes, grey and deep-seeing, didn't falter.

"Mulling, don't be a fool. You know what happened. You know a man was killed. I happen to know you were in the thing somewhere, and you've proved it. I can't keep away from the police. They've got to know. And there's just one way"—the words came out like ice, and Mulling was shivering—"to stop yourself being hung. And that's by talking. If you *did* try to save the thing happening, tell us who did it. It's your one hope."

Mulling was very quiet now; he was like a man who saw death and knew it was unavoidable, and whose fear was suddenly numbed because of it.

"I can't talk," he said dully. "I daren't. If I did he'd kill me, Kerr, he'd kill me!"

"Would he? You'd have police protection, and you'll stand a better chance of getting away from him than the police. You've just that thin chance, Mulling. And remember—hung from the neck until you are—"

He stopped.

For the fear had flooded back through Mulling's mind now and the man had suddenly thrown himself forward, his eyes blazing, his hands clutching at Kerr's coat.

"I'll tell you—but you must protect me, you must! I'll tell you if you'll promise—"

"Of course I'll look after you," Kerr said, and he didn't allow the triumph that he felt to reveal itself in his expression. "Who was it, Mulling?"

Mulling hesitated.

He seemed to be fighting with himself, as though trying to remake the decision, to alter it. But his lips opened. He didn't look at Kerr; he looked past the man from Department Z.

"He'll never forgive me," he sobbed. "But—his name is Mannopoli. Mannopoli! And you'll find him at—"

He stopped; and it was as well for Kerr that he had been

looking at the man's face. For he saw the change of expression and he guessed what it was. He saw the spasm of fear across Mulling's eyes, and as it came he jerked himself backwards, off the desk, towards the wall. As he was going he rooted to his pocket for his gun; as he was going he saw the flash of flame and heard the roar of the shot from an unsilenced gun. He even saw the way Mulling crumpled up.

But before Mulling slumped down, Kerr's gun was in his hand and his finger was on the trigger.

Two shots—one from the door, one from Kerr, stabbed out simultaneously, or so it seemed. But there was a fraction of a second's difference, and Kerr won. His bullet bit into the arm of the man in the doorway; the attacker's bullet went wide.

Kerr caught a glimpse of him.

A tall, abnormally lean man, with satyrishly sharp features and a yellow tinge to his skin. His mouth was twisted; the expression in his eyes was unspeakable. Kerr saw that before the man pulled the door to; and Kerr's second bullet pecked into the wood.

"Blast!" said Kerr, and moved from the desk like a shot. But as he was moving he heard a key turn in the lock; he stopped half-way and swung round, but he saw at a glance that there were no windows in the small office. The only way out was through the door, and that was locked.

There were ways and means of picking it, but Kerr didn't try. The gunman had a sixty-second start, quite enough for him to get too far away for Kerr to follow him. He could hear the bellowing of voices and the occasional shriek from one of the maids as he hesitated, but he ignored it and the crumpled figure of Mulling, and reached for the telephone.

The operator answered quickly and he snapped the word "Police." The grimness of his voice brought speed, and a gruff, somewhat dismal response came quickly, almost as though the owner was prepared to grouse at being disturbed when he was off duty.

"Michford police-station speaking."

"Special Branch Z," said Kerr, and it was enough to make sure the man did what he told him, to erase his scowl. "Tele-phone to the nearest police radio station for a call to bring in a man named Mannopoli—Mannopoli—six-feet one—very thin—sharp features—dressed in grey—wounded right hand or forearm—eyes light grey." He paused between each word, giving the man at the other end time to take notes, then added quickly: "Last seen in Michford village. Have you got all that?"

"Yes—yes, sir." The constable seemed thunderstruck. "I'll—I'll get the message out at once, sir, at once!"

"Try to do it quicker," said Kerr. He added, "Thanks," and rang down. Then he called the number of The Maples.

Fallow's resonant voice answered, but Craigie was on the line very quickly. Kerr related the affair baldly. Craigie made little comment until the other had finished. Then:

"Are you all right?"

"Yes."

"But Mulling's dead?"

"Yes. There are some papers here."

"I'll come over," said Craigie. "You might telephone to London for Davidson and Carruthers. Tell them to be ready, and describe our man. Will you do that?"

"Yes," Kerr promised, and he rang down.

It was obvious—and had been for some minutes now—that there was nothing at all he could do for Frederick Mulling. That the man had been killed with the address of Mannopoli on his lips was a bitter thought, but the name itself gave the Department something concrete to work on, and Kerr was telling himself as he sighed and then put through the call to London that the chase might not be a long one after all. Yet there was something unpleasantly direct about the way in which Mannopoli used a gun and bombs. Kerr could have swallowed the gun, but the other thing was too much.

He was not long being connected to the Mayfair number of a certain Wally Davidson. Kerr guessed—with reason—that the local operator had listened in to his chat with the police and had decided that he was a man who demanded respect.

A slow, somewhat lackadaisical voice came over the wires; to look at and listen to Wally Davidson was one of the laziest men living. Actually he was as capable as most men of acting, and his laziness was an affectation. Kerr knew him reasonably well, and liked the man.

"Davidson?"

"Hallo, Bob. What are you popping up for?"

"C. wants you to get ready," Kerr said, maintaining the regular Department rule not to mention Craigie's name. "A man named Mannopoli. Mannopoli—"

"Spell, can't you?"

"Wally, I'm in a hurry, so take it in phonetically. Mannopoli. Six-feet-one." He repeated the description he had given the policeman, while Davidson grunted "Mm" after every item. Then he went on: "Be ready for trouble any time, old man. The others and I'll be up there fairly soon, I fancy."

"I'm not sorry," said Davidson gently; "I'm tired of doing nothing, and criminals aren't what they were."

"In your young days they were probably effective," murmured Kerr, "but it's so long ago I don't remember. You've no idea where Carruthers is, have you?"

"He and me," said Wally Davidson, "are meeting later. He's been out with a bit, but she's got a headache, and he 'phoned me. We were going to do a stag crawl—"

"You'll be wiser to get some sleep while you can," said Kerr.

"You're a swab," mourned Davidson. "So damned blunt, old

man, and I can't get used to it. You want to finesse a bit more. I
—" Mr. Davidson broke off suddenly, and—in London, of
course—grinned, for Robert McMillan Kerr had hung up his
receiver. Kerr hadn't time for trivialities, and in any case he
did not feel like them at that moment.

Two bodies—or, more correctly, two killings. Neither of
them pleasant. He could just see Mulling's open eyes, staring
at nothing, glazed and horrible. He shuddered; and then the
banging came on the door of the office.

"Hallo," called Kerr.

"Open the door, please. Open the door!"

"It's locked," said Kerr. He recognized the sharp voice of
the little woman, and he thought kindly of her. She certainly
kept her head, and most of the others were probably flat out
by now with shock and excitement. Certainly it was a day of
days in the life of the 'George,' even if Mulling would neither
benefit nor suffer from the inevitable notoriety.

The woman hesitated, and then called again.

"I'll get a master-key if you'll wait a minute."

Kerr waited until she returned, and he stood at the door as
she opened it, preventing her from looking inside. Whether
she understood why or not he didn't know, but she looked at
him keenly and then stepped a couple of yards away.

"You're not hurt, sir?"

"I'm afraid Mr. Mulling is, badly. Has the doctor arrived
yet?"

"Yes. He's upstairs now. What—what happened?"

It was the first time she had evinced the slightest curiosity,
and Kerr warmed to her again.

"Mulling was shot," he said. "Did you see the man?"

"I—I tried to stop him, sir, but I failed." She held up her
right arm, and he saw the ugly bruise on it. "It's a friend of Mr.
Mulling—"

65

Kerr's eyes glinted.

"He's been here often, has he?"

"Every month, regular as clockwork."

"Thanks a lot. I'll probably have one or two questions to ask before long. You'll be in all the time, of course?"

"I'm always on duty," said the woman, with a frosty smile, "although what'll happen now I *don't* know. Would you like a drink, sir, before you see the doctor?"

"It's an idea that's got a lot to commend it," said Kerr, and when she stared he smiled—a rare, transfiguring smile—and added: "Yes, please."

He turned back to the office to wait for it, and he told himself he needed it, although he hadn't realized it before. As he moved he saw the trail of blood-spots along the floor of the passage, and he wondered how badly he had hurt Mannopoli. He half wished he'd gone up to the doctor first, but he realized that the man could do nothing. Even a post-mortem would reveal no new characteristic of the death of Mulling.

He glanced down reflectively at the body; it was queer, but Mulling's death had affected him very little, perhaps because he believed the man had raised no serious opposition to the bomb outrage.

He saw something gleaming yellow, half in and half out of Mulling's vest pocket, and he took it between his fingers. One end was spattered with blood, but otherwise it was unmarked. It was a small, diamond-shaped card, a rich yellow colour, and he wondered idly what it was.

Craigie and Toby Arran could have given him a little information; and Craigie was strongly of the opinion that Miss Ellen Granting could have provided a lot more.

6

IDEAS AND OTHER THINGS

There isn't a great deal that we can do," said Gordon Craigie. "We've got the man's name, and a good description of him. We've three coloured cards, all diamond-shaped." He smiled at Toby Arran, but there was not a great deal of humour in his expression, for Craigie was worried by those mysterious coloured cards. "We've those papers from Mulling's office that I'll go through when we get to London: and that seems the lot."

Kerr nodded. Toby Arran slumped down in a chair in the saloon bar of the 'George'—which was closed now by Government orders that were not special to the occasion.

"The police will try to tidy this up?" Kerr asked.

"I've spoken to the Devon Chief Constable on the telephone," said Craigie, as precise as ever, "and he's contacting immediately with Scotland Yard. This place will open as a public-house, but will be closed as an hotel until further notice. I don't think there's much more to interest us in Devon. The regular visits that the woman told us about aren't likely to be continued. But Mort was the third member of the trio all right, and we'll be watching Mr. Mort very closely."

"You're not forgetting," Toby said, "the girl at Fallow's."

"I'm not," said Craigie, "and I'm going to have her watched, but that isn't your job, Toby. I'll send someone else. Are Davidson and Carruthers ready, Kerr?"

"Yes, they'll be there."

"Then we'll get back."

"You're not going to see Fallow again?"

"No. Two local policemen are watching the house for the time being, and that's all we need worry about. Toby's car is out of order, so we'll use mine."

"No, we won't," said Kerr, and smiled. "Gordon, you're getting old. Mr. Mannopoli isn't a gentleman to stop at crashing a car, but two cars will make it awkward for him. Toby and I'll go in front. You'll follow us."

Craigie smiled a little thinly and agreed. Within ten minutes Kerr was at the wheel of a hired Talbot, with Toby Arran next to him, and Craigie in his own car—a Siddeley saloon—brought up the rear. At Craigie's side were the papers that had been taken from Mulling's room.

Craigie himself did not think there was much likelihood of another murder attempt that night. There were limits, he reasoned, even to Mannopoli's accomplishments, and that yellow-faced gentleman had done more than enough for one day. But Kerr wasn't so sure: nor was Arran. Both Kerr and Arran had one advantage over Craigie: they'd seen Mannopoli, and they knew something of the power that his very eyes suggested and his actions somehow confirmed.

And they were right.

* * *

The late Mr. Frederick Mulling had known that Mannopoli was no fool. He had known also that on certain occasions the man could be deadly. But it had never come to him with such force until that evening.

Mannopoli had telephoned him after the visit to the house in Tarrington, given instructions, and expected them to be carried out. Soon after Kerr's arrival Mannopoli had approached the 'George' by a roundabout route, and entered through the rear of the premises. Mulling had told him of his suspicions of Kerr; and Mannopoli, with a callous cold-bloodedness that had appalled the other man, had laid plans for Kerr's sudden demise.

In a case which Mannopoli always left at the 'George,' the little bomb had been hidden; there were several of them in the case Mulling had seen. Mannopoli had set the bomb by the door, after seeing Kerr on his prowl, and then had left the house. He had waited a while, heard the explosion, returned soon afterwards, expecting to hear that Kerr had gone, and had overheard Mulling about to give away his address; already his name was known to the man from Department Z.

What had happened after that Kerr knew, up to the moment that the scared servants at the inn had seen Mannopoli leap into a waiting car—chauffeur-driven—and career off in a southerly direction.

Mannopoli's right forearm had given him pain, and after ten miles had been put between himself and the pub he had dressed it with the first-aid equipment in the car. His chauffeur, a sour-visaged specimen of the tough variety, had watched phlegmatically. He had worked for Mannopoli for years, more than long enough to know that what Mannopoli did mattered to no one. The chauffeur—whose name was Quaife—did exactly as he was told, neither more nor less. Above all things he never asked a question.

"Get back on the London road," said Mannopoli.

Quaife guessed that the police would be on the look-out now, but the car—a Daimler, although no one had identified it at the village—was large enough to hide the man sitting in the tonneau. He got back on the London road without waiting for further encouragement, although he avoided Michford.

Some twenty miles farther on Mannopoli pressed a buzzer in the window frame, and the chauffeur slowed down. Mannopoli snapped an order.

"Turn up the first narrow lane past this corner."

Quaife obeyed; in less than five minutes the Daimler was hidden from the main road, along a lane that was little more than a cart-track. Mannopoli climbed out, and walked towards the corner, where he was hidden by the shadows, and he carried with him two little gadgets like that which had blown Jerry the potman into eternity. It was not the first time Quaife had seen similar playthings, and when his employer handed him one he took it without turning a hair.

"Wait a hundred yards up the road," Mannopoli said. "If I whistle, throw it at the first car that comes afterwards. Is that clear?"

"All clear, sir."

Mannopoli nodded, and Quaife walked off, a stolid figure who disappeared quickly in the gloom. Mannopoli fingered a whistle—smaller but as piercing as the police issue—with his left hand, which was not so badly hurt. The bomb was in his pocket and was likely to remain there for some time.

He didn't know how long Kerr and Craigie would be, but he was prepared to stake a lot on their returning to London that night by road. He was, above all things, a man of exemplary patience. If he had to wait a couple of hours it couldn't be helped.

What had to be stopped was the continued existence of

Kerr and Craigie—and the man Arran, if it were possible to get all three of them at once.

Mannopoli had, as Mulling had known and Mort knew, a complicated organization in which crime was the leading factor. But his activities were much more complicated than either Mort or Mulling had ever conceived, and he had come to Michford prepared to put a particularly grandiose plan into action.

Thanks to Mr. Mort and his letter it had miscarried, and other plans were endangered.

Mannopoli had learned many things from that. Craigie, for instance, was suspicious of Mort. Craigie and Fallow had a working arrangement—Mannopoli's lips twisted at that thought—and the British Intelligence was likely to be awkward. In his activities as a member of the 'M' syndicate—Mort, Mulling and Mannopoli—he knew nothing of the Department, but in other respects he knew a great deal about it, and he knew it was a simple question of kill or be killed: not necessarily in person, but certainly in the way of ambitions. Mannopoli, who loved money among other things, saw a sum approaching seven figures disappearing if the Department really got on his tail, and he wasn't going to take half-measures. He had already seen enough of Kerr and Arran to know that the Department's reputation was not a thing of legend. They were dangerous men.

They weren't as dangerous, Mannopoli thought, as he was.

But the night was chill, and he was beginning to curse the delay. In half an hour only seven or eight cars had passed the spot where he was standing.

It was an advantageous spot, for he had chosen a place near a sharp bend in the road, where drivers in both directions had to slow down to five or ten miles an hour for safety's sake. He could therefore see the drivers and the passengers, and have ample time to use the little gadget that was warming in his pocket.

Half an hour; it was now well past ten. Why the devil didn't they come?

Mannopoli forgot them, and thought of Mort.

He'd frightened Mort that day; but Mort would be a great deal more frightened when he learned of Mulling's death. Mort, scared for his life, would be a useful ally, even more useful than he had been up to yet. Yes, Mr. Mort was going to have some worries.

Mannopoli smiled, and the expression on his face was literally diabolic. He fingered the bomb thoughtfully, but resigned himself to wait. Once this was over things would run smoothly; it was just as well that in England only Mort and Mulling had ever known him as Mr. Mannopoli. Other people knew him as Mr. Manne, which would not help the police a great deal. Not that Augustus Mannopoli thought he had a great deal to fear from the police.

"Perishing cold," muttered Toby Arran. "Cut the speed down a bit, old son."

"We're in a hurry," said Kerr. "Why didn't you bring a coat?"

"What the hell's that got to do with you?" Toby was not feeling at his best by a long way, and the chilly drive—they had been going for only five minutes and Michford was but three miles behind them—was likely to be an even worse ordeal than the adventures of Lucy, Liza or Peter—take your choice. But for the green card he might have reflected with pleasure on the face, form and figure of Ellen Granting, but in that direction also his thoughts were glum.

Kerr smiled to himself, knowing little and guessing a lot. He felt sorry for Toby's shivers, but he wanted to get to London just as quickly as the Talbot and Craigie's Siddeley behind them could manage it. Until they were snug in Craigie's office or his own flat he would not feel happy.

Just seven miles ahead—less than five minutes away—Mr. Mannopolis stood in the shadows, holding a bomb; and a matter of a few split seconds farther on Mr. Quaife waited also.

Kerr didn't know; Arran didn't know. They went headlong towards eternity, and as Kerr's foot pressed harder on the accelerator when the road allowed it, their speed increased, and the minutes between them and Mannopoli decreased with it.

"Still cold?" Kerr asked two minutes later.

"Worse. Why the devil didn't we go by train?"

"You and the Devil," said Kerr, "should be good friends by now. I don't know. I wish we had."

"Why?"

"I don't know."

"Don't tell me," said Toby, "that you've got a hunch. You had a hunch once before and it gave me a nasty feeling for a long time afterwards." Toby forgot his shivers and frowned. "Any reason for it, Bob?"

"Just Mr. Mannopoli's face."

"Funny, but I feel it too. The swab's eyes—"

"Unpleasant!" said Kerr.

"Unpleasant my hat! They were the nastiest I've seen, and I've seen some. And he's quick on a gun."

"Yes."

"And slick with time-fuses."

"That wasn't a time-fuse bomb," said Kerr patiently, and he came down on the accelerator as they turned a corner and reached a flat stretch—two miles ahead of which Mr. Mannopoli was waiting. "It was a detonator worked on the concussion principle, Toby, and don't you forget it. I—what? Good God! *I'm* doing sixty!"

Bob Kerr, for once in his life, was taken aback.

The Talbot was touching sixty: the little low-lying Singer Sports that flashed past them must have been touching the eighty mark. It went with a *zoooooom*! And then they saw the red eye of its tail-light, but Toby Arran had seen something else.

"Bob." His voice was tense.

"H'm?"

"I've seen that car before, to-night."

"*Have* you, by God! Mannopoli's?"

"No-o." Toby seemed to be having trouble with his larynx, while Kerr came heavier still on the hired Talbot and blessed the fact that it was capable of seventy-five if not more. "Er—at The Maples.*Fallow's* car."

"Fallow's? You're sure?"

"The girl was driving it," Toby Arran said simply.

To Bob Kerr that piece of information meant little; to Toby Arran it meant a lot. He'd glimpsed the girl's profile as the car had passed, although from that alone he would not have recognized her. But coupled with the Singer which he had seen on Fallow's drive and later in his garage, there could be no mistake.

"I see," said Kerr. "It's odd. What shall I do?"

"Catch up, drat you." Toby knew it was the only thing to do, although for his part he would have willingly let the car get away. After all, it *might* be a legitimate run; eighty miles an hour at ten-thirty at night was a bit thick, but it wasn't a crime.

"Craigie's dropping behind," said Kerr. "His bus can't do

much more than sixty. But still—"

The speedometer was showing seventy-eight now, and the sports car in front was within a hundred yards. Very slowly they caught up on it. Both Kerr and Arran felt an urgent need for seeing the girl, for making sure there'd been no mistake. If she was on the road to London in a blazes of a hurry, Kerr was prepared to wonder why.

"She's slowing down," Toby said, after a pause.

"A nasty bend in the road along there, if I remember rightly," said Bob Kerr. "She'll have to slow down to twenty, anyhow. And by the same token so will we."

"Anything nasty behind it?" Toby asked, and he wasn't thinking of the waiting of Mr. Mannopoli.

"A sharp S bend. Craigie'll catch us up here, anyhow. I wish you could have a word with her."

"What for? I can't ask her what she's doing."

"All right; I can," murmured Robert McMillan Kerr, and he slowed down to fifteen miles an hour as he took the sharp bend less than ten yards behind the Singer. He didn't see Mr. Mannopoli. He couldn't have seen the thing in Mannopoli's hands, or the whistle at Mannopoli's lips. He did know that Craigie was less than ten yards behind still, that the girl was less than ten yards ahead. A trio of cars which, if the bomb came, would be smashed to smithereens.…

Mannopoli saw three things at the same time.

He had the bomb ready for hurling; he saw the light-painted Singer in the lead, car and occupant very clear in the headlights from Kerr's car. He saw Kerr and Arran, sitting in the front of the Talbot, illuminated from the headlights of Craigie's car. His lips were a thin gash across his face, and his eyes were vile. Then he saw the Singer's driver's profile.

He went icy cold.

The girl—Granting! She was here!

It flashed through Mannopoli's mind like lightning. If he threw the bomb, the girl would go as well as the men. In that split second he had to decide which was worth more—the death of the men or the life of the girl. Just a split second; the three cars were racing now, the Singer passed him, the Talbot on a level and Craigie's Siddeley was very close behind.

And Mr. Augustus Mannopoli, his face working, lowered his arm and didn't let the bomb go. Nor did he whistle. Mr. Quaife saw the cars flash by, and murmured to himself they were cutting some speed, they were.

And the Chief of Department Z with his two agents were safe for the time being. It wasn't likely they would ever know the hairsbreadth between life and death at the moment they had turned the last curve of the S bend.

Mr. Mannopoli, his thoughts even blacker than his expression, muttered something that could only be called an obscenity out of politeness and called a high-pitched, recognizable cry, for Quaife. Then he trudged slowly, wearily, up the muddy lane towards the Daimler. He had an idea that life was going to be difficult.

"That girl," said Bob Kerr, "knows she's being followed."

"Does she?" Arran didn't seem enthusiastic.

"She does. She travels fifty; so do we. She goes up ten; so do we. She drops twenty—for no reason at all on a flat road— and of course we do. She has a head on her shoulders, has that young lady."

"And a damned pretty head, too."

"Looks," said Kerr, and the single word was enough. He was one of those peculiar men who preferred brains to beauty. "I wonder if... *Hallo!*"

For the Singer, now fifty yards ahead, had sent out the turn-right indicator yet showed no sign of turning. It was slowing down, and Kerr followed suit, frowning. The Singer stopped, and before Kerr had a chance of passing the girl was out of her seat and standing in the road, vivid in the Talbot's headlights.

"*Blast* her," said Kerr, and jammed on his brakes.

Toby Arran didn't. He could see the girl's astonishing beauty, even in that garish light, and he believed she was smiling. It would be a long time before he forgot the episode outside the bathroom.

He kept in his seat as the girl approached. She was dressed in a dark leather coat, a small hat on her fair hair, and she looked a picture. She *was* smiling.

"I thought perhaps it was you," she said, speaking to Toby but glancing curiously at Kerr. Her self-possession was a thing to marvel at.

"Nice of you," said Toby, for some reason nettled by her manner. "Miss Granting—Mr. Kerr. Er—speed-fiend?"

"Any objections?"

"No one," said Toby, "should risk losing life or limb quite like you did. Particularly you."

She smiled, and Kerr could see why she had made such an impression on the little man.

"No? You weren't doing badly." She had a habit, as Toby had learned earlier in the evening, of putting questions that were devilishly difficult to answer. Toby was preparing an inanity when Kerr broke in. He was smiling, but she hardly knew what to make of his smile; others had felt the same about Bob Kerr as he had looked at them, head cocked a little on one side, and the gleam in his grey eyes reflective.

"In a hurry for something special?"

Two things were in Toby's mind. One that she'd probably

flare up at the question; two that Gordon Craigie—who had slowed down and whose car was now stationary—would be even more thoughtful about Miss Ellen Granting. Damn it.

He was relieved of one thing quickly.

"As a matter of fact," she said to Kerr, "I am. A friend of mine has been taken ill suddenly, and Mr. Fallow let me take the car. There isn't a train for another three hours. But I thought you were following me, and I couldn't resist making sure."

"Oh, *that's* all right," said Toby, immensely relieved. She had a legitimate excuse, and that was all he wanted to know. At another time he might have wondered whether it was the truth or not, but he preferred to believe her now. "Well—we won't detain you. Unless you'd like me as a relief driver?"

"Thank you, no," said Ellen Granting, and her smile was dazzling, even if it was a little tinged with sarcasm. "Perhaps we'll pass again on the road. Good night. Good night, Mr. Kerr."

She turned and reached the Singer, climbed in quickly, and started off. Craigie repressed his curiosity, Toby his annoyance, and the three cars moved along, slowly at first and then gathering speed.

Kerr was thoughtful, his mind full of ideas. The girl was interesting. She was on the way to London, and it was just possible her motives were not all she made out. Fallow was all right, but the girl, the green card, and particularly her reaction to it, all wanted some thinking out.

Toby Arran was mentally defending her, and yet puzzled. He didn't like this affair: 'murderous' was a mild word for it. He didn't want her murdered. Yet if she was mixed up in it somewhere, there was a fifty-fifty chance of her life ending abruptly.

And Gordon Craigie was thinking—also about Ellen

Granting—that he would look into her past more closely than he had done. He knew she'd been with Fallow for two years. He also knew that she had travelled the Continent a great deal before she had gone to the Devon village. And he too was worried by those three diamond-shaped coloured cards.

He was more than inclined to think that they represented identity-cards of some kind. The girl would be recognized if she showed the green one; Mulling the yellow; Mannopoli the blue. It was a little fantastic perhaps, but it suggested possibilities that Craigie didn't like. For if there was a large organization behind Mannopoli and the night's crimes, and members of it were known by colours and not by name, this was going to be the devil of a case.

Craigie didn't know that the girl had saved his life, nor did either of the others. Their thoughts would have been even more muddled had they done so.

They were at Salisbury when Bob Kerr made the next discovery.

For a hundred miles or more they'd been within easy distance of the Singer. Now, on a straight stretch of road that lasted for several miles, they saw nothing. Not even the swaying glow of the headlights, which had been their guide when the car had been out of sight before. Kerr swore under his breath, for he had hoped to follow Miss Granting to London; now he wouldn't have the chance. For she had turned off the main road, and they had no idea where she'd gone. She had, in short, sold them the dummy; that trick seemed her speciality.

7

PLANS GO AWRY

The three members of the Department Z reached London in the early hours of the morning, and even Gordon Craigie, who was a man reputed to be able to do without sleep, admitted that he was too weary to do anything until he had had a nap. He settled in one of the two large armchairs in the Department's only office, while Kerr took the other, and Toby Arran, glum, cold and miserable, went on to his flat. There had been a time when Toby had lived with his brother, one Timothy; Timothy was his twin, but Timothy was now married, and a partnership that had lasted thirty-four years and more was broken.

Toby tried to cheer himself as he entered his flat with the thought that Penelope Smith—now Mrs. Tim Arran—had not been eyed without suspicion by Kerr and Craigie during the particularly hectic venture which the Department had battled through against Gregory Marlin and others. In the records of the Department the affair had been called, somewhat ironically, the *Carriers of Death*. Toby didn't think it had carried any more death than this job was likely to; confound it, why couldn't he get that girl's face out of his mind? He'd never—literally never—been smitten before.

Toby went to bed, and dreamed.

Gordon Craigie and Kerr slept, without dreaming, in their respective chairs. A dim light was burning in one corner of the long, high room which served as Craigie's domestic quarters as often as it was used for Department work. For that reason the room was very different near the fire—which was alight most days and nights—from what it was at the far end.

This far end was furnished with a few filing-cabinets, several chairs—none of them comfortable for Craigie was something of an ascetic—a large, plain desk, bare of papers but adorned with three telephones.

The domestic end was furnished—if the word could be used with any accuracy—with the two large arm-chairs, a cupboard built in the wall, a small expanding bookcase filled with classics, all well thumbed, and other odds and ends that might have been found in any bachelor's flat. That night it was tidy; during the day a small table was usually strewn with oddments from the cupboard, from jam upwards, with collars, ties and other etceteras to make it look a mess; but Craigie usually tidied up before going out, and consequently it was immaculate that night.

Dawn was breaking when the telephone jarred the silence that had been broken by the even breathing of the two men.

Craigie opened his eyes and blinked; Kerr didn't open his eyes but cursed the row. Craigie yawned, stretched his arms above his head and, as the telephone jarred again, rose from his chair and walked towards it. By the time he had reached the table, he looked as if he had been awake for hours.

Kerr listened to the short conversation, his eyes still closed. But he opened them as Craigie replaced the receiver.

"Our job?"

"Ye-es. Nothing much. I'm told that Mannopoli was reported in Hampshire, but the police patrol lost him."

"Which suggests," said Kerr, stirring himself and looking, in his disarray, broader and shorter and grimmer than ever, "that he's in or near London."

"He'll more likely be here than anywhere else," admitted Craigie. "I'll ring for something to eat, Bob, while you wash and shave."

Kerr went out of the office—whose doors were manifold and all operated on the sliding principle by an electric push in Craigie's desk—to a bathroom near by. When he returned Craigie had contrived to get bacon and eggs and coffee, with new rolls. Kerr asked no questions, and they set to. And then, the meal over, Craigie said a lot in a little.

"We'll go through the papers."

It was a long job and a wearying one.

Mr. Mulling had kept a vast array of papers, account-books and other things. All of them purported to concern the George Hotel, Michford. Craigie saw very quickly that some of the accounts were entered in green ink and others in blue. The green figures were larger than those of the hotel takings; and each ledger entry was topped by one, two or three letters —never more than the three.

"A code," Kerr said.

"A simple one, I fancy," murmured Gordon Craigie thoughtfully. "Look, Bob."

He took a plain sheet of paper from a drawer in the desk and ran through the ledger pages, taking the letters at the top and jotting them down one after the other. They ran:

A.F.
A.M.
A.R.

A.R.M.
A.F.R.
A.R.G.
B.U.L.
B.E
C.A.
C.H.I.
C.Z.
D.
E.
F.I.
F.R.
G.
G.R.
H.O.
H.U.
I.
I.T.
N.
N.O.
P.O.
P.O.R.
R.U.
S.W.
S.W.E.
Y.

He finished, and tossed the sheet over to Kerr; but Kerr saw more from his Chief's eyes than from anything else.

"H'mm. Initials standing for what?"

"Think of a word beginning with 'Cz'," smiled Craigie.

"I don't think that I'll trouble," said Kerr. "I— Great Scott! Czechoslovakia! Countries, are they?"

"I'd be very surprised if they weren't," said Craigie. "A.F. for Africa, A.M. America, A.R. the Argentine, and so on. And I don't like it."

There was a tension in the office, grown suddenly electric. Kerr's face was set very hard, and Craigie was pursing his drooping lips. Neither of them spoke for several seconds, while Kerr stared at the sheet of paper and all that it might mean.

He saw beyond it as Craigie did.

He realized that if they were right—and there was not much likelihood of anything else—in the newly prosperous 'George' at Michford, that sleepy old South Country village, Mr. Frederick Mulling had been keeping accounts that covered a world-wide area. *World-wide!* If these letters meant what they appeared to, then hardly a country in the world was missing from the list.

Kerr realized something of what it meant.

Join a world-wide organization of this kind to the deadliness of the man named Mannopoli, and he could see the possible horror of it. True, there was nothing else. He didn't know whether the figures here represented 'trading' profits of some kind, or whether the figures themselves represented a code. All that was vague. But he could see the possibilities, and allied to that man with the sharp features and the yellow skin he didn't like them.

Nor did Craigie; but the Chief of Department Z found a smile and folded the paper thoughtfully.

"That's going to help, Bob. Now—you'd better get out and get busy. See Miller first, and ask him to have a look-out kept for Miss Granting. Then Carruthers and Davidson, and tell them to stand by. One of them"—Craigie looked thoughtful—"one of them might know Mort, and get into Mort's circle. Make sure, will you?"

Kerr rubbed his chin.

"I believe Carruthers does know Mort slightly. He thinks he's poison; and he thinks Mrs. Mort is—"

"Mrs. Mort is the angle he wants," Craigie said, and it was a remarkable fact that Bob Kerr needed no more explanation.

He left Craigie's office and went into Whitehall, thence into Parliament Street. Scotland Yard seemed dreary and grey; a few uniformed policemen who looked too warm—for the weather had changed and the nip in the air of the previous day was missing—and a few cars were lined up outside. Kerr went to the main entrance, up the stone steps, through the glass doors, and was saluted by a sergeant on duty.

"Is Mr. Miller in?" he asked.

"In his office five minutes ago, sir."

"Thanks. I'll see him."

He walked along the stone passages, and the hustle of the Yard grew more apparent now. Footsteps were echoing ceaselessly; half a dozen men passed him briskly, most of them holding buff-coloured forms. Many doors were open; men were talking either on the telephone or off it. Kerr passed the Chief Inspector's room as an acquaintance walked out, and he confirmed that Miller was in. Miller's office was two doors along.

Kerr tapped on the door and entered, and Superintendent Miller, the officer usually detailed to work with Department Z, looked up and smiled.

"Won't keep you a moment, Kerr."

Kerr sat down in a leather arm-chair and lit a cigarette. He looked round the room, but his gaze centred on Miller, a big man, inclined to be fleshy, with a dusty countenance and dusty hair. It was a fact that Miller looked as though he should have been in a mill or a bakery and a long way from Scotland Yard. He was an untidy man by nature, although he did his best to avoid creating that impression, and he looked, Kerr told himself yet again, as though he had been lightly dusted with flour.

Miller signed a paper with a flourish and pressed a bell.

"Well, Kerr? You're on this job?"

"You've heard about it, then?"

"Who hasn't? We're after the man named Mannopoli, and we're checking up on twenty-odd men of the name in London. Not that I expect to have much luck."

"You can't be sure," Kerr said. "But *twenty* Mannopolis in London? The name's a freak in itself."

"So's London," said Miller, with his rather obvious humour. He was a dour, stolid man, likable, astute, efficient and yet not over imaginative—which was perhaps a good thing. "There are nearly thirty of them registered, and the Lord knows how many who aren't. Had any luck?"

"Not much," said Kerr. "But here's another job for you. You know that Fallow's in this thing—John Fallow?"

"Yes, Craigie said so. How'd you get on with Fallow?"

"I didn't see him, but the others had no complaints."

"He's a sound man," said Miller, and from Miller that was praise. "What about him?"

"He's got a niece or something—their relationship is a bit vague—named Granting. Ellen Granting. She left Devon last night, and we saw her on the road. She lost us at Salisbury. Will you see if you can trace her?"

"Yes. You want it kept quiet, of course?"

"As quiet as you can," said Kerr. "We don't want the little lady alarmed just yet."

Miller chuckled, for he knew the meaning of that 'just yet', and he wondered who the girl was.

"And, of course, you're still watching Mort?" added Kerr.

Superintendent Horace Miller said that he was. He said it

in no very affable voice, for he didn't like Mr. Mort, that financier who knew just where the law was, and didn't hesitate to cross the line if he could do so with safety. Of all the men who had contrived to commit crimes of money without breaking the law, Mr. Julius Mort was the most successful and the most persistent offender. Coupled with that knowledge was the fact that Miller had once executed a warrant for Mort's arrest and later been forced to release the man for lack of evidence, and it was easy to see why Miller wasn't affable. That was some years ago, before he'd been raised to the Superintendency, and Mort had contrived to get the then Chief Constable to rap Miller's knuckles.

"Right-ho," said Kerr, who'd heard the history, and smiled. "I'm going to see Carruthers at his flat, and if anything should come in I'll be there for the next half-hour. Good-bye."

"Good luck," said Miller, and waved his hand before taking a document off a pile in front of him and beginning to read it. Mr. Miller was working at routine stuff, and he liked that no more than he liked Julius Mort.

Kerr left the Yard and decided to walk to Carruthers' flat.

Not for the first time, as he stepped out briskly, he wondered whether he'd get through this affair. There had been a period when his life had not been worth a moment's purchase, and this case was practically a parallel. He forgot it, and thought of the theory Craigie had formed of the green-ink entries in Mulling's book.

First a green card; then green ink; and blue and yellow cards to mix; Kerr needed no telling that blue and yellow, even mixed by an amateur, made green. Did that mean anything?

He smiled to himself for it occurred to him that if he wasn't careful he'd be going colour-blind, and that wouldn't help him. He reached Carruthers' flat—in Broome Street—and walked up the stairs towards it. Carruthers' man—Hobjoit by name—opened the door, bowed, and said that Mr. Carruthers was expecting him.

"What-ho!" said Bob Carruthers a few second later, and they shook hands. Carruthers was beaming; Carruthers beamed so often that the expression seemed permanent. He was an exquisite young man with very fair hair, light-blue eyes and sandy skin. He was dressed in silver-greys and looked dressed to kill.

"Ornamenting the flat as usual?" asked Kerr.

"Now listen, Bob," said Mr. Carruthers, "do what you like, say what you like, but keep it clean. What's all the fuss about?"

"I don't know yet."

"And tell the truth," said Mr. Carruthers as an afterthought.

"That is the truth," Kerr assured him, and chuckled. "You've met Mr. Mort, haven't you?"

"The Julius of the ilk?"

"Julius."

"If I meet him again I shall probably stifle him," said Carruthers—whose other name was also Robert. "Why?"

"You're going to make him a friend of yours," said Bob Kerr. "Know his wife?"

Carruthers didn't speak, but his expression said a great deal. He did know Mrs. Mort, and he was not enthusiastic.

"Out with it," chuckled Kerr.

"The gigolo hunter," Carruthers said, and lit a cigarette as though to counteract something unpleasant in his nostrils.

"I don't know her," Kerr said reflectively. "She's pretty warm by reputation."

"Ex-Follies," said Carruthers, as though that explained everything. "Lousy with money, and there you are. She's a looker for her age, I'll admit that."

"How old is she?"

"Forty or thereabouts, although I've heard her claim to be twenty-nine."

"And the ménage is a weird one?"

"Weird," said Carruthers, "is only one way of expressing it. She's positively surrounded by the money-hunters, for she's free with her money. She gathers the artistic set—save the word—and half Bohemia on occasions, to say nothing of Bloomsbury. On the three occasions," added Bob Carruthers, sitting down and stretching his legs before him, "when I've been at Mort's place in St. John's Wood, it's been a *Ran-Tan* on a small scale. Mind you"—Carruthers looked severe—"I'm not suggesting the woman's immoral."

"Certainly not," said Kerr.

"Queer thing," said Carruthers, "but I don't think she is. Faithful to Julius and all that. She likes a fuss made of her, and the handsomer the fusser the better she likes it."

"Any preference for colouring?"

"Colouring of what? Cosmetics?"

"Fussers, idiot."

"I've got you," said Carruthers, and didn't even smile. "No-o. No. Can't say I've heard the rumour. What's all your interest about, Bob?"

"How'd you get your knowledge of the lady?" countered Kerr.

"I have an aunt," said Carruthers, and left the subject as though there was nothing more to be said; but Kerr wasn't satisfied by a long way.

"Aunt who? And where connected with the Mort ménage?"

"Lives three doors away," said Carruthers. "But be a man, old son, spare me this history. What's on your mind?"

"You know Mrs. Mort?"

"*I* know Leila," said Bob Carruthers definitely enough.

"Has she ever shown"—Kerr smiled—"any favouritism towards you?"

"Thank the Lord I haven't been near enough."

"Try and get there," said Kerr gently.

Carruthers stared. It seemed to take several minutes before the words sank in, and even then he didn't seem prepared to admit he'd understood them properly. He scowled, waved his cigarette and looked offended.

"Haven't you heard what I've said about her, blast you?"

"I've heard," said Kerr, chuckling, "that you can hold your own with the best of them where the ladies are concerned, my son. If you can't pigeon-hole Leila Mort, you ought to be shot."

"But, damn it—"

"Business," said Kerr, and chuckled at the expression of disgust that crossed his friend's face. "It can't be helped, old son. Craigie wants all he can get on Julius Mort, and the best way is through his wife. It's lucky she's the type she is, and that you know her."

"And do you know," said Carruthers, "I joined up with Craigie because I liked fun. When has this confounded business got to start?"

"Will she be at home this afternoon?"

"I expect so."

"Try and see her. Get"—Kerr smiled—"fresh. But take a hint, Bob. Be careful. You don't know me; you've never heard of me. Clear?"

"It's clear," said Bob Carruthers glumly; "I wish it was as true that I hadn't heard of you, damn you. Leila Mort—oh, my Lord! I don't think I can stand it!"

"You might learn to like it," murmured Bob Kerr, and he heaved himself out of his chair. "I'm going round to see Davidson. Let me know if any message comes, will you?"

"Right-ho, old son. Love to the children and all that."

Carruthers beamed, happier in mind now, and went to the front door with Robert McMillan Kerr.

He nearly went farther.

The car was passing along Broome Street slowly, as though its driver was looking for a number. It was a small saloon, and it looked harmless. Neither Kerr nor Carruthers saw the man in the rear, nursing the gun; but Carruthers saw the first flash of yellow flame and heard the wicked *spit!* as the bullet pecked into the wood just behind his head. Kerr ducked and jerked himself backwards; Carruthers was a split second after him, but even as they closed the door the bullets were cracking through the glass, into the hall against the walls. Seven of them in quick succession; and then the hum of the engine as the car gathered speed.

While Bob Kerr and Bob Carruthers sat on the floor and regarded each other, they did not think that the situation possessed much humour.

"Close," said Kerr.

"They'd followed you," said Carruthers.

"So you can't handle Leila Mort after all."

"That's one blessing, anyhow. You weren't hit, were you?"

"I haven't learned about it yet if I was," said Kerr, getting slowly to his feet and examining the broken glass of the door thoughtfully. "That's particularly nasty, Bob, and the other tenants will be asking questions. Fight 'em off, will you?"

Some thirty seconds later Carruthers scowled and wished Bob Kerr to perdition. For Kerr, the immediate danger passed, hurried out of the house while six other flat tenants came, in ones and twos and all indignant, to know what had happened. Carruthers was a glib-tongued man but even he wasn't the master of a liverish colonel and a woman of sixty who wanted to look forty, at ten-fifteen in the morning.

* * *

"If they're watching me," Kerr said to Gordon Craigie some thirty minutes later, "they're watching Arran, Carruthers, possibly Davidson, and you. I don't like the look of it."

"I didn't from the start," said Craigie. "If I knew a little more what it was about I wouldn't mind so much. But I haven't a hint yet."

"What about questioning Mort?"

"Not wise, I fancy, but we might try it later. Well, be careful. You can't think of anyone else for Leila Mort, can you? Someone not likely to be known."

"Sorry," said Kerr. "I— Damn that 'phone!"

Craigie didn't damn it; it was much too useful. He picked up the receiver and listened; Kerr saw the way his expression changed, heard him snap: "The address, quickly. Eighteen, Dummett Street, Chelsea. Thanks. I'll send someone."

He put the telephone down and looked at Kerr, and his eyes were unusually grim.

"That girl Granting. Says she's just seen Mannopoli go into a house in Chelsea. Get round, Bob; you heard the address. I'll have some reinforcements on your tail."

8

18 DUMMETT STREET

Bob Kerr had not used his car that morning, but now he wished that he had. Mannopoli was in London, and he'd actually got the address. Whatever happened, the man mustn't get away, but by taxi it would take him half an hour or more to reach Chelsea; he couldn't expect a cabby to drive as he would want to.

As he hurried down the stairs outside Craigie's room an idea flashed through his mind, and instead of hailing a cab he ran towards the Yard. Not for the first time luck was with him, for Miller was on the steps. His eyes widened as he saw Kerr.

"Hallo?"

"I want a fast car and a good man."

"Take my bus," said Miller promptly. "The green one over there. I'll send a man down in a couple of jiffs. Heard anything?"

"Craigie'll 'phone. Mannopoli—eighteen Dummett Street, Chelsea." Kerr snapped the words and then turned across the courtyard towards the line of private cars. Miller's green one was a two-year-old Riley, and he knew from experience that it could move. He was in the driving-seat and had taken the car out of the line when the man Miller had hastily summoned came hurrying down the steps of the Yard. A youngish fellow, well-dressed, quick-moving and pleasant to look on. He jumped into the car and Kerr let in the clutch.

"Name's Parrish," said the new-comer.

"Parrish," said Kerr, "do you carry a gun?"

"Miller said you might have a spare?"

"I haven't, as it happens, and that's a nuisance." Kerr swung round into the Embankment and then across Parliament Square, his jaw set, his eyes narrowed and very hard. All the time he was thinking of the fact that Mannopoli was in Chelsea. Unless, of course, the girl had lied.

Obviously Craigie hadn't thought that likely.

Kerr couldn't imagine her lying for any reason; it seemed madness to believe it possible. She was perhaps closer to the heart of this affair than it had appeared at first, but that didn't mean she was working for Mannopoli. Moreover, she might have told the truth when she had talked on the previous night of the urgent call to a sick friend.

These and a dozen other thoughts flashed through Kerr's mind as the Riley threaded in and out of the traffic along Victoria Street. The man at his side said nothing; he seemed keen and alert, a vigorous young man who had probably been trained at the police college; he had something about him which suggested it.

"Sorry about that gun," Kerr said. "Go steady when we get there."

"Likely to be any shooting?"

"Not likely not to be. Damn these roads." They were at Victoria now, and soon they would be running through Sloane

Square and the roundabout that someone who knew nothing about town-planning had created some centuries before. "Do you know Chelsea well?"

"Reasonably."

"Dummett Street?"

"Off the Embankment, turn left from King's Road just before you reach the railway bridge."

"As far away as it could be," grumbled Kerr, and he made even greater efforts at the wheel, not worrying unduly about the thirty-mile limit. The seconds seemed to drag; every momentary pause made him clench his teeth. Mannopoli was in Chelsea and he *must* get the man.

They flashed past Chelsea Town Hall, and a couple of seconds later the man named Parrish snapped:

"Turn left."

Kerr obliged. A few hundred yards took them to the Embankment, and there he turned right. The third road to the right again was Dummett Street; a newly painted sign announced the fact, and Kerr sent the Riley screeching round. He slowed down a second later and searched for the numbers. As he passed thirty-eight he knew that he wasn't far from his objective. He was feeling like a cat on hot bricks, although he didn't look like one as he pulled the car up outside number ten and then jumped out.

"You'll stay here," he said. "There'll be others along before long, and the sooner the better. If I'm not out in ten minutes, tell them to get busy."

"All right," said Parrish, who looked disappointed and yet knew how to obey orders.

Kerr walked quickly but without appearing to hurry towards number eighteen. It was like every other house in the street, a tall one—four storeys at least—with a grey stone facing and a small garden at the front. There was a basement, and to reach the front door he had to climb half a dozen whitened steps. He reached the door and pressed the bell. His thoughts were recurring one after the other.

Of course, the girl might have been lying. Or there might be a trick. Whether or no, he'd find out whether Mannopoli was here, and if he were—

Kerr didn't usually feel chilly in the middle, but he did now. The utter ruthlessness of the yellow-faced man was frightening; for all Kerr knew, the first thing he'd get would be a bullet. He was actually ready to jump to one side as the door started to open; it was a fact he hadn't heard footsteps along the hall, and that made him worry.

He had something of a shock.

The man in the doorway didn't look capable of using a gun; he was small, dapper, oiled and scented; so much was obvious in the first second. He was exquisitely dressed, with an exaggeration that made him look theatrical. Kerr even believed he had colour on his cheeks, and was prepared to swear to the corsets; no man could have a waist like that from nature alone.

"Good morning, sir." It was a high-pitched falsetto voice, accompanied by an ingratiating smile and an upwards lilt at the end to make the question.

"Mr. Mannopoli in?" asked Kerr, and he contrived to do what he had done occasionally before—sound and look like a policeman.

"Mr. Mannopoli?" The exquisite young man frowned and yet smiled at the same time. "I'm afraid I don't recognize the name, sir. And next door I know the name is—"

Kerr's foot was past the level of the door as he spoke again.

"I've good reason," he said, "for believing Mr. Mannopoli to be here, my friend. I'm coming in."

The little man looked as though he would have liked to protest; he didn't. He saw Kerr's gun and he dropped back. Kerr told himself that the man was scared enough to suggest that he'd never been threatened with a gun before. But his colour remained, and Kerr's guess at rouge was confirmed.

"I—I beg your pardon!" Even in face of a gun he had to be polite.

"Sorry," said Kerr. "This isn't a hold-up in the ordinary sense. I've information that a man named Mannopoli is here, and I must make sure. Police."

"Po-lice!"

So the fellow was scared of the police as well as the gun. Kerr wondered what he'd struck, but didn't spend much time guessing. Time was flying too fast already.

"Yes, police." He pushed past the man and shut the door. Like the late Mr. Mulling, this creation didn't seem to have the guts to make any strong protest. "Is this all one house, or are there flats?"

"It's—all—one."

"Good. Take me round."

He made an ostentatious show of the gun, and it had the desired effect. The fellow turned tail, but his body was shivering. His long, wavy, marcelled hair was an offence, particularly where it grew over his ears. Kerr grinned to himself, and wondered whether he'd have any luck. It might be that he would unearth something to interest Craigie.

He was walking in the first room—an empty one—when the cry came.

It was low-pitched and yet feminine. There was fear and there was pain in it. It lasted only for a split second, but there was not the slightest doubt but that it came from the next floor; and Kerr's thoughts raced to Ellen Granting.

"Upstairs," he snapped, and he thought the dandy was

going to faint. The man half turned in protest, and it was then that Kerr saw the gun he had in his hand. Kerr didn't hesitate. He crashed out his left fist and caught the man full on the jaw. His victim yelped and went clean off his feet; then he thudded to the floor, and was very, very still.

Kerr didn't waste time looking at him.

There was more than enough on his mind now. He knew there had been reason for coming to 18 Dummett Street. The little dandy had been armed, others might be armed. But the girl was here somewhere; he was prepared to swear to it. And she was in trouble.

He went up the stairs two at a time and yet with a softness that would have surprised most people. On the first landing he stopped, his lips compressed. There were four doors leading from it, two open, two shut. No sound came from anywhere, no hint that anyone else was here.

Kerr looked into the open rooms and made sure they were empty. The others were a different problem, but he couldn't afford to waste time. The question was—would Mannopoli still be here, as well as the girl?

He slipped a skeleton-key from his pocket and inserted it in the lock. He wasn't an expert at the cracksman job and he made more noise than he liked, but he had the door open at last. He flung it back, with the gun instead of the key in his right hand.

And then he saw Ellen Granting.

She was stretched out on the floor, full-length. Her face — the first time Kerr had seen it excepting in the garish light of the car headlamps—was turned upwards. She was deathly pale, and there was an ugly swelling bruise on her forehead, which suggested why she was unconscious.

But that wasn't all.

Her dress—a flimsy floral creation—had been ripped from

the shoulder to the waist on the left side, although on the right it hadn't been touched. Her white skin gleamed in the light from the window, excepting at a spot just above the waist; and there the red blood was welling from an ugly gash that seemed a sacrilege.

Kerr didn't know how deep it was, didn't dare to wait to see. She was breathing regularly if softly, and that had to suffice him. Mannopoli had done this; he must get Mannopoli—

Kerr's eyes were like fire as he looked away from her and swung round towards the door—

And then he saw Mr. Mannopoli, standing in the doorway, his gun in his left hand. It was almost as if Kerr's life had been turned back, and this was Mulling's room, with Mannopoli standing by the open door. The only difference was that the girl, stripped as she was, was lying on the floor, instead of Mulling being crumpled in a heap on his chair.

Mannopoli's gun was just as unpleasant as before.

Kerr's eyes didn't move from the other man's, although he felt the shivering feeling in the pit of his stomach that he had experienced while he had waited on the porch of the house. He had expected to find Mannopoli; the girl had told the truth, and somehow Craigie's immediate acceptance of her statement was proof enough for Kerr.

But he hadn't expected to find Mannopoli like this.

It was a queer fact that the man could inspire what was, after all, fear. Kerr had never experienced it before and he didn't like it now, although reason told him he had little or nothing to worry about. His own gun was in his hand; he was as good a shot as Mannopoli. And yet....

Kerr shook his head, like a bull, and his mind cleared. Mannopoli spoke almost on the instant.

"We've a little more time this morning," he said, with his hard, clipped sentences.

"Fine," said Kerr, and found a smile. "But not much."

"My time, Mr. Kerr, is my own." The swine was being polite; he looked almost as if he knew what had passed through Kerr's mind. "Unless you've any suggestions, of course?"

"None at all," said Kerr, and was glad that he had not done what he had been tempted to do a few seconds before. He had been going to tell Mannopoli the police were coming. He didn't. Mannopoli seemed to want to talk, and Kerr wanted to gain time. What could have been better?

"Excellent," murmured Mannopoli. "Now—you've been a nuisance, Kerr. You got on to Mulling very well, and Craigie upset me by sending that man to Fallow. I'd like to know just what you've learned."

"Isn't that," said Kerr, "an idea?"

Mannopoli's expression wasn't pleasant.

"Let's have no cross-talk. What do you know?"

"That you are wanted for murder," flashed Kerr. "Or had you guessed that?"

Mannopoli drew a deep breath. Kerr noticed that he kept his right arm up to his chest, and guessed it was heavily bandaged after the wound of the previous night. He was wondering whether Mannopoli seriously thought he would talk, whether Mannopoli would shoot, and how long the police would be. More, whether the girl was fatally wounded. Where in hell did she come in on this game?

"I think you're being foolish," said Mannopoli slowly, "even if you fancy it's clever, Kerr. Or funny. One more chance—"

"It's getting grim, isn't it?" asked Kerr, and he sat on the arm of an easy-chair with a nonchalance that surprised even himself. His gun and Mannopoli's were both raised; if it came to a shooting-match there wouldn't be much in it. "You've bitten off a lot more than you can chew, Mannopoli. All the police of the country are looking for you. All stations, ports and flying-fields are being watched. You haven't a ghost of a chance of getting out of the country."

"I don't want to get out of the country," snapped Mannopoli.

"Then I've learned something," said Kerr, and he laughed.

For a moment he thought he'd gone too far. Mannopoli's eyes blazed, and Kerr's finger was almost on the hair-trigger of his gun. And then, very clearly through the house, came the *rat-tat-tat* on the door downstairs.

Mannopoli seemed to rise on his toes; and when he spoke his voice was a snarl.

"So—you weren't alone, weren't you?"

"Don't be a ruddy fool," said Kerr. "Would I come here alone? You're caught Mannopoli. It's come more quickly than I thought it would, but it's come all the same. Drop your gun and—"

It was then that Mannopoli did a queer thing, a vile thing that made Kerr swear. For the man shifted the direction of his gun *and pointed it towards Ellen Granting*!

Kerr fired; and for a second time he won.

His bullet took Mannopoli's already slightly wounded right arm; Mannopoli's bullet pecked the carpet a couple of inches from the girl's head; and then the man turned on Kerr like a madman. He forgot his gun, forgot everything, and went berserk. Wounded in both arms though he was, he bore Kerr back by sheer frenzied force, and for a moment Kerr had all he could do to beat the fellow off. Mannopoli's eyes were glaring into his, his mouth was open, his sharp and pointed teeth were bared. He kicked, fought, brought his knee into Kerr's groin, and all the time he was snarling and swearing.

Kerr got clear at last, and then hit his man.

He hit three times, and each time Mannopoli took the blow, shook his head, and then rushed in again. The fourth time was enough. The man swayed on his feet, his eyes rolled, and then he dropped across the body of the girl; there was something in their proximity that seemed obscene. Even Robert McMillan Kerr was affected by that girl's beauty.

But Kerr still had no time to waste.

He made sure Mannopoli was unconscious and then hurried down the stairs. The knocking was imperious now, and outside he had glimpsed two police cars and the man named Parrish. He opened the door, to find Parrish on the doorstep.

"You're all right?" The youngster seemed on tenterhooks.

"Yes, thanks," said Kerr briefly. "Get a doctor quickly, will you? And have this house combed. I don't know how many there are in it, but few of them are pleasant. I'll be on the second floor for a few minutes."

Parrish nodded, and snapped an order to a plain-clothes man behind him. Kerr hurried up the stairs towards the room where the man and the woman were lying unconscious. They were both still there—for a moment Kerr had been possessed of an absurd fancy that Mannopoli might have been foxing—and he breathed with relief. It occurred to him to wash the girl's wound, but the doctor wouldn't be long, and it didn't look too dangerous.

The thing was—what would he find in the house?

He decided to 'phone Craigie first, and went downstairs in search of a telephone. As he reached the hall, the front door closed behind the fourth plain-clothes man—excluding

Parrish—who had come with the rescue party. Miller certainly hadn't wasted time, and that fact was a comfort.

"Any different orders, sir?" Parrish asked.

"No. The cars aren't right outside this door, are they?"

"No, sir. A couple of houses along."

"That's fine," said Kerr. "Get the man away upstairs and bind his ankles. He'll be dangerous if he wakes up, even though he is wounded right and left. Leave the girl where she is."

"The—girl?" Parrish looked startled.

"Yes," said Kerr grimly, "the girl. Leave her where she is but have a man in the room in case she comes round. How long will the doctor be?"

"I've sent for the Divisional-surgeon, sir. He shouldn't be more than five minutes."

"Good," said Kerr.

He nodded, and went into the room that led from the hall —the room where the dandified little man was still lying, for Kerr's fists weren't playthings. In one corner he saw the telephone, but before he had reached it a car drew up outside.

Kerr half turned, expecting the doctor, but he didn't expect him for long. Divisional-surgeons, in Kerr's experience, didn't arrive in Daimler cars driven by chauffeurs, and there was nothing vague about this Daimler.

Kerr left the telephone for a few minutes and approached the window. He hid behind a curtain and watched, with increasing wonder every moment. The chauffeur had jumped like an electric lackey from his seat, and was now opening the door. There was a pause, followed by a yap, a definite yap; and in the chauffeur's arms was a poodle of the gingery type that Kerr detested.

A woman was coming, then.

She came a moment later, and Kerr whistled beneath his

breath. She had a stateliness that might have been regal had it not been slightly overdone. She was dressed in furs, and she looked—in the vernacular—worth a million. She was good looking up to a point, and even at that distance Kerr could see her wide, incredibly brilliant eyes—monstrous eyes.

It was like watching a play, and Kerr was so intrigued that he forgot everything else.

The dog came first, on a lead, some yard and a half in front of the chauffeur. Its little pug nose seemed to typify the disdain of the woman who followed. They reached the gateway of number 18 Dummett Street, the chauffeur opened it to let the dog and the woman pass, and they waited for him to go up the steps and ring the bell. By that time they were out of Kerr's sight, and Kerr moved into the hall, ready to burst into a chuckle.

The rat-tat-tat was imperious, only to be expected. A footstep sounded in the hall—one of Parrish's men—but Kerr reached the door first and waved the other aside. He opened it and, his face set poker-fashion, waited.

The woman was standing with the dog in her arms. Her face was composed and he could see that in youth she had been startlingly beautiful. She still had the features, even if she owed a great deal to art. But her eyes hadn't altered; they were the largest Kerr had ever seen, and close to their brilliance was even more incredible. Kerr had a hard job to keep stiff-faced.

"Good afternoon, ma'am."

He expected her to stare him up and down; instead she looked surprised, and even a little put out. He waited, and she drew a deep breath.

"I beg your pardon. This *is* number eighteen?"

"It is," said Kerr.

"Then you are—?"

"I happened to be near the door," said Kerr, and he was

hoping hard she would name the man she had come to see. But she was either clever or innocent, and she said nothing.

"Er—you want to see Mr. Mannopoli?" asked Kerr.

"I do not," she said. "I want an explanation of this, my man. My name is Mort—Mrs. Julius Mort—and I wish to see Mr. Gabrell at once. At *once*, do you understand?"

9

MRS. MORT HAS A SHOCK

When Robert McMillan Kerr had been introduced to other members of the Department called Z he had felt, because of a life which had been solitary, almost aghast at their flippancy. He could be flippant himself, but what he hadn't been able to understand was the ability of some of them—Davidson, Carruthers, Toby Arran and others—to laugh a few minutes after they had seen death.

He understood now.

Working for Craigie was a strain that could have had no equal anywhere else. When a game—they called them games for convenience—started, it was tense and relentless from beginning to end. It was a literal fact that no one could be sure whether this minute would be their last or whether they'd live to see the end of whatever affair was attracting Craigie's attention.

So it happened that laughter came not callously but as a relief from tension. Without that relief the men could not have stood the strain. Their humour, in the opinion of many people, was not of the highest class. It had a heaviness about it at times which suggested that it was laboured; but that didn't matter. It served their purpose and they were glad to use it. A man who could not laugh, be flippant and if necessary be callous on the surface, was unlikely to last long in the service of the Department that demanded everything once a man had joined it.

Mrs. Mort's arrival was a case in point.

Kerr had had something under two and a half hours' sleep since he had started for the village of Tarrington. Most of the time he had been on the go; he had seen two men killed, others wounded, and the girl with that ugly wound in her side, perhaps the more lasting in its effects on his mind. He needed a reserve of mental strength as well as physical; and the reserve was presented by the yapping poodle, the chauffeur, and Mrs. Julius Mort.

In addition to that, Mrs. Mort was interesting indeed to Robert McMillan Kerr.

He smiled—the first time his face had relaxed since he had opened the door, and even the woman could not fail to see the remarkable transformation of a face that in repose was almost forbidding.

"Ah. Mrs. Mort, of course. My name's Kerr, Mrs. Mort."

"Kerr," she said, and glanced at the dog, not perhaps with intention. Then her wonderful eyes searched the Department agent; they might be beautiful eyes but they could be withering. "I don't know you."

"I know," said Kerr, and he could not resist the temptation to try to make this woman lose her temper. He liked people to lose their tempers. So many said things in unguarded moments that they would never have done otherwise.

"You—" She drew herself up proudly, and now Kerr was able to see that she had a figure of the type so often called magnificent, for the chinchillas swelled upwards and outwards. "Are you being insolent, sir?"

"I don't think so," said Kerr, and it occurred to him that Mrs. Mort wasn't used to being kept on the doorstep, but it wouldn't hurt her for once. Yet he could not bring himself to dislike, on sight, the imperious wife of Julius. She looked so much what she was, and there were lines about her mouth and nose which suggested that she could be both pleasant and human.

Mrs. Mort had had enough just then.

"Where is Mr. Gabrell?" she snapped.

"I don't know," said Kerr. "Is he a small man, with long hair?"

"He is. I mean," corrected Mrs. Mort hurriedly, "there is no need for further impertinence! Where is he?"

"Come in," said Bob Kerr.

His mind was working fast all the time, and he was wondering whether it was possible that this woman knew more about her husband's business than was generally believed. He believed he would soon find out. She swept past him as he stood aside, with the poodle cuddled in her arms, and her chin—a pointed chin that did not go with the other rounded features of her face—held high. She continued to sweep as far as the open door of the room where the dandy was lying in an unconscious heap.

And then she stopped. It was as if a sailing-ship had been suddenly brought to a standstill by a vicious squall of wind. Her arms went outwards, the poodle dropped, squealing blue murder, Mrs. Mort staggered, and Kerr stepped forward quickly to stop her from falling. But she needed no support, for after a moment while she had stared hard at the unconscious man, she turned very slowly, very majestically. Kerr admired her poise and her self-control.

"What is the meaning of this, sir?"

"Mrs. Mort," said Bob Kerr suddenly, "I owe you an apology. I am a police officer, and some peculiar things have been happening in this house. Your arrival at this moment was, to be frank, suspicious. I wanted to try and see whether you had any idea of what had been happening. That is all."

She nodded; her self-control was still admirable although she had completely forgotten the poodle, which had landed on all fours and was now squatting, sniffing and glaring malevolently towards its mistress.

"I see. A very unusual way of behaving, Mr. Kerr, but as you are a policeman..." She shrugged her shoulders and seemed to infer that no one could expect better things from a policeman. "Who attacked Mr. Gabrell? He's not"—fear flooded her eyes suddenly, fear and concern—"badly hurt? He's not—"

"He'll come round very soon," Kerr assured her. "But I don't know that I can set your mind at rest any further, Mrs. Mort. He will be immediately arrested; you can, in fact, consider him under arrest now."

She was puzzled, angry, indignant; but he didn't think she was frightened.

"I am afraid I don't understand."

"He threatened an officer of the law with a firearm," said Kerr, exaggerating a little, "and he'll have to explain why. But if you'll excuse me, Mrs. Mort, I've a lot to do. There has been a shooting here and we're extremely busy. If you care to wait until Mr. Gabrell recovers consciousness, do so by all means."

"I will," said Mrs. Mort. "Thank you. And send a maid to me, will you?"

"As far as I know," said Kerr, "there aren't any maids. I haven't heard or seen any, and I think I would have done if they'd been about."

"But that's absurd! There should be several!"

"Then they've been given a holiday," said Kerr, "or they've been frightened away." He bowed, and for a second time the woman was surprised at the way he could behave when he wanted to, and left her in the room; he didn't leave her for long.

Parrish was coming down the stairs, and Kerr beckoned him.

"Send a man in there," he said. "There's a woman—a Mrs. Mort. Tell her the man's under orders to stay there. If she leaves, have her followed. She'll go in the Daimler."

"Right-ho," said Parrish, and he looked as if he would gladly have done the job himself. For his part Kerr was beginning to wish that there were one or two of the Department men in the offing. The police were good fellows and capable, but they had one great disadvantage: they acted according to regulations. There were no regulations in Department Z.

Kerr went and telephoned Craigie, and he learned one thing before he started talking.

"Toby and Wally are on the way," said Craigie. "Had any luck?"

"We've got Mannopoli," said Bob Kerr, and he chuckled into the silence that followed; if there was one thing Gordon Craigie hadn't been expecting, that was it, and for once in his life he showed a hint of excitement.

"How the devil did you manage it?"

"It's a bit of a puzzle," said Kerr, and suddenly his mind clicked back into action. The interview with Mrs. Mort had stemmed the tide of his thoughts more than it should have done. "Here's the story, Craigie. I came here—knocked one man out—heard the girl yell—"

"What girl?"

"Ellen Granting."

"*She's* there, is she? Go on!"

"I found her," said Kerr, very grimly, for he was reliving those few seconds, and he seemed to have a picture of the girl's outstretched body in his mind's eye all the time. "Lying on the floor, stripped to the waist on the left side, with a bump over the head and a knife wound in the side."

"Badly hurt?"

"I don't know, but I don't think so. Anyhow, Mannopoli came into the room just after me. He can move very quietly. He wanted to know how far we'd got. I foxed him, of course, and then the police came. And"—Kerr paused for a moment—"this is the queer thing, Gordon: he didn't shoot me when he heard the knocking and knew he was caught. He tried to shoot the girl."

"Did he?" asked Craigie, and it was obvious from his tone that he was getting a lot of shocks that morning.

"He missed," said Kerr, characteristically omitting to say why, "and I had a second's start of him and caught his forearm. He went mad, Craigie. Only word for it. I K.O.'d him at last, of course, and the police are with him now, upstairs. How's it sound?"

"Incredible," said Gordon Craigie frankly.

"My thoughts exactly. If the man's the leader—and we've been thinking he is—we've got him. Whatever the fuss was about it's over, and we can rest again."

"We won't rest so soon," said Craigie. "I'll come over, Bob. Keep Mannopoli at the house, and the girl. All right?"

Kerr agreed that it was all right, and was about to ring off when he bellowed. The noise was not pleasant to Craigie's ear and Craigie said so.

"Sorry," Kerr chuckled, "but I forgot something of interest. The name of the man I knocked out in the first place is

Gabrell. He had a visitor a minute or two ago and she's still here. A Mrs. Mort. Mrs. Julius Mort."

"You forgot that?" murmured Gordon Craigie gently, and Kerr smiled. "I'll be over. Tail her if she looks like going."

"I've asked a policeman to do it, if Davidson or Arran doesn't arrive in time."

"All right. I don't think she'll go far, but she might touch interesting places. It's queer, Bob, I don't feel much happier."

"It's just as queer," said Bob Kerr, "that I don't either. A nasty feeling that I'm sitting on gunpowder. However, we'll see and you'll get over as soon as you can. I'll run through the place for papers."

"Do. Particularly anything in coloured ink, or with that series of letters. Good-bye."

Kerr rang down thoughtfully, and then went out of the room—opposite that in which Mrs. Mort and her boy friend were sitting or lying. Gabrell was probably still unconscious, and the policeman wouldn't be a help to amours in any case. Mrs. Mort was having a dull afternoon in some ways.

He had been so engrossed in his talk with Craigie that he hadn't heard the door open and close. But as he reached the hall Parrish came running downstairs, his eyes shining. Parrish was a young man who always seemed to be running.

"I say, Mr. Kerr. The surgeon's here, and would like a word with you.

"I'll come up," said Kerr, and acted on his words.

The Divisional-surgeon, in the room where Ellen Granting was lying—on a couch now instead of the floor—was a short, stout man with a decided Scottish accent—an unusual mixture. He eyed Kerr, and spoke abruptly.

"Ah! I thought you'd better see this, Mr. Kerr, before it's covered up. The wound, of course, the wound. Peculiar, and I thought perhaps it would have some meaning for you."

"Meaning for me?" asked Kerr in surprise, and then he looked at Ellen Granting's side, and his mouth suddenly went dry.

He forgot the medico; he forgot Parrish and another curious policeman. He forgot everything but that bare, red wound. It seemed incredible. Damn it, it *was* incredible!

But the wound, purely a surface one, was horrible. A patch of skin had been completely removed—a patch in the shape of a red diamond, perhaps two inches along each side.

A red diamond! Deliberately cut into the girl's flesh.

What could that mean?

Kerr felt sick, and he turned away. The medico did not need to ask whether he had seen anything of interest. He pursed his lips and bandaged the girl's waist calmly and expertly. Kerr's nauseation lasted only a few seconds, and then he longed for Craigie to come. He wanted someone to talk to, someone who might be able to understand a little of what the thing meant.

He couldn't think clearly, but he did his best.

He learned that the girl was likely to remain unconscious for an hour or two—she was suffering, the doctor said, from slight concussion—and that Mannopoli was awake now but sullen and silent. He was lying on a bed in another room, with his ankles bound, and with two policemen watching him. It was almost impossible to be careful with that gentleman.

Kerr went through the house, looking for papers, but he had little or no success. Tradesmen's bills—chemists' and tailors' in particular—social invitations, visiting-cards and an occasional counterfoil of a cheque comprised the yield after he had been through all the rooms on the first and second floor.

And then Craigie arrived. He came on the heels of Davidson and Toby Arran, who slipped into the background.

"Nothing happened?" he asked.

"Mrs. Mort's still here and the little man Gabrell is still unconscious; so's the girl."

"Badly hurt?" demanded Toby Arran.

"It's a queer thing," said Kerr awkwardly, and he explained just what had happened, and just what the medico had allowed him to see. Just as the sight had struck a paralysis through his mind for a few seconds, so the narration seemed to react on the others. Then Toby Arran broke the silence with an outburst of vituperation that would have broken anything.

"But she's not badly hurt," Kerr went on slowly. "All the same, she ought to be. Mannopoli tried to kill her."

"You're sure of that?"

"I shifted his aim; the bullet touched the floor a couple of inches from her head. And when he saw what I'd done he went berserk. Literally berserk. He *needed* her to die!"

"It certainly looks like it," said Craigie.

"And that means," Kerr went on heavily, "that she knows something."

"And," broke in Toby Arran quickly, "that he's afraid she might talk."

"She will talk," said Bob Kerr very grimly. "That young lady has been holding out on us, but we owe her a lot for leading us to Mannopoli." He hesitated, and then went on: "What about the Mort angle, Gordon?"

Craigie fingered his chin.

"We'll take it slowly," he said. "Mrs. Mort came here to see this fellow Gabrell. Gabrell used a gun—or tried to—on you. That suggests Gabrell knows Mannopoli and wanted to stop you finding him here. All right?"

"That's about the ticket," Kerr admitted.

"Fine. Now—does Mrs. Mort know of the Gabrell-Mannopoli connection, or does she come here for Gabrell alone? We'll have to find what we can about that man, and if we put him under arrest we'll probably learn a lot. You say he's the type to get scared very quickly?"

"Very quickly indeed."

"H'm. Well, we'll follow Mrs. Mort—you can do that, Toby— and meanwhile I'll get someone to do what we hoped Carruthers would manage. We could badly do with someone in the Mort ménage."

"But with Mannopoli caught," Toby Arran objected, "the shindy is probably over."

"I wish I could think so," said Gordon Craigie. "In any case we've got to find what it's about and what's happening."

They were sitting in the room opposite Mrs. Mort and her—they suspected—paramour. The police were still going through the house, confiscating all papers. Craigie's quiet voice had been almost monotonous, Wally Davidson was feeling thirsty and telling himself he hoped they'd get out soon. Kerr was wondering whether the job would come to a dead end like this—

And the scream came.

It was something so sudden, so piercing, so filled with horror that not one of the four men moved for ten seconds. It came once—twice—thrice! from the room opposite them, and it was followed suddenly by a wailing and a weeping that sounded more delirium than hysteria; that came, they knew, from Mrs. Mort.

Kerr moved first, and the others were still in their chairs when he reached the door, flung it open, and raced across the passage. They hadn't seen him whip the gun from his pocket, but they did see him open the other door; beyond him they saw Mrs. Mort, her eyes distended and the wailing still coming; but they didn't see what caught Kerr's eyes.

Kerr ignored the screaming woman and looked at the

outstretched body of the man he had knocked out something under an hour before. The trouble with Mr. Gabrell, however, was that he was no longer just unconscious. He was dead, for a bullet through the brain has a distressing habit of causing death. And the policeman who had been playing gooseberry was in little better state, although Kerr saw he was breathing.

Kerr felt sorry for the woman as he looked at her, and yet his voice was very hard, and his eyes didn't alter. They were remorseless, and she tried to avoid them.

"I'm sorry, Mrs. Mort, but you must calm yourself. Just what happened? And what did you see?"

"But—but it was terrible! Terrible! To go out like that—to die like that! I can't believe it, I can't!" Her voice rose again, and she half rose from her chair. Kerr took her outflung arm and steadied her.

"Please," he said. "It's important."

"But like that—like that!" She was wailing, a high-pitched, horrible sound, and she looked a travesty of the well-preserved woman who had entered the house and had been annoyed by Robert McMillan Kerr.

Kerr did the only thing; he smacked her face.

It had more effect than anything else could have done. For a moment she eyed him as though she didn't know what had happened. Then the light of sanity came back to her eyes.

"What—what did you say?"

"How did it happen?" asked Kerr very gently, and he knew that he would have no more trouble with her.

"The man was at the window. I looked round and saw his face. He was holding a gun, and—and he fired twice. Twice!"

"I didn't hear the glass break," Kerr said.

"No—no! Poor—poor Cecil had asked me to open the window just a minute before. If I hadn't opened it..." She shrugged, and Kerr saw the tears in her eyes. "But there it is."

"Would you recognize the man if you saw him again?"

"I—I don't know. He had a hat on—"

"Did the policeman who was with you see him?"

"I don't—think so."

"I see. Well, I may have to worry you again, Mrs. Mort, but if I can spare you any trouble, you can be assured I will." It didn't sound like Kerr as he talked, very gently. "I'll send a man home with you, to make sure you're all right."

"Thank you—thank you. I…" She broke off and turned her head away; and it was a fact that she had been devoted to the man who was named Cecil Gabrell and looked a lot worse even than his name.

Kerr escorted her to the door, where Toby Arran took over. Then Kerr went into the room where Gabrell had been shot. The fat Scotch doctor was examining the body, and Craigie was watching him, while Wally Davidson, forgetful now of his thirst, turned out the pockets of the dead man's vest and coat.

The vest yielded the card which they had almost expected. But what Craigie hadn't expected were the letters on the back of it. It was green—a darker shade than that which they believed Ellen Granting had lost—and on one side were the written letters: P.O.R.

"Which suggests," said Gordon Craigie slowly, "that Gabrell was the Portuguese agent, and he was killed to stop him from talking. Mulling died for the same reason; and Ellen Granting, but for the grace of God, would have gone too. It's bad—"

"Because Mannopoli certainly didn't do it," said Robert Kerr, and his voice was strained. "There's someone else all right."

10

INTRODUCING TOMMY

Mannopoli hadn't killed Gabrell; so much was certain. Therefore someone—Mannopoli's agent or another agent of that gentleman for whom Mannopoli worked—had shot the man through the window. Therefore again the Department was in a spot. In previous jobs it had discovered reasonably early whom it was fighting. Now they knew of no one, even if there were several possibilities. It was a fact that the shooting of Gabrell and the policeman affected the Chief of Z and his star agent more than anything else had done.

They wouldn't have minded so much if they could have had any idea what it was about. That was the snag. Sudden death; a large, effective and deadly organization; a man like Mannopoli who seemed nothing more than a cipher; these things were worrying.

"Not," said Wally Davidson, "that I'm going to worry." They were out of the house now, and walking towards Craigie's car; there had not been so many cars in Dummett Street since the first house had been built. "I'm thirsty, and there's a pub at the corner, old sons. Coming?"

"Drink alone," said Kerr, "and get back to your flat as soon as you can. We might want you in a hurry."

"I shall not drink alone," said Davidson with dignity. "It's like you, Kerr, to suggest it." He looked aggrieved, and lazier than ever, but his eyes were twinkling. "I'll go and see Tommy."

"Tommy who?"

"Rumsden. He paints and lives in Chelsea, a couple of hundred yards away, if my memory serves. So if there's nothing at the moment, boys, I'll snatch him out."

"What kind of a man is Rumsden?" asked Craigie, pausing with a hand on the handle of his car door. He was still thinking of finding someone who could enter the Mort ménage.

"Thoroughly to be recommended," said Davidson. "Packs a punch, looks pretty when he wants to, heaps of oof, and I'm told he's an artist. Single. So long."

"Sound him," said Craigie; "we need someone new."

"I'll sound him," promised Davidson, "but I warn you he's a serious artist and he may not take kindly to being dragged from his work. What are you going to do?"

"Think," said Bob Kerr, "but not of you." He smiled, and Davidson walked off, covering the ground more quickly than he appeared to.

Craigie had come in his Siddeley, and Kerr no longer needed the police car. At a more reasonable speed they returned to Whitehall and went through the paraphernalia of getting into Craigie's office.

Only Craigie knew how to get in from the outside, and when he wasn't there no one had access to it. It was built so that it seemed to be solid wall, and the sliding-door principle would have surprised many people who passed the walls every day of their lives. Craigie could not take chances, and at times there was information in that long room which would have been worth millions to the right—or from Craigie's point of view the wrong—man. But they entered at last, and Kerr sat down.

Craigie took out his meerschaum, to which he was unreasonably devoted, and stuffed it thoughtfully.

"Well, Bob. Suspects."

"Suspects," said Kerr, and sighed. "Well—Mort for one."

"I'm beginning to think even more deeply about Mort," admitted Craigie. "I wonder whether he is in this thing farther than we think?"

"He's in it. And he's the only live man to our knowledge who's left. Of course there must be others. Hundreds," said Kerr in an expansive mood, "of others."

"Well, we'll start with Mort. What about his wife?"

"Think she's in it?"

"I don't know." Craigie was thoughtful. "It's queer that she should have come to the house where Mannopoli was, but it may be that Mannopoli had fixed up the friendship between her and Gabrell. She was upset enough by the man's death."

"It must have been pretty grim for her," said Kerr.

"Ye-es. Mrs. Mort is on our long-shot list, then. It's a pity she couldn't give a description of the man at the window."

"It's a greater pity that the blind oaf who was watching outside didn't notice the man slip into the gateway," said Kerr feelingly.

Craigie nodded, and wondered what the man—a detective who had come with the police reinforcements—would say when he was interrogated by Superintendent Miller. Miller didn't like mistakes on a grand scale, and the man who had been left outside to watch the premises had certainly made one.

He had admitted that his attention had been attracted by

an organ-grinder complete with monkey at the end of the road. He had seen a man pass him, wearing a big trilby hat—which fitted in with Mrs. Mort's vague description—and a minute or two later he had seen the man still walking along the same side of the road. He had realized the man must have stopped, for he would have been at the end of the street by the time the detective turned had he kept moving, but the detective had assumed that the monkey—complete with organ-grinder—had been a source of attraction to more persons than one.

In the minutes the policeman had spent watching the entertainment, the other must have slipped into the gateway of number eighteen, fired at the two men through the open window—using a silenced automatic of .22 calibre—and then proceeded calmly on his way. Obviously a man of nerve.

"Now," said Craigie, "Ellen Granting's on the long-shot list as well. She's mixed up with Mannopoli. He wanted to kill her, and that suggests she's not in sympathy with the gentleman, but it doesn't mean she hasn't been, some time or other."

"And that's our limit," Kerr said.

"Well—hardly. You've all the employees at the 'George' in Michford. Employees at the Morts' house in St. John's Wood. Servants at Dummett Street and—perhaps—others."

"I suppose," Kerr said, "Fallow's all right?"

Craigie smiled thoughtfully.

"No one's all right," he said, "but we won't go far wrong in trusting Fallow. He sent me that letter the moment he received it, and he could only have had my telephone call asking him to watch Mort for any developments a few hours earlier. Mannopoli tried to kill him—"

"He also tried to kill Ellen Granting."

"Yes, but we know the object with Fallow. He wanted the letter which Mort had sent. At all events, I've sent a couple of men down to Devon, and The Maples is being watched. If anything did crop up we'd know immediately. But our two strong pointers at the moment are the Morts, and the dark-green card with the letters P.O.R. Someone will have to go abroad."

"Want me to?"

"I don't know yet. We'll wait for a few days and see if we can get anything else. I wonder if Davidson can bring this man Rumsden to us?"

"Wally won't be long before he finds out," said Kerr.

He could not have had an opinion confirmed more quickly, for the telephone bell rang soon afterwards and when Craigie answered it he said: "Yes, Wally." He said one or two other things and then returned to the fire, which was burning cheerfully despite the warmth of the day. "He's bringing Rumsden," he said.

"I've an idea I've heard of the man."

"He's a reputation for modernist work," Craigie said—Gordon Craigie often created the impression, unintentionally, that he knew everything. "Dabbles in surrealism, I'm told. We'll see."

"He doesn't sound promising," Kerr said.

"Wally wouldn't have taken me seriously if he hadn't considered it possible we could use him. I'm seeing him here. You'll stay?"

"Yes," said Kerr, and grimaced. "There isn't much anyone can do, anyhow. I wish there were."

"Things will move fast," Craigie prophesied, and they took out the list of letters which they believed was a code of country names, and poured over it.

* * *

Meanwhile Mr. Wallace Davidson and Mr. Akers (Tommy) Rumsden were together in the comfortable private bar of a pub at the end of Dummett Street, Chelsea. Mr. Davidson was, as always, tired, lean, exquisite. Mr. Rumsden looked a mess.

He was one of the few real artists who looked like one. He affected a vast yellow bow tie and a blue collar with shirt to match. His coat was of many colours and his trousers navy blue—the only quiet part about him. His hair was not so long as it was untidy. His nose was crooked—a broken nose, in fact, which had been well doctored—and his face could be generally described as rugged. He was one of those men who looked ugly at first sight and fascinating ever afterwards. His eyes were blue, that sky-blue which seems to be alight all the time. And his voice was a deep bass, a deeper bass than any others Wally Davidson had ever heard. He was glad that he had thought of Akers Rumsden—known for some odd reason as Tommy—for Rumsden was amusing.

He was imbibing frothy stuff from a quart tankard, waving his free left arm and declaiming at intervals against the evils of beer and public-houses. He swallowed the beer like a camel gulping water, and continually came up for more. The more he drank the more bitterly he declaimed; the more bitterly he declaimed the greater the pallor of his cheeks—he was a colourless man where cheeks were concerned. The greater the pallor, the more fiery his eyes, and the more fiery his eyes the wider his smile.

Davidson got a word in.

"You don't like beer?"

"I don't," boomed Tommy Rumsden. "It's a crime, a sin, it's water, anyhow, and it destroys the heart, the soul, and the spirit of a man. Davidson!" He gripped Davidson's lapel. "Have you ever seen the spirit of a man?"

"I've seen the spirit going into the man," said Davidson, and unhinged himself. "I mean, you don't approve of beer or public-houses. That's right?" Davidson made it appear as if he was really much too tired to talk.

"Correct, my son, correct! I do not approve! All publicans are sinners and all sinners should be behind bars." He winked at the portly, beaming host of the pub, and careered on. "Beer is damnable, wine is a mocker—fill it up, George—and between you and me you're going to perdition with every spot you take. Right up, George. And, Davidson—"

Davidson tired of the indirect approach.

"Did you know we'd got an appointment?" he demanded.

"What for?"

"To see some friends of mine?"

"And are they soaking themselves, ruining their lives, destroying their alimony canals—something a bit odd about that word 'alimony' but it'll do—blearing their eyes, risking the life and limbs of the old and the young when at the wheels of their cars, are they—"

"Drink," said Davidson; "we're in a hurry."

Mr. Rumsden poured a pint of bitter down his leathern throat, planked money on the counter, and exhorted Davidson to move fast.

"Do you ever wear different clothes from that?" Davidson asked as they reached the street and Rumsden's two-seater, a decrepit Frazer Nash that should have been off the road years before.

"Certainly not," said Tommy. "What's the matter with them?"

"A bit startling, old son. Oh, the artistry's all right, don't misunderstand me. In fact, you look damned good in them. Do for any circus. But for this place we're going—Whitehall and whatnot—important people, y'know—they're a bit hit-you-in-the-eye."

"In these," declaimed Mr. Rumsden rumblingly, and ignoring the startled gaze of three housekeepers and a maid near by—"or naked."

Davidson looked shocked.

"But this place we're going to, old son. Equally out of place both ways. Not that they'd object. Be damned amused, in fact. But we don't want to attract attention. So if you'll slip to your flat and change—"

"In these," said Mr. Rumsden more loudly than ever, "or as Nature made me. And it made a good job." He plucked at his tie and looked prepared to divest himself.

"Come as you are," said Davidson bitterly, "and if you're thrown out don't blame me. Tommy, be serious for a moment."

"H'm—h'm," said Tommy, and proved he could be.

"This is likely to be dangerous. Bumped off in the twinkling of an eye and whatnot. Sure you're ready for it?"

"Ready for anything," said Tommy, "just as I am. Here we go."

Some twenty-five minutes later Wally Davidson, who was large for the Frazer Nash and bony, swore that never again would he drive with Akers Rumsden. Akers Rumsden, in fact, was the worst driver in London and its environs, and had Wally been a J.P. he would have demanded a Government test. He had said similar things most of that bumpy way, and Tommy had ignored him.

They parked the car a hundred yards from Craigie's office— which was approached through a small doorway in a street off Whitehall—and went along. Davidson didn't know whether they were being watched; the best he could say was that he didn't think so. He wondered how Craigie would take the flamboyant clothes of Mr. Rumsden, and wondered also whether he had been wise to introduce the artist to the Department.

They walked up to the first landing and Davidson pressed a bell hidden under the handrail. After a pause, during which Mr. Rumsden grew restless and mentioned that he was thirsty, the door opened. The sliding of it surprised Mr. Rumsden. He stood eying it reflectively, as though wondering whether thirst was an illusionary thing.

"Come on," implored Davidson.

"In there?"

"Yes. It's a door, isn't it?"

"That's a comfort," said Mr. Rumsden, and he crossed the threshold of Department Z for the first time.

He might have been its most frequent visitor.

He seemed a changed man as he stepped into the room, saw Craigie, half in and half out of his chair, and Kerr likewise opposite him. He blundered across the room towards Craigie and took that worthy's thin white hand.

"Well, well, well! It's a pleasure to meet you, and I've always wanted to. Don't trouble to get up, it's not worth it. Wally introduced me. As for you, sir"—he turned on Kerr and his grin was colossal—"fame is your lot. Flying through the air like a bird, fearless in face of disaster, courageous in face of all risks, what greater pleasure than to meet Bob Kerr, what greater honour than to shake his hand?" He pumped Bob Kerr's hand. "Wally, who the hell is this other fellow? You'll forgive Davidson, sir; it was his upbringing. A backward mind developed very slowly, and his greatest attainment is the devouring of beer. Wally, who the devil is—"

"Tommy," said Mr. Davidson weakly, "this is Gordon Craigie!"

"If you knew, why the hell didn't you say so? Now—you want me, Mr. Craigie. Yours to command. I'm a busy man but for Wally I'll do anything, preferably between two and six, the shut hours. What?" Mr. Akers Rumsden beamed.

Gordon Craigie chuckled, and Bob Kerr smiled, although he was a little thoughtful as he regarded the flamboyant Tommy Rumsden. Was Tommy too jovial? Or was his imagination playing still more tricks?

"Davidson's given you an idea of what kind of work you'll be doing," Craigie said.

"He spoke of death," said Mr. Rumsden sepulchrally, and hitched up his trousers.

"Ye-es. It's risky. But the particular job I want you to do needn't be—"

"Then why," demanded Mr. Rumsden, "pick on me?"

"—If you're careful." Craigie decided to ignore most of Mr. Rumsden's irresponsibilities. "Later you'll find it difficult, but for the moment I want you to get acquainted with a Mrs. Mort."

"*Mort!*" For the first time since he had entered the office Rumsden looked taken aback. "At Gretley Place?"

"That's right." Craigie looked sober. "You know her?"

"I know of her," said Mr. Rumsden, and regarded Davidson reproachfully. "You knew this was coming, didn't you? She'll fall on my neck, and—no, I can't do it. I just can't. I'll die for you, but I won't join Leila's hounds."

"Leila?" asked Craigie.

"Don't you know her as Leila?" asked Mr. Rumsden. "I've had some three dozen letters in the past year, inviting me to an At Home, or a Cocktail Party, or a Sherry Binge, or a Private Entertainment, all signed by Leila Mort. That's her method. She gets an eye on some poor devil and keeps at him until in desperation he goes. If he is weak-minded, he stays. If he stays he's done. It's worse," said Mr. Rumsden with horror, "than the effects of beer. Wait a minute. Here is one, actually a signed invitation to visit Mrs. Leila Mort. Look, I tell you!"

From his many-coloured coat he drew a letter, dog-eared, torn in one corner—to make a spill, Mr. Rumsden explained obligingly—and typewritten. It was an invitation, dated some three weeks before, to a Sherry Party at Gretley Place, and it was signed by Leila Mort.

"Do you know," said Kerr as though in a dream, "I thought I remembered that woman. She used to send me those things."

"Lion-hunting," said Rumsden. "She loves to be surrounded by people who are famous, and once she gets her talons in…A friend of mine," diverged Mr. Rumsden, "rather likes the woman. Says she means well, and serves good beer if you prefer it."

"It couldn't have suited our purpose better," said Craigie.

"You're not seriously asking me to accept this?" Mr. Rumsden retrieved the letter and glared.

"That or another one, for that's probably dated. Yes, I'd like you to. That's if you care to join us."

"What's the game?" asked Mr. Rumsden flatly.

"I don't know," said Craigie, and gave a brief outline—omitting most of the things that he and Kerr knew but which were not public property. He also used Mrs. Mort's visit to the Dummett Street House as the reason for his interest. As he talked Mr. Rumsden seemed to muse, and as he finished Mr. Rumsden took a crumpled cigarette from his pocket in his shirt and tapped it lightly on his thumb.

"I'll buy it," he said. "I'll barge over like this. Give the dear a shock. She loves—so she said in one of her letters—originality, and this coat was made specially, let me tell you."

"It looks it," said Bob Kerr.

"It's a good, serviceable coat," said Mr. Rumsden. "If I get blue paint on my fingers I wipe it on a blue bit. Yellow ditto. Red also, and so on. See?"

He pointed to an occasional daub of paint, which had merged so well in the colour scheme that no one would have dreamed it was not part of the cloth; and even Kerr was satisfied.

Some five minutes later, charged with certain orders by Gordon Craigie, whose Department he had just joined, Mr. Tommy Rumsden left the office with Davidson. Mrs. Mort would receive a visit in the near future, and up to a point it was nicely arranged. But Bob Kerr was thoughtful, and Craigie saw it.

"What's the trouble?" he asked.

"It's odd," said Bob Kerr, looking at his fist. "I *did* have those letters from Mrs. Mort, but it's queer we should have picked on a man, by accident, who had *entrée* to her place. And there's another queer thing."

"Go on," said Craigie.

"This game," said Kerr, eying his chief, "is a colour one of some kind. Rumsden's a colour specialist. What do you make of it?"

"I don't know," said Craigie. "I thought of the first but not the second. All the same, Rumsden can do no harm—we'll make sure we don't tell him much—and if he's all right he might do a lot of good. A fool of that nature will walk where angels fear to tread, and if he's really with us we couldn't have picked a better man. Meanwhile—"

"*Damn* that telephone," said Robert McMillan Kerr, for he hated the thing, and in Craigie's office it was rarely quiet for two minutes on end. There were times, in fact, when three were ringing at once, although only one was going now.

Craigie went over and listened. Kerr had heard some sensations after that same process, and watching Craigie's face he had an idea something was coming now. And he wasn't far wrong. For Gordon Craigie replaced the telephone and swung round, his eyes blazing.

"Mort's left London," he snapped. "He left by air, and he's half-way to Paris by now. Bob, that's your job. You *must* get him."

Bob Kerr was standing by the door very quickly.

"Ring Paris," he said, "and get someone to watch for him over there. I'll go to the Hôtel Metropole for messages, and I'll be there in a couple of hours. You'll 'phone Heston, of course, to have the bus ready for me?"

"And I'll send Toby Arran after you," said Craigie. "Good luck."

Robert McMillan Kerr, until lately flying-ace and speed-record holder, left the Department and started on the chase of Mr. Julius Mort. He felt it in his bones that it was going to be a dull one, and he took the sudden change of plans without a grumble; sudden, unexpected things were always happening to agents of Department Z.

11
PARIS AND OTHER PLACES

K err did not look like a man who could move at withering speed. He seemed on the steady side, in fact —the type of man who would prefer not to travel at more than forty even on a straight road. Yet, as Tommy Rumsden had been eager to point out, he was a master of speed in the air, and he proved it that day.

He also proved that he wasn't slow on the ground.

Within five minutes of the message reaching Craigie, Kerr was in Craigie's car, in Whitehall. For a second time that day he took little or no notice of road regulations, and two policemen saw the number of his car only just in time to prevent themselves from trying to stop him; to stop Kerr in that mood would have been next door to impossible, but they didn't know that.

He owned a small 'plane that was always in readiness at Heston, and Craigie would have telephoned the mechanics to get it fuelled and wheeled out of the hangar. Kerr's thoughts were divided between three things. First, getting through the traffic; second, whether Toby Arran would keep him waiting;

third, just where he would find Mr. Julius Mort in Paris. Mort's sudden disappearance—or more accurately his flight, which looked suspiciously as though he expected the police would be after him soon—seemed to suggest that Mort was even deeper in this affair than the Department had suspected.

That was the devil of the whole job; who the hell could they suspect as the king-pin of this game? It *must* be something out of the ordinary, something really big. Even Mannopoli—whose mental balance Kerr suspected to be a little lop-sided—wouldn't use bombs or do other things to the extent that he had unless the organization for which he was working was a big one.

What was it doing?

If Kerr could have glimpsed only a facet of the activities he would have been happier. He needed something to bite on. Well, this jaunt served the purpose reasonably well, and there wasn't time for grousing anyhow.

He wondered whether the girl had recovered consciousness yet. He couldn't get the picture of her out of his mind. Mauled as she had been, there had been a composure about her features that was little short of astonishing. Kerr had heard her cry, piteous, entreating.

Now he frowned.

It was surprising that her expression had shown no hint of the fear and pain she must have experienced. Certainly she hadn't. He had never seen a more serene beauty.

Odd, devilish odd. Well, when she came round Craigie would talk to her, and it was possible that she would have a great deal of interesting information to pass on. It was quite certain that Mannopoli had tried to kill her, and nearly as certain that he had wanted to make sure she couldn't talk.

Mannopoli was a prisoner too; he *might* talk. It was queer how some men acted when they were behind bars.

Kerr went perilously near the tail-board of a lorry, whose driver—apparently possessed of eyes at the back of his head—was not polite. By that time Kerr was in Chiswick High Street, and another fifteen minutes would see him at the aerodrome.

Should he go on if Arran hadn't arrived?

The contingency didn't arise, as it happened, for Toby Arran was waiting. Kerr had expected many things, but that was the last. He showed his surprise, and Toby perked his head on one side.

"They told me," he said, "that you could move fast. I'm beginning to doubt it."

"All right," said Kerr; "I'm pilot."

"Now look here," said Toby, who was never really happy in the air, "don't get rough, Bob. No offence meant."

"How did you get here?" They were walking towards the aeroplane, a four-seater cabin 'plane, sleek and grey with its two great engines purring and the propellers whirling in a windy circle.

"By tube," said Toby, with a chuckle. "Craigie told me to hurry, and I popped down to St. James's Park, and here I am. It's quicker than by road."

"All right," said Kerr, and not for the first time it occurred to him that he often went to an immense amount of trouble to do things that were actually simple. He didn't say so, for Toby would probably crow, and Toby crowing would be insufferable.

They climbed in the cabin; mechanics pulled the chocks away from the wheels, and Kerr released the brakes. The monoplane went forward, slowly at first and bumping a little; and then it swooped upwards towards the blue heavens, as smoothly and calmly as a great bird. Kerr climbed faster than usual from a take-off; soon Heston was a vague haze behind them, and the nose of the monoplane was pointing towards the East Coast.

Kerr explained, and went on:

"Craigie's telephoning our men in Paris to watch for Mort, and we're going to the Metropole to pick up messages. Mort *might* stay in Paris; I'm more inclined to think he'll use it as a jumping-off place for other, better lands."

"He would," Toby sniffed. "I haven't been to the Follies for a year, Bob. Could do with a lift-up."

"You're going to Paris," said Kerr heavily, "on business."

"Carry on, Sergeant," murmured Tobias Arran; and then his expression grew serious, and he said very slowly: "Ellen Granting, Bob. Was she badly hurt?"

"You've been told no," Kerr said.

"I know. You might have softened it down a bit; I'd rather you didn't."

Kerr didn't immediately reply. He was amazed at the effect that Ellen Granting had on Toby Arran. It was almost as if the man were falling in love, for Kerr knew the signs.

Kerr hoped it wasn't true, but if it was it couldn't be helped.

"I told you just what the position was," he said. "She'd had a bit of skin cut out of her side—not very deep—and she'd been hit over the head. I fancy she'll be up and about again in a couple of days, with nothing more than an occasional twinge to remind her that the thing had ever happened."

"Hump!" said Arran, and he was so silent for a few minutes that Kerr thought he was day-dreaming. He wasn't, for he went on at last in a harder voice than Kerr had ever heard from him before. "There's something foul about that wound in her side."

"I know," said Kerr.

"I'm damned if I can understand it."

"I don't understand anything," said Kerr, and then it occurred to him that Toby was brooding, and that he might easily get morbid. He plunged into a recital of Mr. Tommy (Akers) Rumsden's introductions to the Department, and his power of description was so vivid that Toby Arran laughed; and from that moment the atmosphere was more cheerful.

They sighted the sea after twenty minutes' flying, a shimmering surface with scintillating lights on the tops of the waves that looked like a myriad diamonds. A clear blue sky emphasized the serenity of the waves and the green fields that ended abruptly. Arran glanced at the speed-indicator, saw they were touching two-fifty and whistled under his breath. Kerr certainly knew what speed was in the air.

And Kerr wasn't the only one.

He noticed the other machine first. It was behind them almost in a straight line, and he had seen it several times and wondered. He knew that few machines flying over England touched two hundred and fifty miles an hour, and it was a disturbing fact that this one was gaining. The monoplane—called, he had told Toby, the *Grey Queen*—was very nearly at its limit, but the other bus—a biplane—was still on its tail.

Kerr opened the throttle a little wider, and the needle quivered towards the two-seventy mark. There was no appreciable difference in the *Queen's* speed; and after three minutes' flying there was no appreciable change in the gap between the two 'planes. If anything the biplane was nearer.

Kerr broached the subject.

"We're in for trouble," he said, and he jerked his head towards the rear of the cabin. Arran glanced round and saw the biplane for the first time. He didn't alter his expression but he felt an unpleasant sensation in the pit of his stomach.

"After us, are they?"

"Looks like it."

"Will you fight?"

"If necessary. I don't like taking the *Queen* against a biplane, but she's a beautiful little bus and she usually does what she's told. Ever handled a machine-gun?"

"Have I not!" exclaimed Arran, and he felt more cheerful. Action was a big thing. "Got one?"

"Under your seat, two of them. Tommies."

"You believe in being ready for trouble, don't you?" murmured Arran with a chuckle.

"I'd be in it if I wasn't," said Kerr, his eyes on the mirror that showed him the approaching 'plane. He waited until Toby Arran took out a familiar snub-nosed Thomson machine-gun—Tommy for short, although neither of them thought of Rumsden—and then went on. "Have a look through your glasses, Toby. You might see how many there are in the cabin."

Toby Arran obliged. He focused the glasses, and was surprised at the way in which the biplane seemed to grow nearer. He scanned the faces of the occupants for a few moments, and although they were tiny he was reasonably sure that he had never seen any of them before. He was able to say that the biplane's cabin held four men, and that was the main thing.

"Four, eh?" said Kerr in a tight voice. "That means they can tackle us on both sides, old man, and I don't like it. I can't use a gun while I'm here, blast it. And they're faster than we are."

"Much?"

"Thirty miles an hour, I fancy. I'm going to slow down. We might as well start the funny business if there's going to be any."

Arran nodded, and yet he felt doubtful. The unpleasant feeling at the pit of his stomach had gone; he had a gun, and even in the air a chance was a chance. But:

"Supposing they aren't after us?"

"We'll see," said Bob Kerr, and he eased off the throttle.

It happened quickly, too quickly. The *Queen* dropped to a hundred miles an hour, and the biplane seemed to leap on top of them. Toby Arran was watching with his glasses all the time. The four faces loomed larger, gigantic now; and none of them faces that Toby could feel any affection for.

And then he saw the snout of the Tommy poking through a slit in the biplane's cabin window!

"You're right," he snapped, and he had the Tommy in his hands in a flash. "Shall I open the window?"

"The left one," said Bob Kerr.

The words were hardly out of his mouth when the other 'plane opened fire. The *tap-tap-tap* of the machine-guns, the stabs of flame, and the pecking of bullets on the undercarriage of the *Queen* seemed to come simultaneously. And as they rattled Kerr swung the 'plane round to the left in a screeching bend.

At the same time he increased the speed, and the *Queen* leapt ahead. In a flash they were out of range of the other machine.

Or so Toby thought, until the second gun started. The bullets were dropping short, but Kerr hadn't been wrong when he had said that the others had the advantage.

"Hold tight," Kerr said. "We're going over them. Let them have it when we're there."

Kerr's coolness was a thing to marvel at. Arran was tight-lipped now, and he realized the dreadful possibilities of this duel in the air. It had come so quickly that he had hardly had time to think about it, but he knew that if they lost it would be the end.

Kerr didn't seem to give it a second's thought.

He knew his job, and he could handle the *Queen* like a toy. After that racing bend he straightened out and then pulled back on the stick. Flying conditions were perfect and he knew he could rely on his bus to do just what he wanted.

The *Queen* went upwards.

It was travelling so fast that the biplane seemed to drop behind them; and now Arran, still nursing the Tommy, could see that Kerr was smiling, a tight-lipped smile of little humour but of great satisfaction. He saw too that the biplane's nose was pointing skywards, that it was climbing too; but Kerr didn't give it a chance.

It was the most ruthless, devastating thing that Arran had ever known, and he played his part in it almost detachedly, as though he couldn't control his own actions.

The *Queen* raced forward; for a moment it looked as though the two 'planes must collide, and then Arran saw that the monoplane was well above the other; the biplane was beneath them, its left-side machine-gun working fast but ineffectively. Arran saw that he could pour a broadside into the gaping cabin; and Kerr's voice snapped the order at the same moment.

"Let it go."

Toby Arran touched the trigger of the Tommy and kept it there. Wind cut through the open window, flame blew back in his face, the stink of cordite was in his nostrils. But the bullets snapped out, *tap-tap-tap-tap-tap* all the time. Ceaselessly and remorselessly he hurled them into the cabin, and he saw the glass pierced, saw first one then another of the men drop away from the window. He could see the pilot trying frantically to get out of range—

And then the flames came.

They came with a terrific burst, and the *Queen* was caught in the gust of wind that they created. A split second later the flames were streaming from the tail of the biplane as it dropped—dropped—dropped towards the sea, smoke adding now to the horror of it, a great black pall that hid the red anger of the flames.

And then the biplane hit the water.

They heard nothing of the crash; they saw the sea cleft as though in two, a great yawning crater, a wild seething foam; the biplane's nose went first; and then it simply dropped out of existence.

It just wasn't there; but the water was swirling and breaking below, where it had been; the smoke was still a black pall, while a few odd pieces of débris were tossed and turned in the thrashing waves.

Toby Arran said afterwards that it had been the most horrible thing he had ever seen. The way in which the biplane and its occupants had been wiped off the face of the earth was something that turned him. He dropped back into his seat after he had looked away, and Kerr, glancing at him, saw that he was very pale.

Kerr had seen things like that happen before; he had seen aeroplanes taken by the wind and storm and dealt a similar fate, and in this case he could feel nothing but a grim satisfaction. Either the biplane or the monoplane would have suffered that fate; he'd won, and that was all there was to it.

Arran stirred himself, took a swig at the whisky in his flask, and colour returned to his cheeks. His voice was a little unsteady.

"They're certainly after us, Bob."

"And they didn't lose any time," said Kerr. "We were watched and followed from Heston. That biplane must have taken off ten minutes after us—it was standing outside the hangar when we were there."

"Did you recognize anyone?"

"No one at all. More mystery." Kerr's laugh was a bark. "Anyhow, they're four less, and they can't go on forever. Paris and Mr. Mort is the next thing to worry about. A spot of your whisky, Toby; I haven't got my flask."

From which, Toby gathered, Bob Kerr was more affected than he made out to be.

Some three-quarters of an hour later they flew over Paris. Both from the air and on the ground the country was familiar to the fliers, and they landed with no more exhilaration than they would have landed at Heston. Memory of the fight and its end was dimmed now. They wanted Mort, and to get on the tail of the game.

A slim, red-haired man with very full lips was waiting near the customs sheds as they left the aerodrome. There was something familiar about him to Toby Arran, who eyed him several times. Apparently disinterested, the red-haired man scraped the ground with the ferrule of the walking-stick he was carrying, and Arran saw, after several squints, what he was doing. He smiled.

"Robert, my son, there's a friend. The red-haired cove making Z's in the dust. Come over. It's all right, I've seen him before."

The red-haired man lost no time in introductions.

"I had a call from Z," he said, when Arran had spoken the password. "Mort's at the Bristol at the moment, but he's telephoned reserving a seat on to-morrow's *Golden Arrow*."

"Good," said Toby, and Kerr snapped:

"Is the Bristol watched?"

"One of our men's there. A short fellow, but broader than Arran. Wearing a blue trilby and carrying yellow pigskin gloves."

"Are you coming?" asked Kerr, already beckoning a cab.

"No, I'm staying here in case of new arrivals."

"Keep staying," said Kerr, "but they won't come." He didn't wait to enlarge on his words, but waved cheerily at the red-haired man, whose smile was one of amusement. Arran waited with Redhair until the last minute, and then leapt for the cab.

The Bristol was crowded; the two men from England had passed the man in the blue trilby and the gloves—with, of course, other things—and their cabby had delivered them, after many narrow shaves and more noise than seemed possible, outside the munificent entry to the hotel. Kerr signed as 'Mr. Kerrick,' and Arran omitted to sign at all; such things were easy.

"I ought to have asked Redhair for Mort's room number," Kerr said.

"I did," beamed Toby, "while you were walking to the cab. And here's the master-key. Efficiency is our watchword, eh? Going straight up?"

"This is a job," said Bob Kerr very grimly, "when there isn't time to argue. We're going to put the fear of God into Mr. Mort, and if he's not religious we'll try the fear of the devil. Where is he?"

"Suite ninety-seven. On the third floor."

"A suite for one night, eh?"

"Remember he's a millionaire and probably a regular visitor," Toby reminded him. "What's the scheme?"

"I'll go in, and you'll keep watch while I'm doing it. You'll hang around, of course." They reached the lift, and didn't enlarge on their plans until they were on the third floor, which, as usual, was deserted. By the time they had reached suite ninety-seven, their campaign was clear in each man's mind. Kerr was relying again on those downright methods that so often had taken him past corners which would have been sticky for most men. Thanks to Redhair and the master-key, getting in Mort's room would not be difficult, and Kerr proposed to introduce himself to Mr. Mort without a by-your-leave.

Toby Arran saw the broad back of his friend disappear, and wished he could see the fun. He was standing at a corner of the passage, so that he could see the room where Kerr had gone, the lift and the stairs at one and the same time. Or within a split second of each other—a thing that Toby considered made no difference.

He was wrong.

He saw the lift come up, and saw the little Frenchman who stepped out and walked rapidly past him, muttering under his breath. The Frenchman was muttering in French which was not polite, and Toby, following him with his eyes, wondered what had upset the little gentleman.

And then he stopped wondering.

He didn't see the cosh; he didn't hear a sound until it thudded on the back of his head like a ton weight. A single gasp forced itself from his lips, but he didn't realize it. He dropped like a stone, and would have thudded against the floor had not the man who had used the cosh grabbed him.

The man was a large one, and muscular. His face was what might be called nondescript; his actions weren't. He picked Toby Arran up in his arms, stepped to the nearest door, opened it and bundled Toby inside. He waited just long enough to fasten cord round Toby's wrists and ankles and stick plaster over his lips, sealing them unpleasantly. Then he went out, going towards suite ninety-seven. The little Frenchman who used bad language was waiting outside it, and together they opened the door and walked in.

They saw the back of Robert Kerr and the front of Mr. Mort; the front of Mr. Mort was unpleasant to look on, for that fat millionaire was dreadfully afraid.

12

HOT WORK

B ob Kerr was not a believer in superstitions; had he been
he might have had some faith in sequences, particularly
the popular sequence of threes. For on this affair, of which he
knew so very little beyond action, he had already been
surprised twice when he had been in a room to which he had
no legal access; and this was the third room, and the trio of
events was likely to be completed.

But if Kerr wasn't suspicious he was observant, and he saw
the way Mr. Julius Mort kept glancing towards the door.

He had reached one opinion since arriving in Paris; he
didn't believe Mort was the man he was looking for. He didn't
believe this financier could have been the inspiring genius of
those deadly attacks any more than Frederick Mulling.

Very little had passed between them.

Mort had been in the first room when Kerr had entered.
He had started up, and his face had slowly turned colour.
Normally it was florid, but it had become a pale pink. He was
very fat, and every ounce of that fat seemed to quiver.

But he kept glancing towards the door, and Kerr slipped

his hand in his pocket. His left hand. The right was holding the gun which had been such an unpleasant surprise for Mr. Mort.

Kerr had spoken twice, Mort once. Thus:

"I've come," Bob had said, "from England; I've just finished with Mannopoli, and now I'm after you."

And Mr. Mort had muttered:

"I—I—don't know what you mean. I—"

"You soon will," Kerr had grunted; and then, following Mort's gaze and seeing the hint of relief in the man's fish-like eyes, he had realized the men were standing in the door-way. He took two steps from Mr. Mort and turned round. His gun was still in his right hand, and he drew his left, apparently empty, from his pocket.

The very large man and the very small man faced him. Neither of them was handsome, and neither of them looked pleased to see him. The Frenchman was furtive, narrow of eye and sallow of skin. The other man was a Dane or a Swede; so much Kerr was sure. He was a vast hulk of a man, and his brutishness suggested a certain cunning. There wasn't any cunning about the gun in his hand.

"Hallo," said Bob Kerr.

The big man grinned unpleasantly and took a short step forward. His English was guttural but good.

"Caught you, eh? Drop that gun, mister!"

"Mine or yours?" asked Kerr affably, and as he spoke he opened the palm of his left hand.

It was a simple gesture, almost that of a man who wanted to free his fingers from cramp. The big Swede—Kerr after-wards confirmed that guess—didn't even look at it. Nor did the Frenchman. Neither of them saw the little phial that flew from Kerr's palm, but they heard the tinkle as it broke at their feet and with one accord they swung round, convinced it came from behind them.

Kerr's first shot took the Swede's gun out of his hand without touching his fingers, and his second went through the Frenchman's forearm. Kerr liked forearms. Both men yelled; the Swede lurched forward, venom in his eyes, and then he choked.

Mr. Mort choked too.

Bob Kerr, holding his breath to save himself from swallowing the gas from the phial—what a clever thought of Craigie's it had been to give him the phials!—grabbed Mort's arm and dragged him towards the door which led into the next room of the suite. Once in, he banged the door and pushed Mort forcefully towards the bed. Mort reached it and struck against it, and then sank down. He hadn't the strength to stop himself.

"So you've some friends here?" asked Kerr, and without waiting for an answer he stepped across the room and clouted Mort across the head with the butt of his gun. He hit hard, with intention. Mort yelped once, his eyes rolled, and then he sagged farther downwards. Kerr didn't wait to see him quivering, but slipped a small thing that looked like closely woven fabric from his pocket, put it over his mouth and nose and then went back into the first room.

He was smiling as well as he could behind the mask. The Frenchman had fallen first, and across his little body sprawled the Swede. Both of them were right out, and both looked as though they had known a dreadful fear just before losing consciousness. Kerr stepped to the window, flung it open wide, and then considered.

Mort would be unconscious for ten minutes, and this brace for half an hour. Toby had been on guard and had therefore been caught napping. His first job was to find Toby.

He removed his mask and went out, but he had no luck at first; he reasoned quickly and then, thanking the red-haired man more than ever, decided to use the pass-key on every room in sight. He wondered what would happen room by room, but he didn't wonder for long.

In the first a middle-aged and fleshy Frenchman settling down to an afternoon nap sat up from his bed like a jack-in-the-box and swore. Kerr apologized profusely in fluent French and went out. In the second a large, spreading woman who was certainly not French was examining herself in a large mirror, a full-length mirror. She screamed. Kerr hurled a dozen frantic apologies and banged the door to, breathing hard. He hoped to God no one had heard that scream, and he listened for a few seconds, on tenterhooks. But the woman was either shameless, on reflection, or was too shy to confess the truth; she created no further disturbance, which was a relief.

Kerr regarded the third room thoughtfully. Heaven alone knew what he would find in there. If he could safely have tapped on the door the situation would have been more decorous, but if Arran had been pushed into one of these rooms it was by no means certain he was alone. So Bob Kerr opened the third door, drawing a deep breath as he did so....

And he stood on the threshold like a man turned to stone.

And the woman who was sitting back in an easy chair and smoking was as motionless. Her peignoir was a long way from effective, but Kerr hardly realized it and certainly she didn't care just then. She was more startled than she had ever been in her life, and for a moment her beauty seemed haunted and her expression strained.

While Robert McMillan Kerr closed the door behind him without asking permission, and regarded Ellen Granting with eyes that could not have been harder.

That girl was here!

Kerr recovered his self-possession first, but the girl wasn't far behind. She didn't move, but he saw that her muscles relaxed. She made no effort to spread the peignoir further, and the flimsy things she wore underneath were little help. She hardly seemed to care; Kerr wondered fleetingly whether she was doing this deliberately. There were better ways of antagonizing a man than revealing curves and other things; she was certainly lovely, and her flesh was like mother-of-pearl.

"So you're here," said Kerr slowly. "You recovered quickly, didn't you?"

She moved now; she stood up, and she smiled. Gad, but she was a vision!

"Yes—I'm here. And so are you. You move fast, Mr. Kerr."

"I've reasons for it."

"Haven't I?"

"I'd like to know them."

"You might—one day."

"All things are possible," said Robert McMillan Kerr, and he walked across to the single bed in the room and sat down. Her eyes didn't leave his. "When did you leave London?"

"By the afternoon air-liner from Croydon."

"Does Craigie know you've come?"

"Is Craigie my keeper?"

"Is this," asked Bob Kerr with a smile that was really of amusement, "your favourite back-chat, Miss Granting?"

"I've never tried it before," she said, and she stretched her arms above her head and yawned; she was like a young animal, lovely, graceful, almost feline, and certainly

147

unashamed. "Do you make a habit of bursting into rooms like this?"

"I've done it often before," said Kerr. "Not always so pleasantly."

He waited; he was smiling, and he was a remarkably attractive man when he smiled. She seemed to realize it; there was something very alluring about her, and for the life of him Kerr couldn't be sure whether it was entirely natural or whether she was deliberately putting herself out to destroy his critical faculties.

"You can be human," she said, and she laughed. Her teeth gleamed as she laughed, and Kerr had to harden his smile.

"I'm often human," he said; "it's a question of finding it out, that's all. Er—did you come to Paris for a special reason?"

She shrugged her shoulders, and her eyes were gleaming.

"That friend of mine who was taken ill," she said, "was removed to Paris, and of course I had to come after her."

"Of course," said Kerr, and his voice was gentle. "So the other story was pitched, too?"

"Hadn't you guessed."

"Pretty well, but it's good to be sure. Now—you'll forgive this instance—but you're in a peculiar position and I'm in an awkward one. I don't want to be harsh, but I want information."

"What about?" Her expression was inscrutable.

"Mannopoli."

Her lips tightened a little, and he had an idea she was angry or frightened. It was impossible to be sure which.

"I can't tell you anything about him."

"Did you know he tried to kill you?"

"I know," she said, with a sudden vehemence that surprised him, "that he would kill me if I talked. Now do you understand?"

"I've heard a lot of things," said Kerr, "but I've never met a man who could commit murder from a prison cell—or a hospital ward, whichever Mannopoli's in. You knew the police had him?"

Ellen Granting did not answer immediately. Kerr saw her expression, and wondered what was passing through her mind. Her clear eyes were frightened—yes, frightened was the word. And when she spoke her voice was very low.

"Mannopoli is capable of anything," she said.

The words made Kerr feel cold. In themselves they confirmed the impression that he had formed of the man; and then there was the slow, deliberate way in which they had been spoken. One thing was certain: this girl knew a great deal about Augustus Mannopoli, and was aware of the man's odd power of exciting fear.

But Kerr forced himself to speak.

"I see. And you're so frightened of him that you won't talk?"

"That's it." She wasn't trying to exercise the thing called it now; she was deadly serious, Kerr believed, and he drew a deep breath.

"Then I'm badly afraid," he said, "that I'll have to make you. I've got to know."

They stood there for perhaps twenty seconds, their eyes narrowed, Kerr's lips set, hers parted. She was breathing fast, her breast was rising and falling, and the lace on the top of whatever the peignoir covered was quivering; an absurd thing to notice. Her eyes were very direct; Kerr had never seen any so clear, and he could well understand why Toby Arran had been bowled over. He'd have to do something about Toby Arran soon.

"I can't talk," she said at last, in a high, strained voice.

"You've got to."

"You can't make me!" There was something courageous about her defiance, and something that caught at Kerr's heart. He hated this job; it was the devil, dealing with women. And this one had had enough to cope with during the past day or two. Her side must be strapped and bandaged even now.

"I can," he said, and she understood just how he could; she could see past his expression, and his face was set, and knew that nothing—nothing!—would stop him from making her talk. Force must be used if necessary. He *had* to know.

Murder was rife; Craigie believed—in fact *knew*—that this affair had complications outside England. Anything, everything might be at stake. Yes, he *had* to know.

And then she seemed to break down.

The fear in her eyes was naked, the catch in her voice was rending. She took a half-step towards him; and then before Kerr knew what was coming her arms were about his neck and she was pressing against him, her eyes so close to his that he could see every lash, every fleck in their grey. He could feel her heart thumping, the pressure of her hands and arms.

"No, no, no! You mustn't make me talk, you mustn't!"

"It's for your good," Kerr said, and it was typical of him that he didn't move, but his muscles were tensed. He looked stiff and cold; he felt his own heart thumping, so very close to hers, and he knew that it would have been easy to fall—for whatever she wanted, whatever she asked him to do. But he daren't.

"I tell you—"

"I'm sorry," said Kerr; "you've got to talk."

For a moment she eyed him as though she didn't believe any man could have withstood that appeal. And then she sobbed, a harsh, racking sound, and drooped back into the chair, her face covered in her hands.

"It will—mean the end for me," she said, and her voice was very unsteady.

"I'll look after you."

"You can't! Against Mannopoli no one could. He's too powerful. Good heavens, don't you realize he's an organization in a dozen countries, he has friends in every sphere, in every Government, everywhere? Don't you know how powerful he is, how quickly he kills, how—" She stopped for a moment, and Kerr waited, on a tension now that she had said so much to confirm what he and Craigie had feared. "You don't know, of course." Her voice was dull and all trace of hysteria had gone, although she still looked badly frightened. "Well, this is all I know. Three years ago I—I lost my head. Don't think that's meaningless, it explains everything. I made a fool of myself, came over here and—was left stranded. I was penniless. The only relation I had in the world was John Fallow, and I'd never met him; I wouldn't appeal to him for help."

She wouldn't, Kerr thought, but it was only a fleeting fancy through his mind. His eyes hadn't altered, but inwardly he was exultant. This was what he had wanted for—how long was it? Three days? It seemed years! Forgotten was Toby Arran, Mr. Mort, the Swede, and the Frenchman. The girl was all that mattered just then.

"I met Mannopoli just after that," she said. "And—I told him how I was placed." Her eyes didn't flicker. "In Paris," she said, "money can be earned easier than anywhere else by a girl whose looks aren't against her. I thought Mannopoli was that type. He wasn't. He gave me money and told me of an address at which to go. At the address I was given a supply of—of green diamond-shaped cards—"

"The devil you were!" exclaimed Kerr. He couldn't resist that interruption, although it didn't seem to affect her.

"Yes. Mr. Craigie found one somewhere. Well—I was sent back to London. I'd had to make a statement of all my relations and friends. I didn't know why. For a time I was living in luxury. And then—I was told to go to John Fallow, and ask him to let me live there. I didn't like it, but Mannopoli came to the hotel where I was staying—and I didn't hesitate long after that."

She shivered; the past seemed to be in the room, and Kerr believed he could understand what she was feeling.

"I went to Tarrington. Fallow was kindness itself. And I *forgot* why I'd gone there. For two years I heard nothing. And then, a few weeks ago, I was sent for. I went to London and saw Mannopoli again. He told me to get certain things from Fallow's safe, and I had a month in which to work. I hated it, but I knew I'd have to do it."

"Did you get what he wanted?"

"No, thank God! Arran came before that. I don't know much about it, but I gathered that Mannopoli didn't want anyone to know Mort was concerned in any—criminal affair. Mort had written a letter or something to John Fallow. That's all I know. That's all I know!" she repeated, and her voice rose, for Bob Kerr looked as though he hadn't heard her.

But he made good the omission.

"It's a lot," he said. "It's a great lot. Now listen, Miss Granting. No one but Craigie and I know you've told me this. No one. But there are a few questions you might be able to answer."

"I'll try." She was composed again now, and she walked across to the wardrobe and slipped her arms into a more effective dressing-gown. Kerr felt relieved. "What are they?"

"First—do you know any of the addresses from which Mannopoli has been working in Europe?"

She shook her head slowly.

"I only know that he's stayed here sometimes."

"You know what countries he's connected with?"

"Practically every country."

"Do you know any of his agents, other than Mort?"

"I—" began the girl; and then she stopped and looked towards the door. Kerr followed her gaze, and though he was half prepared for it, he cursed inwardly.

The handle was turning, very slowly.

The door opened a fraction of an inch; a little more. Kerr slipped his gun from his pocket; the girl watched, wide-eyed, and terrified now. And then, very softly, came Julius Mort's voice.

"Ellen, are you there?"

Mr. Mort was conscious, and still badly afraid! There could be no mistaking that. The girl's lips parted, but before she could speak Kerr had reached the door and flung it open. Mort darted back, but the gun stopped him going too far.

"Come in," invited Bob Kerr jovially. "*You* might do more than your lady friend, and talk. I'll be able to handle you, anyhow. *Come in*, I said."

Mr. Mort advanced slowly, his eyes on the gun. Kerr didn't see the expression, that might have been of gratitude at the way he had lied, that passed through the girl's eyes.

"How are the boyfriends?" asked Kerr cheerfully. "Come *right* in, and close the door. You"—he motioned with his free hand towards the girl—"get back in your chair. I've had more than enough of you. Mort—"

He didn't go any farther.

He could have cursed himself a moment later, for as soon as he felt the pressure in the small of his back he knew what it was.

The girl had held him up; the girl was poking a gun in his ribs!

"Drop your gun," she said, and her voice was very firm.

Kerr hesitated. Should he shoot Mort and take a chance?

153

He believed she had been telling him the truth, he believed that she was doing this to convince Mort she hadn't talked, to make certain Mort carried no tales. But—he wasn't sure.

He had an idea it wasn't a moment for bluffing.

He released his hold on the gun, and it thudded on the floor. The pressure in his ribs relaxed, but the thing of greatest interest was the change in Mr. Mort.

Mort seemed a new man! He padded across the room and then before Kerr had an idea of what was coming, he brought his podgy fist into Kerr's face. The Department Z man staggered back, but on the rebound he leapt forward, his eyes blazing. Damn the girl, damn Mort! He'd—

The thing hit him on the back of the head, and he didn't know any more just then. He went out. As he did so the girl dropped the gun which she had used as a club, and stood back, staring, apparently aghast. Mr. Mort didn't. He chuckled unpleasantly, and his relief was a thing to marvel at.

"You're a good girl, Ellen, a very good girl. I couldn't have done better myself. Slip along to my room and get some sticking-plaster. Lorens will have some in his pocket—he's uncon-scious, but that needn't worry you."

The girl hesitated; and then she obeyed. Mort chuckled, even more unpleasantly than before, and knelt down. He made an excellent job of tying Kerr's wrists behind him, and his ankles with a length of cord that he took from his pocket, and by the time that the job was finished the girl reappeared. She had the sticking-plaster and Mort made a good job of sealing Kerr's lips. Kerr and Arran might have been twins in treatment.

"Good," said Mort, who seemed to have forgotten his earlier display of cowardice. His eyes were on the girl's, and she shivered. They were unpleasantly cold. "It's a lucky thing for you he didn't persuade you to talk, my dear, otherwise you might have been branded very differently."

"Don't talk about it," she said tensely. "What—what are we going to do?"

"We're going to Berlin, of course, as arranged. The Hotel Frankfurt, and I'll see you there at midday to-morrow. Now" — Mr. Mort gave an order and looked as though he regretted its necessity—"get some clothes on and hurry away. This place isn't safe any longer. Hurry, my dear!"

He patted her shoulder in a fatherly fashion, and she shuddered. He smirked, and walked out; but not until she had shot the bolt of the door did she slip off her dressing-gown and, stiff because of the wound and the plaster on her side, start to dress. She looked very grim, very capable and very beautiful; she appeared to have forgotten Bob Kerr.

13

THE MORT MÉNAGE

M rs. Julius (Leila) Mort had returned from Dummett Street after the murder of the man named Gabrell very close to tears. It was natural that her secretary immediately sent for the doctor; it was natural that the man from Harley Street gave Mrs. Mort a sedative and sent her to bed. Because she was sound asleep for the rest of that day she knew nothing of the stir that Mort's sudden trip to France had created in the household.

Mort's affection for his wife was a thing of doubt, but he certainly kept her in luxury. The house at Gretley Place was a home fit for a millionaire; one trod on priceless carpets and looked at priceless daubs; very few things in the Mort ménage were not valuable. If a painting of dubious ancestry contrived to get in, it did not remain for long. Mrs. Mort had one favourite axiom—she always liked things *good*.

Something under an hour after Gabrell's murder, Julius Mort reached the house, went upstairs past bowing footmen— such things were still possible even in London—and snapped an order to Riddle, his valet.

"I'm going to Paris. Flying from Croydon in an hour. Get everything ready."

Riddle was curious, and yet knew his employer well enough to realize he mustn't show it. Mort looked worried, he thought, but that was nothing out of the ordinary these days.

"For how long, sir, shall I pack?"

"A couple of weeks."

"Mrs. Mort, sir, is in bed under doctor's orders. Shall I give instructions for her to be called?"

"No!" snarled Mort. "I'll go and see her."

He didn't; and Riddle knew it; but no one cared.

Among the dozen servants who watched him hurry out of the house and climb into the Rolls which was waiting outside, some fifteen minutes later, was Mrs. Mort's secretary.

Most people expected Mrs. Mort to have a male secretary; she disappointed them. Perhaps it was because she could bear no one near her at whom she couldn't snap, and she did not make a practice of snapping at anything in trousers if it looked presentable. Consequently Mary Wayne did the job, and did it well.

She looked competent, and she proved her looks did not belie her. She was, in the words of Mrs. Mort, a colourless little thing, and consequently she was not a victim of that lady's vituperative efforts more than once a week. She was slim, nearly thirty, dark, pale, and bespectacled. Her hair was straight and pulled into a bun at the back. Her clothes always contrived to make her look shapeless, and on the whole Mary Wayne enjoyed the joke. She didn't believe that Leila Mort was quite the hussy that most people made out, and she'd found her amenable to reason in most things.

True, Leila would have had a shock had she been able to see Mary Wayne on her 'off' days—those rare occasions when she was allowed to go out on her own and give no definite time for coming back. Mary went invariably to her sister's flat at Notting Hill, played for a few minutes with the Cherub—or her sister's three-year-old son—changed, dressed her hair as it should be dressed, slipped into a dress that fitted her, took off her plain glasses and looked like the Mary Wayne who had lived before she had worked for Leila Mort.

There was a story behind it; Mary had learned of the job at Gretley Place, and had an acquaintance who had once worked for her ladyship—a courtesy title that most of her servants bestowed, not charitably, on Leila. The acquaintance had discovered that the only secretary who had worked for Leila Mort for more than three months had been plain and dowdy. She passed this news on to Mary Wayne, with the information that the job carried a really good salary—some three hundred pounds a year—and Mary undertook to get it. She had now been working at the Gretley Place house for three years.

She didn't like the men, but she saw little of them. She had more than enough to do, but she was often able to persuade Mrs. Mort to get her extra help. And, coupled with occasional week-ends of freedom and a few week-days when she could get into the country or go to her sister's—one Jane, who had married a sailor who acted on the Atlantic liner *Jania* as Second-officer Hanson—and enjoy herself.

Of all the people at Gretley, visitors, hangers-on and servants, she disliked Julius Mort most. Julius Mort obviously didn't mind whether a secretary was plain with a bun or not; but he had experimented only twice with Mary, and thereafter there had been peace.

But when he could he made her life a misery, and she watched him go with considerable satisfaction.

"How long will he be gone, Riddy?" Mr. Riddle, pompous and an ideal valet, was reflecting on similar thoughts to Mary's.

"I packed for a fortnight, Miss Wayne, but you know how unexpectedly he comes back sometimes."

"He's good for a week, anyhow," said Mary, and smiled at Mr. Riddle, who wondered whether she was really as dowdy as she looked. Her teeth were something to think about.

To ease Mary's burden further, Leila was in bed. The girl didn't go out, but she stayed in her own room and read a light novel, the first she had been able to read at a sitting for weeks. Dinner—more reading—bed; and the day had been perfect.

But Mrs. Mort woke up next day with a vile head and a worse temper, and purgatory had begun. Mary took it cheerfully enough; she could understand it in a way. For one of Mrs. Mort's private entertainments were due that afternoon, and Leila would naturally want to look her best.

The private entertainments were innocuous enough. An orchestra, two or three top-of-the-bill artistes from the variety stage, preferably a couple of celebrities, a troupe of chorus-girls, anything alcoholic, a general fug and a bad morning to follow. In Mary Wayne's mind that summed them up, and the afternoon's affair was not likely to be any different from the general run.

Mary knew that Mrs. Mort knew Cecil Gabrell; she saw the report of his murder; and she understood even more fully why her employer was in a bad mood. Consequently she was more cheerful than usual with her employer, and ten minutes before three-thirty—the time the first guests were to be expected—the older woman smiled for the first time that day.

"You're very patient, Mary. I won't forget it."

"I've got a job to do," said Mary Wayne. "But are you sure you feel well enough?"

"Don't I look well enough?" asked Mrs. Mort.

"You look"—Mary searched for the word that would please Mrs. Mort, and found it—"divine." It wasn't far wrong, for

Leila Mort was dressed in maroon, which showed her colouring to the best advantage, and she looked not a year over thirty. If her make-up was a little on the heavy side, it was only to be expected.

"You so often find the *right* word," said Leila Mort. "Now I'll go in. You'll come with me, Mary, and make sure Holt doesn't go wrong. I wonder if anyone *new* will come to-day?"

Mary wondered too, and doubted it. She believed that Mrs. Mort's clientele had just about reached its high-water mark. Those who had been once and hadn't liked it would never come again, and those who arrived would probably have a favour of some kind to ask before the month was out. On that point, Mary was a cynic.

At twenty minutes past four, as a famous pair of comedians finished their turn and made even Leila laugh and forget her celebrities and her troubles, Holt—the butler, who was even larger and more pontifical than Riddle—threaded his way towards Mary. That meant trouble; they all brought their troubles to Mary.

"What is it, Holt?"

Holt looked worried and nervous.

"There's a man—a *gentleman*—asking for Madam," he said. "In the hall."

"What has he done wrong?" asked Mary.

Holt swallowed a lump in his throat.

"He—he smote me, miss, on the back."

"*Did* he?" exclaimed Mary, and she chuckled, to Holt's disgust. "What name does he give?"

"Rumsden—Akers Rumsden, Miss Wayne. He says that he's had several invitations, but—er—he doesn't *seem* quite the type of man—er—*gentle*man whom Madam would wish to attend. He looks," added Holt gloomily, "as though he comes from Bohemia."

"The country or the place?" asked Mary, and her eyes were gleaming. This visitor seemed out of the ordinary.

"The country, miss." Holt was very firm. "I don't like to turn him *away*, Miss Wayne, in case he *has* been invited, but I'd like you to *see* him, even if the name is familiar. Have you—er —heard of him?"

"I've sent him invitations," Mary admitted, her eyes sparkling hopefully. "All right, I'll come, Holt."

"Thank *you*, miss." Holt steered off majestically and much relieved, while Mary Wayne followed him as the orchestra played a soft, low waltz that had something of magic in it, and seemed to lend itself to the occasion.

The ballroom at the Gretley Place house had been converted for the afternoon and early evening into an oasis. It was so obviously an oasis that even a man who had never been to a desert would recognize it; even a stream was bubbling from the "spring" in the floor and trickling away—where, no one knew. The palms were waving in a gentle electrically created breeze, the orchestra looked like a Bedouin group, and the air was so hot that the Sahara would have been envious had it been present. But most of the guests looked cool enough, a mixed gathering with most of them immaculate.

Mary stepped out of the room to the hall; and then she stopped. It was enough to startle anyone.

Mr. Tommy (Akers) Rumsden had done himself well. The navy-blue trousers of the previous day were replaced by sky-blues that looked like pantaloons. Otherwise he was the same. His untidy hair looked longer than ever, his pale face was fierce, and his arms were waving wildly as he talked to Holt.

"It's an outrage," declaimed Tommy Rumsden violently, "positively an outrage, and as for you..." He advanced towards Holt menacingly, and Holt gave ground. "As for you..."

Mary recovered herself, straightened her face and stepped

forward. Perhaps it was Rumsden's appreciation of art that made him see past the bun and the horn-rimmed glasses. He stopped waving immediately, and bowed. It was the most perfect bow Holt, in all his experience, had ever seen.

"Mrs. Mort? *Rumsden* is the name, one Akers *Rumsden*. Time and time again I have promised myself this pleasure, and now"—he glanced towards Holt and scowled—"and now this—"

"I'm Mrs. Mort's secretary," Mary said easily, "and Holt has to ask me to meet all new guests, Mr. Rumsden. You'll understand, I'm sure, that we have so many gate-crashers. I—"

"Then why," demanded Mr. Rumsden, glaring at Holt, "doesn't he keep them out?"

Holt opened his lips fish-fashion, and then decided silence was the better part of valour. Mary forced back a chuckle and went on quickly:

"If you'll come this way, Mr. Rumsden."

Mr. Rumsden extended his arm until she was hooked, and then went into the ballroom. He didn't show the slightest sign of surprise at the oasis; he might have lived all his life in houses decorated as this had been for the occasion.

"Jolly crowd," he said in a more than audible whisper, and Mary Wayne took a chance.

"Do you *have* to behave like this?" she asked.

Mr. Rumsden seemed thunderstruck. He stopped in the middle of the room heedless of fifty curious pairs of eyes, and regarded the girl. He frowned and then he smiled; and in the most incredible whisper which she could only just hear, he said:

"Good Lord, no! Tell you the truth, someone wagered me a pony—fifty quid—that I wouldn't come to one of Leila Mort's shows and stick it out for the whole affair. A pony's a pony. Will you give evidence for me, if necessary?"

Mary Wayne had to keep a straight face somehow, and yet she would have loved to laugh, a loud, gurgling laugh to shock the rest of the gathering, including Mrs. Mort.

"Of course. But do behave."

"For you," said Tommy Rumsden, "anything. No effort too great, no effort too small. Which is Leila?"

"Standing by the palm over there."

"Which palm?"

"The one near the orchestra."

"Is that," asked Mr. Rumsden with a sniff, "an orchestra? I thought it was part of the landscape. Who's that little woman with the white hair?"

"That's Ruth Framer, the artist."

"Stage artiste, darling; don't forget my honourable profession. Does characters, doesn't she? Good, I'm told. We'd better get the job finished so that she can do her piece, but before reaching Leila let me say one thing and ask one question. It's an incredible piece of luck to find you here—"

"We haven't met, have we?"

"What the devil does that matter; you're the star of the whole thing. God! Not a man without a stiff collar! So remember, my dear. Er—what was the name?"

"Wayne."

"Don't misunderstand me. The name I shall call you by?"

"You certainly won't," said Mary Wayne; "Mrs. Mort might overhear you. And she's already more than curious, so get that other question out and let's hurry."

"All good things," said Tommy Rumsden, "come to an end. Do you keep beer?"

"Beer?" Mary was startled.

"Now look here, I took that bet because I was told you supplied anything in tankards. Don't say it was a lie. You know what I mean, sweetheart. The curse of the nation. Beer to drink."

"I think perhaps," said Mary quickly, "we could find some." They were three yards from Mrs. Mort now, and Mary looked up with a tight-lipped smile—the smile she reserved for Leila. "Mrs. Mort, you'll be so glad that Mr. Rumsden, Akers Rumsden, has managed to come. Mrs. Mort," she assured Mr. Rumsden, "is such a *great* admirer of your work."

"I never work," said Tommy, taking Leila's hand and bowing low. "Art comes by inspiration—what greater inspiration could I have than this? I've waited ages, Mrs. Mort, to see you."

Mrs. Mort, who had been inclined to view the new-comer with suspicion, melted. Praise, praise, praise, and she was happy forever; the thought was Mary's.

"It's delightful of you to come, Mr. Rumsden. Ruth Framer is just about to give us some of her *unparalleled* character sketches, and if you care to sit here"—she sank down on a settee and smiled invitingly—"I'm sure we shall be fascinated together."

"Ah-ha!" said Tommy Rumsden, his eyes on Mrs. Mort's lips. "Who is to be the fascinator? Ruth Framer or...But I must compose myself."

He composed himself, sitting back in the settee, one leg over the other, his chin in his hand and a scowl on his face. Obviously he was concentrating. Ruth Framer obliged Mrs. Mort and brought more than a modicum of applause. Mary Wayne watched, caught Rumsden's eyes occasionally and turned away quickly, while the private entertainment went on, and Rumsden had his beer.

He called it a jolly show when, at half past seven, the guests started to go. Mrs. Mort pressed him to stay to dinner; Mr. Rumsden said he couldn't that night, but he'd be delighted to dine later on. Mrs. Mort suggested the following evening, and Mr. Rumsden accepted. Mr. Rumsden, in consequence, felt satisfied.

At half-past eight that evening Wally Davidson and Tommy Rumsden slipped through the little door in the turning off Whitehall and, a few minutes later, sat opposite Gordon Craigie. Craigie was at his desk, and looking worried.

"Did you get anything?" he asked Rumsden.

Rumsden—dressed normally now—shrugged his shoulders.

"It's early days yet. But Mort's decision to dodge off rather upsets my little hopes. All the same, I'm down for dinner to-morrow, and that's promising; I was approved."

"Yes," said Craigie thoughtfully. "That's good going. Be careful, Rumsden. What kind of a crowd did they have?"

"A big one. Most of them nonentities, but an occasional man or woman who mattered. I saw Fosgill, the Canadian minister, over there, and Garon, from the U.S.A. Senate. Both with their wives. There was someone from Jugo-Slavia too, but I missed the name. No one suspicious, Craigie."

"No-o. But that's interesting up to a point. Anything else?"

"There's a girl there named Wayne. A useful helper, I hope. I propose telephoning her when I've left here, for a bite of supper. Plain-Jane and no nonsense to look at, but a definite winner. I'll find her useful."

"For heaven's sake," said Craigie, "don't go and get tangled up with a girl. There's enough of that bother in this job already."

"Trust Tommy," said Tommy, and he gathered that he wasn't wanted for further details. He left the office alone, and

Craigie looked at Wally Davidson; Wally didn't need telling that Craigie was worried.

"Developments?"

"Kerr and Arran went over to Paris this morning," said Craigie, "and I haven't had a word from them. No sign of Ellen Granting—I'm worried about her."

"How did she get away?" Davidson asked.

"We sent her to a nursing-home," Craigie said, "and she outwitted the man Miller had watching, and just walked out. I haven't heard anything of her since."

"Have you 'phoned Fallow?"

"Yes. He's heard nothing. Hadn't any idea she was connected with Mannopoli, of course. It's a nasty shock for Fallow, but we can't help that. The position is, Wally, that we haven't another angle to go on until we hear from Kerr."

"You're watching Mannopoli, of course."

"He's at St. Martin's, in a private ward, with two men in the room all the time, one outside the door and one outside the window. That's the best we can do with him. I don't think," Craigie said, passing his hand through his hair, "that he'll talk, but we'll try. If only Kerr gets some news quickly we might be all right."

"How big is it?" Davidson asked.

Gordon Craigie didn't answer for a moment, and then he drew a deep breath.

"I don't know," he said. "But—I'm afraid, Wally. We're only on the fringe of it, and I'm afraid it's so big that it might topple us over."

"But, damn it, how?"

"We've been close to disaster before," Craigie said. "War and other things. We've never been so long getting information. This affair *must* have been going on for years, or we'd have met with a less organized opposition. And now we're causing trouble in England, the birds are flying—or dying."

"You mean you think they're all clearing out because it's near the end?"

"That's what I think," said Craigie, "but we'll see. Everything possible's being done. Now—I want you to relieve Carruthers. He's watching Gretley Place and he'll follow Mrs. Mort wherever she goes."

"What time shall I relieve him?"

"Make it midnight, until six o'clock. You'll want a nap."

"I'll manage it," smiled Wally languidly. "By the way—anything from Gabrell?"

"Nothing that's useful. We can't even find his passport," said Craigie, "although I'm sure he's not English. Will you telephone just before midnight?"

"Call it done," said Davidson; he waved a hand and was gone.

About the time that Craigie was talking to Davidson about relieving Carruthers, Carruthers was confounding life. There were a lot of jobs he would do with pleasure, but watching any single house was not one of them. Particularly in these circumstances. Carruthers would have preferred to be up and doing.

He had been assured that Mrs. Mort never travelled except by car; consequently he was sitting at the wheel of a Daimler, dressed beautifully as a chauffeur, and reading the *Daily Express*. He could see everyone who went in and out of the Mort house, and he had seen Tommy Rumsden some three-quarters of an hour before. That had caused his last smile.

The Mort ménage seemed asleep.

Carruthers saw the Rolls that came along the road; he didn't give it a second glance until—some fifteen yards away from him—its driver lost control.

Carruthers didn't have time to wonder whether it was an accident or not.

He just saw it coming, gasped, saw it leap in the air like a live thing—and *saw* it crash into the Daimler.

And then there was a terrible pain in his chest, another in his head—and blackness. It had happened so quickly that he had not even had time to feel afraid.

14

MR. MORT PAYS A VISIT

S ome three hours before the time of his appointment with Ellen Granting at the Frankfurt Hotel, Berlingastrasse, Berlin, Mr. Julius Mort reached the rendezvous. He had already reserved a suite of rooms, but not as Mr. Julius Mort. He was prepared to answer to the name of Mr. Mortimer Julius—a convenient twist that made reasonably sure he wouldn't be taken for Mr. Mort during the short time he expected to be in Berlin.

He was in Berlin even less time than he expected.

Twenty minutes after he had arrived he rang for an attendant and asked for letters. A letter was waiting, addressed to Mr. Julius, typewritten, and on plain, cream-coloured paper. Mr. Mort had been expecting the letter, and yet there was something about it that made him hesitate before he opened it.

Not for the first time he was afraid.

There would be orders here, and orders that he dared not disobey. They might demand risks even greater than he had already taken, and those risks already brought shivers to

Mort's flesh. He had been in a good humour after Kerr had been knocked out by the girl, but he had had time to think since then.

He didn't like thinking these days.

It was a remarkable fact that until the evening when he had sat down and addressed a letter to John Fallow, he had been living a reasonably orderly life. True, he dabbled in crime, but that hadn't worried him, and the organization had been so good that he did not fear any consequences.

Then he had seen Mannopoli at the 'George' in Michford. After that life had been—hell. In the three days that had passed Mort had learned several things, and one of them was the real size of the organization that he and Mannopoli—and Mulling —had built up, or helped to build up.

He was a badly frightened man because he knew that the orders he had to carry out might lead to death; and if he didn't carry them out, it would certainly mean death. Obviously the thing for him to do was to act on orders and hope that the organization was strong enough to save him.

The size of it made him gasp; when he had first learned of it he had refused to believe it was possible. But he had been shown considerable evidence; and, what was more, he was assured that if the plan which the organization had been perfecting over a long period was successful he, Julius Mort, would have nothing to fear from the law, from his associates, or from anyone.

That, thought Mr. Mort, was a delightful prospect.

But he returned to the letter and, with a grimace, tore it open. He was sitting in a comfortable hotel in a room that might have been in England or France for all the difference it revealed in furnishing and general appointments. It was a very comfortable and expensive room.

Mort unfolded the single sheet of paper and, his breath

coming fast, read the brief message. He read it twice, and then he didn't know whether to feel relieved or even more afraid. For the order was indecisive, and yet...

> *Mort,*
>
> *You will report here to night, at eleven-thirty. You will travel by air from Berlin in a machine which has already been detailed. You will go to the usual airport as Mr. Julius, and all arrangements will be taken out of your hands.*
>
> *I shall expect a comprehensive report of activities in England.*
>
> *Daak.*

It was signed like that; just Daak. It was the first time Mort had seen that actual signature, and he didn't like it. Not that there was anything wrong in the writing, smooth and flowing with a hint of the flourishes more common on the Continent than in England. But all the same—Daak. Just like that. It made Mr. Mort shiver, for he had been told so much about Daak in the past few days.

Well, he was wanted with a report. He'd better write the report out, in case he forgot half of it. His memory for detail wasn't as good as it might have been, and so many things had happened in the past few days that anyone could be forgiven for not remembering them all. Mr. Mort glanced at his watch —set to the local time—and saw that he had less than two and a half hours in which to eat and prepare; he must eat, and he wanted to prepare. He pushed unpleasant thoughts as far from his mind as he could, gave orders for a meal to be brought to his room, and settled down.

* * *

About the time when the many countries of Europe had been divided into large or small parts, according to the whims and fancies of certain tired statesmen, the little country of Bania had been completely forgotten, and for a good reason.

Bania was so small that its army's strength stood at a thousand regulars, most of whom were past the usual retiring age. No one in Bania retired. Few people in Bania even moved with the times. It was a little principality, up in the hills between Germany and Poland, and its only town was so inaccessible to general transport that even the Great War had passed it by. And so innocent had been Bania in that holocaust that even the statesmen let it rest in peace.

Daakmann, in consequence, also rested in peace.

Daakmann was perhaps the least-known man in the world to Governments and the Great Powers. He wasn't even the titular head of the Banian Government. Unlike a certain Korra, who had operated against the Department and the world in Lathia, he had never been a popular figure, and as permanent Under-secretary (or its equivalent) to the Prime Minister of Bania, he played an even less conspicuous part than the permanent officials of the British Government.

Daakmann hadn't minded.

From his early days he had seen into the future with a keenness that was little short of incredible. He had anticipated the world War, and closed Bania as well as it could be closed against it. He had anticipated the mess that followed, and kept Bania out of it. It was a small, self-sufficing country. Its people missed a great many luxuries but, never having tasted them, didn't care. They were peaceful folk, mostly agricultural folk, and some of the industries went back—it was rumoured—to the Stone Age. It says enough about Bania to claim that since the War less than fifty American tourists had passed its frontiers; Bania didn't exist for the world in general.

But Daakmann existed, and Daakmann travelled, although not under that name.

He had visited most capitals of the world, and he had learned many things of interest to a man with an ambitious mind. He had seen what money could do; and he had wanted money. And by accident he had come in contact with a gentleman who had called himself Mannopoli.

Mannopoli and Daakmann had many things in common. Among them was a complete disregard of human life—a complete indifference to anything but their own comfort: brains and ambition. At that time Daakmann was forty-eight, and young enough to want to change his life.

Mannopoli was a man of great ideas. He had passed some of them on, and found Daakmann enthusiastic. For his part, Mannopoli had realized the necessity of having a hide-out such as Bania, a place where no extradition laws operated, where a man could be quite safe if he was a friend of Daakmann's. And then Daakmann had revealed himself to have an organizing ability out of the ordinary.

The profits of the thing that Mannopoli had conceived were so vast that to share them made no difference. A thousand people could have had an equal share, and each man would have had more than enough to pay him a hundred thousand a year as interest only. It was, as Daakmann and Mannopoli knew, a big thing.

Oddly enough, Mannopoli had discovered after a time that he depended a great deal on Daakmann for assistance, for ideas, and particularly for the execution of them. Daakmann hadn't failed him yet, and Mannopoli didn't think he ever would.

Daakmann...

He was a small man as men go; five feet eight, and slim enough. He dressed quietly; he looked a genial, benevolent man of something over fifty. It was only his eyes that made one realize that he wasn't what he looked.

His eyes were amber; large, iridescent, like a wild beast's. One glance from them, when he was in anger, made men shiver.

And there were his hands.

They were long and thin, yet out of proportion to his arms; the hands themselves seemed almost as long as his forearm. They were white and slim—and powerful. Servants had seen Daakmann strangle a wolf-hound without seeming to exert himself, and had crossed themselves to cast the Devil out of him.

They hadn't succeeded, for if the Devil was in Mannopoli it was a hundred times stronger in Graff Daakmann.

The house in which he lived was a big one, but most houses in Bania that weren't hovels were sizable. It was built high up on a hill, some three miles from Bey—Bania's capital —and it commanded a glorious view of Poland, Germany and Bania; all around it stretched the mountains of Central Europe, high towards the sky; mists swirled even about the roof of the house on cloudy days.

It was a remarkable fact that the house was also built so that no one could approach it without being seen. The road that led to its gates was steep and three or four acres of land surrounded it. Only powerful cars could get right up; most of them had to stop, and the passengers walked the hundred yards between the stopping-point and the iron gates of Daakmann's house. None of them minded. Few people went to see Daakmann unless they were afraid of him or on business; and those on business knew enough not to cross him by making complaints.

Thus was Graff Daakmann, known to some as Daak, and Daakmann's house.

* * *

It was dark by the time Julius Mort reached the house, and he was heartily glad that he didn't have to walk far. He had been cared for, as Daak had suggested in the letter, with Germanic efficiency from the moment he had reached the Berlin airfield and introduced himself to the officials as Mr. Mortimer Julius. The 'plane had been of the large cabin type, although Mort had been the only passenger; its comfort had been such that even Julius, who was perhaps the most easily frightened man alive, did not feel any anticipatory tremors of a crash.

The landing had been smooth; if there was anything about the job that Mr. Mort didn't like it was that he had no idea where he was. He didn't know where Daak lived. Daakmann, in point of fact, could have been found only by Mannopoli and two others, despite the organization which he controlled, with some thousands of members and a hundred sub-offices throughout the world.

The country was hilly, that much the short car-ride had told Mortimer. He'd passed through no towns, and from the flying-field to the moment when the car pulled up outside the front door of the house something under fifteen minutes had passed. Mort knew that and nothing more.

It was a dark night, with a chill wind blowing across the hills. He shivered, for he was clad for autumn, not winter, and wondered how long it would be before the door was opened. As he waited the wind whistled about the eerie, lonely place, and shadows which were more of the imagination than anything else sent unpleasant prickles up and down Mort's well-covered spine. Had he been less concerned with these he might have noticed the thing above. He didn't. Nor, oddly enough, did anyone at Daakmann's house, although three people were employed there to look for anything that might have been even a little out of the ordinary.

The aeroplane, flying at least ten thousand feet, was visible only because of its navigation lights; its engine was dulled by distance and the wailing wind. The only thing it did out of the ordinary was to circle round and round, instead of flying straight over the house on the outskirts of Bey.

Mortimer Julius, heedful of nothing but the cold, snapped his fingers, and, hey presto, the door opened! Mort might have been pleased had he not been surprised. It had opened so silently and so suddenly that he jumped.

"I—er..."

"You are expected," said the man at the door.

He was a big fellow, coarse of face and unpleasant of eye. His lips were thick, wet and slobbering. He waited for Mort to pass and then closed the door as silently as he had opened it.

Mort was in the house of Graff Daakmann—or Daak— only the fourth important member of that organization which was worrying Craigie and others to cross the threshold.

It was a big place, a cold place. A single electric lamp burned in the lofty hall. A few old paintings hung on the walls, the floor was bare of carpets and brilliantly polished. The staircase leading directly opposite the front door had a carpet, and Mr. Mort trod the stairs with something like confidence. The slobbering-lipped man preceded him.

Silence: movements muffled now by the thick pile; gloom; Mr. Mort's nerves; everything combined to make him feel like shouting aloud to convince himself this was real. What would Daak be like? Where was this place? He...

"Ah!" exclaimed Mr. Mort, for the man in front of him stopped, and they almost collided.

They were on the first landing, and there were three doors leading from it. The first door was open; the second, on the right of the landing, was closed. The coarse-faced man knocked on it, and someone called, "Come in," in rather a high-pitched, expressionless voice.

The man with the slobbering lips opened the door, bowed to whoever was inside the room and called:

"Mr. Mortimer Julius."

And Mr. Julius Mort entered the room, and came face to face with Graff Daakmann—whom he knew as Daak. Mr. Mort saw those yellowish eyes fixed on his as though the man sitting behind the long desk were reading his very soul—and he felt sick.

Daakmann didn't offer to shake hands; he knew of Mort from Mannopoli, and it occurred to him as strange that this fat, podgy, pig-like man should be a millionaire, and should have made the whole grandiose scheme possible in so short a time. Daak neither liked nor disliked people who worked for him, and Mr. Mort left him cold; but he certainly entered into nothing that might have been called friendly conversation.

"Ah! Mort, eh?" His voice was guttural but his English perfect. "Sit down, Mort. I've wanted to see you for some time."

"I—I have, too," said Mr. Mort. "You, I mean, not me. I..."

"Of course, of course. But surely"—Daakmann was very suave—"you only knew that I existed three days ago."

Mr. Mort swallowed hard and tried to smile.

"Ha—yes—ha-ha! Three days is a long time, eh, Daak?"

"*Herr* Daak," said Daakmann.

"Of course, of course!" Mr. Mort looked as though he would gladly go down on his knees to apologize. "Hard to know what—Mr.—M'sieu—Herr Daak—quite a lot, ha-ha!"

"Yes," said Daakmann, and smiled. Somehow his thin lips and the smile reminded Mort of Mannopoli—he wished they didn't. "Well, now—England. What have you to report?"

"Report, yes," said Mortimer, and swallowed again. "I—er—from when?"

"From three nights ago, yes?" Daakmann smiled again, and Mort continued to wish he wouldn't.

"Well—er—damn' beastly time, Mr.—Herr Daak. Poor old Mannopoli—in prison, of course. You knew that?"

"I knew that," said Mr. Daakmann, and the fact didn't seem to worry him. "But perhaps, Mort, you would care to put it in your own words. From the moment that you were foolish enough to send that letter to Fallow."

Mort liked the 'foolish' even less than he had liked some of the other things, but he stammered through a recital of those things which he thought Daakmann would want to know. Throughout the whole time Daakmann didn't move; he had his hands folded on the desk in front of him and he kept his amber eyes fixed on the fat, perspiring face of the Englishman. When Mort concluded he still didn't speak. Mort looked worried more than ever.

"And that—er—is about the lot. Can't think of—"

"Tell me," said Herr Daakmann, "is it true you are a millionaire?"

Of all the questions Mort had expected, that was the last. He simply gaped, and then he realized that probably Daak wouldn't like it, so he managed to find words.

"Er—yes. Of course. Didn't Mannopoli tell you?"

"I was wondering," said Herr Daakmann with a wolfish smile, "whether he had been correctly informed. How did you make your money, Mort?"

"Well—er—stocks and shares—and things. And *things*." Mr. Mort managed to smile, and his effort was ghastly.

"The things being illegal, eh? Well, I've no quarrel with you about that," said Herr Daakmann, and he smiled for the first time in a manner that suggested a little humour. "Well, what you've told me is most interesting. Now for some instructions. You know something of what you are expected to do?"

"Yes. But I hope," said Mort in a very thin voice, "you won't ask me to commit murder. I—I don't like committing murder."

"The only time I allow murder," said Herr Daakmann as if he was discussing taking sugar in coffee, "is when it is necessary for the furthering of our little scheme. Unfortunately those people in England discovered something, and it was necessary. That letter to Fallow—"

"But—but I didn't know then!"

"Oh, you've been forgiven, Mort, otherwise…" Herr Daakmann turned his left thumb down, and the gesture was unpleasant enough to make Mort shudder yet again. "But the interference makes it necessary to get to work quickly. We have allowed three days, in fact, and most of those days you will be in the air."

"In—the—air?"

"In an aeroplane," said Herr Daakmann, and he looked puzzled—just as he had looked when he had wanted to know whether Julius Mort was a millionaire. "I shall give you a list of the people you will call on. Twelve countries in all. You will give them the time, and the procedure will be confirmed by post. You will just tell them what time the thing happens. Is that understood?"

"Yes—yes, of course. You—you'll tell me the time?"

"I shall," said Daakmann, and he chuckled. "You can know now. Midnight, English time, three days from now. The twentieth of September. Is that clear?"

"Yes, yes, quite clear! It shall be done, I assure you! I assure you!"

"I shall find," said Daakmann, "whether an extradition warrant has been issued for you, and if it has you will have to travel under a *nom de plume*. If not—as Mr. Julius Mort. Now—we will go into my office, Mort, and get those addresses."

Julius Mort, who was by nature a cunning man—hence his millions—was just beginning to realize that Daak wasn't likely to bite, that he'd been brought to this queer place simply to be given a list of names and addresses, and he felt happier. He even felt bumptious, and wished he'd emphasized the part he had played in stopping Kerr and the man Arran in Paris. Very astute he'd been then, very astute indeed.

But he had another shock before long.

Herr Daakmann stood up and leaned his hand on his desk. The sliding noise that followed made Mort jump, so did the sliding door that appeared in the wall behind Daak; that gentleman laughed, his guttural, unpleasant laugh.

"We must keep these things secret, Mort, from prying eyes. Come along."

Mr. Mort entered the 'office,' which he would have called a laboratory, although one wall was fitted with a desk and some filing-cabinets. Mort's eyes were on the laboratory fittings, but Daakmann went to one of the cabinets, pulled out a drawer, and selected a card. He sat at the desk and wrote a list of names and addresses down on paper for Mr. Mort; and when he looked up he saw Mort's interest was elsewhere.

"Very understandable," said Daakmann. "You're interested, of course, in how the world will be put to rest on the midnight of the twentieth of September?"

"Of—of course." Mr. Mort was shivering, and his eyes bulging. "Is—is the stuff in here?" He approached the bench.

"Some of it," said Herr Daakmann—"just enough for our immediate requirements, Mort. I—*Mort!*"

His voice hardened; there was such an expression in it that

Mort went as rigid as a poker. Daakmann was staring at him, his eyes blazing pools of venom. And all Mr. Mort had done was to pick up a little glass phial that had been on the laboratory bench.

"Put—that—down—gently."

Mort just stared—at the man and then the phial. He had it in his hand, and now he lowered it very slowly, stiff with fear, to the bench. That was the stuff—in there! That was the stuff!

And then Mr. Mort sneezed; and the phial tinkled into a thousand fragments on the bench.

15

STRANGERS IN BANIA

The low droning of the twin engines, the ticking of a small dashboard clock, and the soft breathing of two men were the only sounds that disturbed the silence of the cabin. Beneath the monoplane was silence, darkness only broken by an occasional light; about it that same darkness. And here and there between breaking clouds the unexpectedly bright gleam of a star. But for the most part the monoplane was flying blind, and Toby Arran didn't like it.

Toby had never been happy in the air, but to Bob Kerr it was second nature. He had dropped below the clouds from time to time, and each time he had seen the distant beam of headlights—like little pencils from the height at which he was flying—moving slowly along the ground. And then suddenly they had stopped moving; Kerr had tickled the rudder bar into a half-turn and watched the ground below when Toby thought he should be looking where he was going.

The lights were switched off; the darkness was complete, saving for a dim white glow from two or three different points near the spot where the car was standing.

"Mr. Mort," said Bob Kerr in an unusually gentle voice, "has arrived, Toby."

"Any chance of making a landing?" demanded Toby hopefully.

"There's a good chance of breaking our necks if we do," said Kerr cheerfully, "and less chance of ever taking off again if we managed to get down safely. All the same, the policy is to go down, isn't it?"

"H'm," said Toby. "Well, you're boss, old son. Mine but to do or die. Make it a quick one, won't you?"

"The landing or the end?" demanded Kerr, who had never appreciated Toby Arran quite so much as he had in the past twenty-four hours.

"Whichever's the safer," implored Toby. "Any idea where we are?"

"Over Germany, I think, near the Polish border. There-abouts, anyhow. Hilly country too."

"Go on," murmured Toby, "make it bright and cheerful while you're at it. Are we going down?"

"I'm losing height," said Bob Kerr thoughtfully, and he was pushing forward a little on the joystick. "But I don't know whether we can manage it."

"Mort's 'plane landed at an airport," said Toby. "Why can't we go back to it?"

"Because we'd never locate this place again," Bob Kerr returned, "and that's on the important side. Keep cheerful, Toby. I've been in worse spots than this, and it's a fine night."

"Och aye," said Toby Arran, and apparently resigned himself to the inevitable, while Kerr took the monoplane down by easy stages, wondering whether he dared switch on his headlights or whether if he flew low enough he'd be able to make a landing without them. It had been done before, but he'd seen enough to know that the country was uneven, and he had no more desire than Toby Arran to come a cropper. Croppers at night in what might be hostile territory weren't just what the doctor ordered. But he went down slowly, watching all the time, and getting as near those three dim lights as he could. For those lights bespoke a house, and the house which Mr. Julius Mort had recently entered.

Kerr didn't have time for thinking; Toby did. Anything was better than nothing, and it was pleasant to brood over the times when things had looked black and yet turned out on the credit side. The last time they had been in the air, for instance; and that ruthless fight over the sea. Toby still shuddered when he saw in his mind's eye seething waves where a moment before there had been a biplane.

They'd got out of that, and other things.

He couldn't remember much after he'd reached Paris, until an attendant had opened the door of the room which had been his temporary prison. A maid, who had promptly fainted. But she had screamed first, help had come, and some three hours later, after Mort had left the Bristol, Kerr and Arran had explained themselves as well as they could, obtained a clear bill from the Sûreté—thanks to an urgent telephone call to Whitehall—and had been ready again for the fray. Neither had been badly hurt—they had to thank Mr. Mort's dislike of murder for that—but both were sore in mind and body.

Kerr had told Arran just what had happened, and hadn't eased up when talking about Ellen Granting. He wasn't sure what to make of Ellen Granting, and Arran—although he would have preferred to have entered a strong defence of the girl—couldn't find it in him to argue. She was playing a queer game, and up to a point a crooked game. Toby didn't like that extract from her history when she had applied to Mannopoli for help. Not the kind of thing, Toby thought, that the Ellen

Granting he believed in would be likely to do. She would just take one look at Mannopoli and reserve her judgment.

She hadn't done that.

If she'd told the truth she had lost nothing by it, but she'd been coerced into joining Mannopoli's crowd. She was afraid of Mannopoli—that rang true if nothing else did—and she was prepared to do his bidding.

The one thing Toby couldn't get straight in his mind was the reason that had inspired her to knock Bob Kerr out.

Kerr had handled her leniently; much more leniently, if the truth were known, than he had wanted to. Her gratitude had taken the form of a crack over the head. Of course she had to convince Mort she was really on his side—

Toby gave it up and brooded.

Kerr, as it happened, was thinking about that blow on the head and—he was only human—what had preceded it. She'd been very lovely, and her appeal when she'd pressed against him made his heart thump now. Had he been wise to make her talk?

Of course he had!

He smiled a little—and Toby wondered what on earth he could find to smile at—and thanked the Fates that the girl hadn't the strength of a man. That blow *had* knocked him out, but he had been more dazed than anything else; and he'd heard—thank God he'd heard—Mort mention the Hotel Frankfurt, Berlin.

When at last he'd been released he had telephoned Craigie, reported everything—even the Frankfurt hotel—squared himself through Craigie with the Sûreté, and hurried to the airport. The monoplane, refuelled and ready for flight, had been waiting. In a little less than an hour after Mr. Mort, Kerr and Arran had reached the hotel. They hadn't shown them-

185

selves. They had waited, seen the visit to the airfield, seen Mort go up and, naturally, had followed him.

He'd landed somewhere near the German-Polish border.

Kerr had flown in circles above the airfield, seen the man move from 'plane to car, and followed.

Now they were flying again in circles, getting lower and lower with every turn; and somewhere in the house below Mr. Mort was talking—or sleeping, or doing something. Kerr badly wanted to get down.

The question was, should he risk disaster?—and when he looked at the situation coldly he knew disaster was the most likely result if he went down—or should he fly around until morning, locate the place, and then report to Craigie?

Kerr did argue with himself; but the result was known before the argument started. He'd go down. It might be too late if he waited; if he and Toby met their finish—well, it couldn't be helped. They'd have tried.

Kerr had an idea, necessarily without foundation, that they'd have the luck. Now, flying less than five hundred feet from the ground, he decided to take a chance and use the searchlights. He was careful to have the nose of the mono-plane pointing away from the house, so that the glare should not attract the attention of the occupants; then he clicked the switch down, and the great beam of light stretched out, a dazzling sea of white carving through the darkness.

Toby Arran gasped and went pale.

Bob Kerr's teeth snapped together; he pulled back on the stick and opened the throttle to full burst. Ahead of them, stark and frightening, a rock-strewn hillside rose sheer from the ground! It was touch and go whether they'd top it or not, and both men knew it.

The monoplane almost stood on her tail; the light curved round in a great arc, on mountainous crags then on clouds;

and then suddenly Kerr straightened out, and said offhandedly:

"Close, Toby."

"Is that what you call close?" demanded Toby Arran, his voice unsteady. "I'd call it a darn' sight nearer than that."

"We missed it, didn't we?"

"All right, all right, but are you going to dowse those lights again?"

"I've never had any leanings towards suicide," said Bob Kerr, "and I'm not going to start now."

The monoplane was at two thousand feet. That hill—Toby called it other things—was well beneath them, and they'd missed it by the proverbial hairsbreadth, or by a matter of twenty feet. Whether they were seen or not, in country like this it wasn't safe to fly without the searchlight; and it was even more risky to land without it.

Kerr swung the 'plane round, and now the searchlight picked out the rock-strewn countryside, Daakmann's house, the steep incline that led up to it, and—Kerr smiled—a flat stretch of land below. It was good enough for landing, and even though they were perilously close to the house the opportunity was too good to be missed.

He pushed the stick down, and this time there was no trouble. He flew round the house, making as sure as he could that the roaring of the engines didn't attract attention; and then the searchlight showed him that the flat stretch of land was ideal for his purpose. It was easily wide enough for a take-off or a landing, and as far as he could see it was comparatively smooth.

Toby wondered whether he was being optimistic and waited. The earth seemed to rise up and meet them; then the wheels touched the ground, the monoplane bumped a little, settled down and ran smoothly along. Kerr shut off the throttle, and they taxied to a standstill.

All about them darkness dropped as the searchlight was switched off, and an eerie silence through which the whistling of the wind came occasionally, shrill and piercing and somehow frightening. They seemed to be shut off from the world.

"It gets worse," whispered Bob Kerr. "Not a sound or a sign; no one in there, Toby?"

"Not that I can see. The light's burning in the corner."

"Odd," said Bob Kerr, and he scratched his chin and wished he dared light a cigarette. "Three rooms on the ground floor lighted and not a sign of anyone about. Two rooms upstairs lighted—ditto. Odd indeed."

"Better bust in, hadn't we?"

"Ye-es," said Kerr. "The gates are open for emergency, and the obliging cove who left the car outside must have known we were coming. Slip back, Toby, and turn it. Make it snappy."

Toby Arran, a different man on the ground from what he was in the air, slipped back brough the dark, silent grounds of the house and climbed into the powerful Benz standing by the gates. He wondered whether the noise of the engine would wake the occupants of that eerie, silent house, and hoped for the best. He was feeling good. Not only was the landing successfully accomplished but the landing-field was good for a quick take-off, and here was the car. The chances of a getaway if there was trouble were a good fifty-fifty, and Toby never minded if he could count on odds as fair as that; he would even take two to one against.

He made as little noise as he could, and turned the Benz so

that they could get in it and run back quickly down the road along which they had walked from the landing-field. Then he made his way back quietly to the window where Kerr was waiting.

Kerr hadn't been idle; the window was open a couple of inches now at the bottom, and as Toby arrived, Kerr pushed it well up. The squeal as it went up was enough to wake the dead; they waited, hearts pounding, but nothing happened.

"I'll go first," said Kerr, and he climbed through.

Toby bumped into him a moment later, and was about to comment on some people being clumsy when he saw why Kerr was standing so still and staring across the room.

It *wasn't* empty.

The man was lying in a crumpled heap on the floor, in front of a chair. A cigarette had burnt a small hole in the carpet, and also burnt his fingers. The expression on his face was one of complete surprise, even though his eyes were closed. He looked as though he had been startled, but not alarmed, before he had lost consciousness. Kerr didn't like the way one knee was doubled beneath him.

"So," he murmured, "they've had other visitors."

"Is he right out?" asked Toby.

"I don't know. Doesn't seem to be breathing. Where's that little mirror of yours?"

They walked slowly across the room and reached the huddled body of the man. His lips weren't moving, although they were parted. His chest didn't seem to be lifting. Toby had slipped a small mirror from his vest pocket, and now he held it in front of the man's mouth.

He pulled it away thirty seconds later, and he felt relieved, for there was a faint mist on it. The man was alive, even if he was very close to the border-line.

"Hitch him into a chair," Toby said, "and leave him. He won't come round for an hour or two."

"Notice anything odd about him?" Kerr spoke as he hoisted the unconscious man up and put him gently into the easy chair in front of which he had been lying.

"Can't say I do."

"Nose and mouth," said Kerr, and Arran looked again.

It wasn't a certainty that there was anything to notice; Toby wouldn't have seen it unless it had been pointed out. But Kerr had seen the slight puffiness at the man's mouth and nose —something like a man with a severe cold. No more, no less.

"Odd—"

"If you say that again," said Toby Arran fiercely, "I'm going home. Not a damned sound anywhere. Think we dare light up?"

"Not yet we don't," said Robert McMillan Kerr. "Someone put that gentleman where he is, and we don't want the dose repeated on ourselves. I've had enough unconsciousness to last me a long time. Block that door open with a chair."

Toby obliged, and they went into the hall. Its dreariness struck them in the same way as it had Mr. Mort: cold—eerie —sinister.

Another door, along a passage that led along the right of the wide staircase, was open, and a gleam of light came through it. Toby waited, gun in hand, by the foot of the stairs. Kerr went quickly, and with the stealth that he could manage when the need arose, towards the open door. No sound came; not even the sound of men breathing. He pushed the door open a fraction of an inch, and then pulled his gun.

Still no sound.

He widened the gap, and stepped in; and then for the second time he had a shock, a big shock; and he seemed to doubt the evidence of his own eyes.

There were four people here—two men, two women. None of them were young. All of them were sitting or lying, with their eyes closed, in chairs or on the floor. One man had obviously been walking from one side of the room to the other, with a glass of lager in his hand—the broken glass was on the floor, the beer a light-brown pool on the polished oilcloth.

Both women were sitting down, their heads lolling backwards. The second man—dressed in uniform, which told Kerr immediately that he was the driver of the Benz outside—was near them. On every face was that same expression of acute surprise; and at every mouth and nose that slight puffiness.

Kerr drew a deep breath and turned away. His whisper seemed to echo about the passage and the stairs like a deep-throated bellow. Toby started, saw Kerr beckoning, and hurried towards him.

"Four more," Kerr said. "Mirror, old man."

"It's doing overtime," Toby muttered, more to get the weirdness of this place out of his mind than anything else.

Kerr tried each mouth; and found each person was breathing. Whether they would breathe for long he didn't know. An idea flashed through his mind and returning to the first room they had entered, he looked hard at the man's face.

"What the hell is biting you?" demanded Toby irritably.

"Face more swollen," said Kerr without hesitation; and a steely band seemed to fasten about Toby Arran's chest as he realized it was true. The man's mouth and nose *were* more swollen.

"Damn it," said Toby in a strained voice, "it's uncanny. I wonder who the hell did it?"

"I wonder where they are," said Kerr. "Now we've got to move. One room apiece on the ground floor; then we'll tackle it upstairs.

They went through the rest of the rooms downstairs and

found nothing. One light was burning in an empty room, but otherwise nothing was in any way out of the ordinary. The eeriness of it, increased by the silence that was broken from time to time by a whining gust of wind, was getting on their nerves. They went upstairs together, and found there were only two floors. That was a relief. Danger wasn't likely to come from below and it couldn't come from above.

Only one room on the first floor was locked—the second on the right. They went into the others, and as they went their sense of wonderment increased. This was fantastic! Five men —hefty-looking fellows all of them—were there, unconscious, with the same puffiness about the mouth and nose. Three of them had been near windows, and Kerr frowned.

"Look-outs," he said. "I wonder if they're armed?"

They were; each man carried two guns, fully loaded Malin automatics—the most up-to-date German models. They'd been on the watch all right, and Toby grimaced.

"If they hadn't been K.O.'d," he said, "we'd have had a warm welcome. Whoever did it did us a good turn. It's damn silly, all the same. All drugged, of course."

Kerr nodded slowly.

"Drugged or something else. Toby—the Granting girl said she had to steal papers from Fallow's place. Fallow was a Government chemist, in the gas experimental stations."

Toby Arran drew a deep breath.

"Gas! You think that's it?"

"I can't think of anything else it might be. We'll smoke now; there's only the locked room left, and no one'll get out of that quietly enough to surprise us." He proffered cigarettes, and Toby lit one thankfully. Then they went to the locked door.

Toby—more expert at lock-picking than Bob Kerr, for he had been longer in the service of Department Z—had the door open in something under two minutes. Which meant, he opined, that it was a tough lock. But the door opened at last, and both men entered the room, guns in hand, although they didn't expect to meet trouble.

They didn't.

They entered a well-furnished empty room, with a large desk in one corner. But there was a hole in the wall—or a sliding door—and past it they could see the laboratory that Daakmann had called the office. They went in quickly; and they saw two men, Daakmann, small, thin, with his amber eyes closed and an expression of malevolence rather than surprise on his face; and Mort. They recognized Mr. Julius Mort, whose flabby face was even puffier, whose expression was one of unadulterated terror. He had been dreadfully afraid.

"Well, well," murmured Kerr, "so this is where it started from."

"Eh?"

"Where it started from. Broken phial on the bench—both men right out—enough chemicals here to kill a town. Toby, I'm beginning to like this less than ever. I wonder"—he looked at Daakmann—"who this gentleman is. There's something about him I don't like, my son. However—"

"Damn!" said Toby Arran distinctly.

After longing for a cigarette for over three hours, the one he had been able to light slipped from his fingers. He bent down to pick it up; it eluded his grasp and he tried again; and then, as Bob Kerr was smiling at him thoughtfully, Toby Arran grunted. As he grunted he collapsed; and Bob Kerr, every muscle in his body rigid, saw his friend's face as he turned over on his back, saw that his eyes were closed and his lips set in that odd expression of surprise.

Kerr stared; he felt very cold, and very grim. So the gas—

released from the laboratory somehow—was thick in this room, close to the floor. It was all right until you went too near to the carpet. It—

Bob Kerr didn't move for thirty seconds; and then, through the silence that had been broken until that moment only by his own breathing, came the sound of a car outside.

16

ELUSIVE LADY

Bob Kerr had had some shocks in the past few days, but this was perhaps the biggest. One thing by itself he could have managed, but Arran collapsing as he had done, followed by the sound of the car, was almost too much. He stood dead still for thirty seconds; and then, drawing a deep breath, he picked Toby Arran up in his arms and carried him out of the laboratory.

Perhaps it was as well he had something to do.

He went into a bedroom directly opposite the office, and rested the little, ugly man there. Then he straightened up, took his gun from his pocket, and went downstairs.

The new-comers might have a key; they might be on the same errand as he was himself. He didn't know. He waited in the doorway of one of the rooms without a light, while footsteps echoed on the path outside and up the steps that led to the front door of the house.

He'd know soon whether they had a key or not.

There were two people—two distinct footsteps. One heavy,

one light—almost like a woman's. Kerr's lips tightened; and then he heard the key being pushed into the lock.

His hand was very steady on the butt of his automatic, and he was prepared to shoot on sight, if necessary. He was well in the shadows, but he could see the door clearly. It opened slowly at first, and then more quickly. A woman stepped through.

She was dressed in costly furs; she was wearing an absurd little hat atop her wavy fair head. She looked incredibly beautiful in the dim light of the hall, did Miss Ellen Granting.

She was here again!

Kerr waited.

The girl looked as though she was thoroughly at home. She stepped in and waited for the man to follow. He came in slowly, almost hesitating, and even Kerr could not help smiling. It was the giant Swede he had gassed in the Bristol, at Paris, and the man looked as though he was scared out of his life.

"Come in, Lorens." The girl's voice was very clear. "Don't look as though he'll bite you."

"He—he might not like it, miss."

"He'll forgive you—or he'll forgive me, which is much more satisfactory. Come in and close the door; it's cold."

"It's quiet," said the Swede, and looked about him fearfully. There was an amazing difference in the pluck of the man and the pluck of the woman. But Lorens closed the door and then stood hesitantly in the hall. The girl frowned. Obviously she had expected someone to hear her. She took two steps towards the room with the open door—in which one man was lying very close to death—and then she saw him. The half-scream that came to her lips startled even Kerr. The Swede strode after her—he didn't lack physical courage—and past her.

"What is it? I—"

And then he saw the unconscious man, and paused in turn.

The girl's profile was towards Kerr, and he could see the expression that mingled horror, uncertainty and surprise. Perhaps surprise most of all. Certainly she had never dreamed that anything like this would happen. Her first words, spoken rather quickly and with her voice higher than usual, brought another smile to Kerr's lips.

"Someone else has been here, Lorens! Someone else—"

"Someone else," said Bob Kerr cheerfully, "is still here. Hands in the air, both of you!"

The girl stared; the Swede swore and took half a step forward. Kerr touched the trigger of his gun, and the bullet nicked a piece out of the giant's ear. Lorens stopped dead still; and his hands reached for the ceiling.

"You too, my dear," said Bob Kerr.

"Mr.—Kerr!" She didn't obey him. "Thank God it's you! I was afraid—"

"Your ear," said Bob Kerr, "is admittedly a pretty one, and it wouldn't be improved with a piece out of it. Put your hands in the air."

"You—wouldn't—dare!" She had changed colour and her voice was very low.

"I'm not," said Kerr, "in love with you. Didn't you know?"

She obeyed at last; her expression was inscrutable; but Kerr didn't think she liked him.

"You forget," he said, "that you tricked me once, my dear."

"I *had* to! If Mort had guessed—"

"Yes, and if I'd guessed you wouldn't have pulled it off, but perhaps it's as well, for we've arrived. You"—he motioned to the Swede—"come here, walking backwards."

The Swede obeyed. Kerr made sure he could see them both, and waited until the giant stood about a foot in front of

197

him. He ran his hands expertly over the man's clothes, and dislodged two guns and a knife—not a bad picking.

"Get back," he said, and the man started to move; Kerr let him take half a step, and then brought the gun down sharply on the base of his skull. One blow was enough; yet another man was added to those unconscious—or worse—in the house of Graff Daakmann, of Bania.

The girl's eyes were blazing.

"You—*swine!*"

"It's not so long since," said Kerr gently, "that you did the same to me, and I haven't started being offensive about it. Your turn."

"I won't move!"

"All right. I'll come to you. Take that coat off."

For a moment he thought she would defy him; and then she sighed, almost with resignation, and obeyed. Beneath the fur coat she wore a cunningly cut but very simple dress of navy blue; he was glad, for it wasn't a hard job to make sure what she carried in the way of firearms.

He found a small automatic in the top of her stocking. As he slipped it out she didn't move or speak, but her expression was no longer inscrutable; she was trembling with anger. Kerr chuckled.

"Modesty hasn't been your long suit," he said, "so I'm not going to apologize." He ran through the pockets of the coat, and found a second gun; her handbag revealed nothing.

He slipped the automatic into his pocket and smiled.

"Not your lucky day, Ellen. And you certainly know how to protect yourself. Did you know Mort was here?"

"I did."

"Still freezing, eh? The last time you were a little warmer, and it might pay you to be this time. Because"—Kerr's voice hardened, and there was no mistaking the grimness of his eyes

—"I'm getting more than a little tired of this game. It's time you told everything, and if you don't start quickly you're going to wish you had."

"You're an expert at handling women, aren't you?"

"Women," said Kerr, "are like men: good, bad or indifferent. And those three things are judged by standard. My standard at the moment is that you're mixed up in a nasty business, and therefore you're bad. You will get"—the expression in his eyes didn't alter, and it would have frightened most women—"exactly the same treatment as a man in the same circumstances. I can't afford to take chances."

"Have you never heard of—"

"Chivalry," said Bob Kerr, "is an excellent thing in its place, but it's not on the cards for to-night. Are you going to talk, or must I get rough?"

For a moment she looked as though she would defy him no matter what happened; and Bob Kerr was by no means sure he could key himself up to make her talk; words were all right, but actions a little more difficult. He didn't trust her, although he couldn't bring himself to believe that she was wholly bad. But he did believe she knew a great many things that would be more than interesting—would, in fact, be vital. And he *had* to learn what they were.

The hopelessness on her face reminded him of the moment when she had started to talk at the Bristol. She seemed to sag. She took a step towards Kerr, and said:

"All right. I'll talk."

And then she flung herself at him.

She was as wiry as she seemed soft, and her strength was incredible. For a moment Kerr was beaten back, and all the time she was punching, kicking, scratching at him. He could have thrown her off without too much trouble—but she *was* a woman. He struggled, fighting to get at one of her arms. He managed it and twisted her away. Just as that outburst of fury had come with devastating suddenness, so did her collapse. She sagged away from him, and would have fallen but for the fact that he still held her arm.

Kerr was breathing fast; yet even then he could not prevent himself from wondering what Toby Arran would have said had he seen that outburst. As it was, the quicker she talked the better.

"You've had all the licence you're going to have," he said, and his grip on her wrist tightened. "Well?"

"You're a devil, aren't you?"

"Supposing I am. I—"

And then Kerr stopped.

He hadn't been able to understand what she was doing. The Swede was unconscious, and she couldn't expect to get any help from inside the house. Yet she had been fencing, as elusive as ever, all the time. And now he realized the probable reason. She had come with the Swede; either there were others outside or there would be soon. She was fighting to gain time, and up to any trick to do it.

Now Bob Kerr was on tenterhooks.

He believed he could make her talk; pain did strange things, particularly to women. But could he bring himself to use force? It seemed a sacrilege. Not, he knew, that it would have made any difference had she been plain. It was a matter of sex, purely and simply, and...

She was smiling now, and seemed to be able to read his thoughts.

"So you can't manage it, eh? I—"

And then she stopped.

She was looking past Kerr towards the stairs, and Kerr was prepared for a trick, and didn't look round. As it happened there was no need, for Toby Arran—*Arran*—raised his voice. *Toby* was about again!

"Hallo, Bob! Visitors?"

"Visitors," said Kerr. "How are you?"

"Can hardly get one foot in front of the other, old son. Absolutely tired out. Who—"

He stopped; Kerr knew he had recognized the girl.

Ellen Granting looked up at him, and Kerr had never seen her smile quite so ravishing. She was clever, was Ellen Granting. But at the moment he was more concerned with Toby Arran.

Toby had been gassed, and he'd recovered quickly. Possibly the stuff had lost most of its strength; probably he was about again because he had not breathed it in for more than a few seconds. But he was on his feet, even if he was not likely to be much use in a rough-and-tumble. It was a relief, and Kerr felt easier in his mind.

"So it's you," Toby said, and his voice was hard; he seemed to sigh. "Come to visit a sick friend?"

"You don't look really fit," she said.

"I said 'friend'," murmured Toby. "Has she talked, Bob?"

"She's just going to."

"Get on with it." Toby could feel what he liked, but he knew they *had* to learn what this girl could tell them. He prayed that she would come out of the game reasonably clean, but she was mixed up in it and she could help them. The Department came first, always.

"You as well?"—her voice contemptuous.

"Me as well," said Toby. "You've had more than enough chances to come clean, my dear, and you haven't taken them. I—"

He stopped.

Bob Kerr's expression changed, and so did the girl's. For

the girl laughed, a low-pitched laugh that was full of grim humour, and she took several steps backwards, watching Kerr all the time. As she did so the footsteps they had heard outside came again; and then someone thundered at the door.

She cried out before Kerr could stop her.

"Be careful there! Careful!"

A sudden silence; an oath; and then a snapped command. The hurrying of footsteps, and then a crash of glass as a bullet was fired through the glass of the door.

Kerr acted almost on the instant.

He knew a lot; he knew where this place was and how to get to it. He knew also that there were half a dozen men at least outside, and he didn't think much of his chance of making a fight and winning it. Toby wasn't fit enough to be much help.

"You did that well," he said, and he stepped towards the girl. He didn't like the job, but it had to be done. He repeated his dose on the Swede, and before she could even cry out she was swaying on her feet, unconscious.

"That makes us square," he muttered. "Toby, can you run?"

"I can try."

"Get out through the window we came in, towards the car. Shoot on sight, for the legs. I'll follow with the girl."

"Damn it, Bob!" Arran was alert enough now, although he had spoken the truth when he had said that he was dreadfully tired. "Leave her and cut for it."

"My dear man, she's precious in more ways than one." Kerr slung her over his shoulder as he spoke, and Toby Arran was already by the open window. Toby climbed out; and as he did so a harsh voice was raised, from the side of the window.

"There they are! Stop! Stop!"

Toby fired towards the vague black shape; the man stopped bellowing and grunted. They heard him fall. Toby was running now towards the gate, and Kerr wasn't far behind him. Behind them footsteps came again, shots through the gloom. A bullet whistled perilously close to Bob Kerr's head, but he didn't seem to notice. Toby, his mind cleared by the keen night air, was three yards ahead, firing occasionally as figures loomed out of the darkness and then dropped down. Voices were raised behind them; lights were switched on all over the house, spreading a yellow glow about the grounds.

But Arran and Kerr, with the girl, were near the gate.

They could see the wing-lamps of one of the cars shining, and they saw also the two men who were moving towards the gate; less than five yards separated them.

Toby touched the trigger of his gun again; and the soft tap of the hammer was all he heard. Empty. *Empty!*

He flung the gun into the face of the nearest man and leapt like a tiger at the other. The fellow was sent backwards by the impetus of the rush, even though he was nearly twice Toby's weight. Kerr took advantage of the slight lull and bundled the girl into the back of the first car. His gun was out of his pocket like a flash, but he didn't have to use it. One man, his cheek cut open by Toby's automatic, leapt at him; Kerr hit him twice and the fellow dropped down.

Toby was mixing it as only Toby could, fists clenched, knees and legs in action; nor was his adversary particular. As they fought the men from the house were racing towards them, and Kerr knew it would be touch and go.

He fired twice, bringing one man down, then he cracked the gun on the back of Toby's adversary's head effectively. Toby was breathing fast, but he muttered:

"Good boy. You driving?"

"Yes—take these."

Kerr slipped two guns—the Swede's—from his pocket and Toby grabbed them. Toby jumped into the rear of the car, missing Ellen Granting's head by a fraction, and crouched low. The car was a tourer, and not too safe, but three shots kept the nearest men back. Kerr, at the driving-wheel, let in the clutch and the engine purred. He switched the headlamps on, and the winding road ahead of him was stark and clear.

The car lurched forward. Toby muttered as he banged his chin but kept firing. He knew that the big thing to do was to keep the pursuit off, and he stopped firing at the men and aimed at the other two cars. Seven times he fired; four times an explosion like a bursting howitzer rent the air, and four tyres were sadly in need of repair.

"Hot stuff," murmured Toby, and he slipped into his seat, breathing hard. It was reasonably sure they wouldn't be followed; as sure that they'd reach the monoplane. And that— what mattered after that?

Toby Arran had enjoyed himself.

Bob Kerr hadn't.

He knew that none of the things that had happened had been avoidable. More than half a dozen men had come to the house, and it was as well the Englishmen had lost no time. But he would have liked to have learned a great deal more.

Well—there was still the girl as a possible source of information.

He pressed harder on the accelerator. The car bumped up and down along the uneven road, the lights shining on the trees that were swaying in the strengthening wind. Above them the clouds had practically disappeared, and although there was no moon the stars shed a gentle light. They were out of earshot of the house now. With luck both cars were out of action until new tyres could be fitted, and that wouldn't happen quickly.

A fork in the road puzzled him for a moment; then he remembered seeing it when they had walked from the aeroplane, and he turned right. He didn't choose wrongly. Very soon the light from the headlamps shone on the grey metal of the monoplane, standing where they had left it. They reached it quickly. Kerr carried the girl into the cabin, switched on the lights, opened the throttle and started, while Toby banged the door of the cabin and collapsed, breathing hard, into a seat.

But he was still happy, for that had been fun and they'd got out of it with colours flying.

A tall, thick-set man with a square head and the hard grey eyes of the typical Teuton brought the Swede, Lorens, round with methods that were rough but effective, and listened to his story.

It wasn't a long one.

He'd come with the woman—Mannopoli himself had told him he could trust the woman—to the house. She told him they were going to see Daak, and he hadn't liked it. But he'd entered—and then he'd found that accursed Englishman in the hall. He hadn't a chance. He'd been shot once—look at his ear.

The square-headed man grunted, but realized there was nothing he could do. He went through the house room by room, and he was increasingly worried by what he found. But his worry was nothing to what he experienced when he saw Mort and Herr Daakmann lying unconscious if not worse.

He was half-inclined to hope it was worse.

Daakmann had telephoned him an hour before to hurry with a strong force of men to the house. Daakmann had been told, by telephone, that Kerr and Arran had followed Mr. Mort in the monoplane; he had wanted to see Kerr and Arran, but he hadn't reckoned on Mr. Mort's sneeze.

The square-headed man—who was nothing more nor less

than the Kommissar of the Banian Police—was extremely worried. He had taken orders from Herr Daakmann; he'd been a long time carrying those orders out, and he'd arrived too late to be of service.

Herr Daakmann wasn't gentle with people who failed him.

But there it was, and it couldn't be helped. The only thing to do, thought the Kommissar, was to get the sick men to bed, to treat them with a certain preparation which he knew—for he had seen some of Daakmann's early experiments with a certain gas—might help to revive them. And wait. It didn't occur to him to fly while the going was good. He had an unpleasant feeling that Daakmann could reach him anywhere, everywhere.

If Daakmann recovered.

There was just one man whom the Kommissar would have liked to have seen—a certain Mr. Mannopoli. Mannopoli was clever, and knew the treatment better than anyone else. But Mannopoli, he had heard, was in England; there was no chance of his arriving, and the Kommissar would have to do the best he could.

At that very moment Mr. Mannopoli was being interviewed by Gordon Craigie in the private ward of St. Martin's Hospital, London. He said little; most of what he said was offensive or threatening. He claimed that he would not be under arrest for more than three days, and that when he was free Craigie, and certain others, would know a great deal about it. He was not frightened; certainly he did not fear the threat of hanging for the murders he had committed. He behaved as if he *knew* he'd never hang.

Gordon Craigie was more worried than ever; the only thing that cheered him was the knowledge that Kerr and Arran were after Mort again and that they might send news at any moment.

* * *

About that time Bob Kerr had realized with a sickening sense of hopelessness that the monoplane had not been properly fuelled at the Berlin airport. For petrol was running very low, and he couldn't keep up in the air more than another ten minutes. He'd have to risk an immediate landing, and this time his hunch didn't give him any encouragement.

But he had to go down.

MR. RUMSDEN MAKES PROGRESS

B ut, my dear Mary," said Tommy Rumsden, "it's one of those things that just can't be helped. It's happened. In forty-eight short pregnant hours I've fallen for you. For the first time in my thirty-two years I'm in love. And it's not a matter to be referred to jokingly. It's serious. Dinner to-night, I insist."

"But..." said Mary Wayne, and stopped, for Tommy Rumsden was not a man to take no for an answer.

"I listen to no buts," said Tommy. "I mean it. Either you come out with me—somewhere hot, somewhere slow, pick which you like—or I spill the beans. I tell Mrs. Mort, bless her, just what a viper she has been nestling to her bosom. That you are in league with her visitors. That you bite the hand that feeds you. What time?"

"I'm not coming," said Mary Wayne firmly. "I can't afford it, Tommy. Sorry."

"H'm!" said Mr. Rumsden judicially. "I may be wrong, but I think that's the first time you've called me 'Tommy'. I'm probably wrong, but I also think you mean it when you say you're sorry. But you should know me well enough, sweetheart, to know that I won't marry a girl who's tied quite so tightly to her employer's apron-strings. Damn it, the honour of the Rumsdens counts a bit, whether you know it or not!"

"We were talking about dinner to-night," said Mary Wayne, suspiciously quickly, and to herself admitting that she liked the fool more than she really wanted to admit. "As for anything else—"

"Damn it, didn't you hear me propose to you? And if a girl can't dine with a man the night she's promised to marry him, it's getting to something. I mean," added Tommy Rumsden warmly, "you just can't do it. It isn't—"

"Don't," said Mary Wayne, very softly.

And Tommy Rumsden, who knew when to stop, stopped. He contrived a chuckle into the telephone which sounded as though he understood, and she could imagine the way his lips were curving at the corners, and then went on:

"If you change your mind, Chelsea 91245 gets me. As far as I know I'll be here until late. Try and come."

"I can't promise," Mary said, "but I'll try."

"And that," said Mr. Rumsden to himself as he replaced the receiver, "says a lot. God, but that girl…Now what was it Craigie said? Well, Craigie can't have everything. I wonder what the old dog's doing, and how Wally's getting on? A queer business this, but my end's turned out to be jam."

He beamed at the telephone as if it were Mary, bethought himself of the way she could smile, imagined what she'd look like if she was dressed as he would have her dressed—Tommy Rumsden was a nice-minded man, and meant it—and told himself she had been hiding her light under a bushel too long, that Mrs. Mort would soon be wanting a new secretary, and that he wasn't the only one to have proposed to a girl within forty-eight hours of meeting. He was convinced of them all.

Tommy Rumsden was cheerful, for he did not know just what things were happening about him.

Mary Wayne was cheerful, for she was almost convinced that Rumsden meant what he said. It was a remarkable fact that he had managed to make her think about him, practically without ceasing, since she had first seen him, outrageous tie and sky-blue trousers and all, grimacing at Holt in the hall of the Gretley Place house.

She had managed to get to lunch with him on the previous day, although she hadn't had time to change, and she doubted whether she would be able to get away from the house again for the evening. That momentary revelation of softness which Leila Mort had revealed on the afternoon of the 'private entertainment' had not lingered. Mrs. Mort seemed more shrewish than ever; Mary, remembering Gabrell, thought she understood.

She turned from the telephone, sighed, walked slowly to her own room, and then remembered that she had some letters typed and ready for Leila Mort's signature; Leila didn't like to be kept waiting too long. She gathered them from her desk and hurried to her employer's boudoir; it was both a boudoir and practically a salon; Mrs. Mort did a great deal of private—but not secret—entertaining there; her select friends rarely troubled to knock.

Mary Wayne had never omitted that preliminary before.

Perhaps it was because Tommy Rumsden's words were echoing in her mind. Perhaps it was because she knew she was later with the letters than she should have been. In any case she opened the door of the boudoir; and as it opened she saw the heavily built middle-aged man who was sitting on a Chippendale chair, and she heard Mrs. Mort say:

"At midnight on the twentieth. The day after to-morrow."

"That's right, my dear," said the middle-aged man; and then he glanced towards the door, and Mary Wayne—who was rarely scared of anything—felt more frightened than she had ever been in her life. She couldn't move; she couldn't even wave the letters to explain her presence. She just stared.

She heard Mrs. Mort's vast intake of breath.

"Wayne! What does this mean?"

"I—I'm dreadfully sorry." Mary forced herself to speak, but her employer's expression—one of sheer, venomous hatred—coupled with the expression in the eyes of the man, was still frightening, and she wished the ground would open up and let her disappear. "I brought these letters for—for signing. I—"

"Never," said Mrs. Leila Mort, "*never* come in here again without knocking, under pain of instant dismissal. I'll send for you when I want the letters. Go."

She even pointed to the door, and Mary Wayne, oddly observant even then, saw Mrs. Mort's breast rising and falling under the stress of an emotion that seemed absurd.

The girl managed to keep her head. She closed the door quietly, after a slight bow, and then walked to her own room with her cheeks burning; and there was only one sentence in her mind.

"At midnight on the twentieth."

Had she been allowed to deliver the letters, had no fuss been made, she would have thought no more of the words. Mrs. Mort obviously was making an appointment. Even conceivably an elopement or something equally foolhardy now that Mort was away. But to behave as she had!

Mary trembled with repressed indignation, sat at her typewriter for ten minutes, staring ahead of her and doing nothing. She could not get those words out of her mind.

"At midnight on the twentieth." What did they mean?

Could they mean anything more than a peccadillo? Mrs. Mort —the Leila Mort she knew—would never have made that fuss; hang it, Mary knew as much about Mrs. Mort's friendships as Mrs. Mort did herself.

She couldn't rid her mind of the single sentence. Couldn't. And while she was trying, the hard eyes of the middle-aged man and the blazing eyes of her employer seemed to loom in front of her eyes. What on earth had she walked into?

She shrugged her shoulders at last and started typing. She typed so fast that she didn't hear the middle-aged man as he passed her door and went downstairs; she did hear the buzzer summoning her to Leila's presence, and from the length of its ring she could guess that Leila was still at boiling-point.

She took the letters, her note-book and pencil, and hurried along to the boudoir, tapping before she entered. Leila Mort called: "Come in."

She was standing by a mirror, looking towards the door. She looked older—and she looked a vixen. Her lips were tight, her eyes still blazing.

"Come—*in.*"

Mary went in and closed the door, ready for anything, and, above all, trouble. She did not feel that she could take it easily. She might get six pounds a week for working for Leila Mort, but there were other things than money.

"Why did you come in like that?"—the words were like pistol-shots.

"I did it unintentionally," Mary said, as coolly as she could. "I'm sorry."

"Sorry! You—"

The older woman took a step forwards, and Mary noticed something else. She was afraid. Afraid! And there was more fear than anything else in her expression.

"Mrs. Mort"—Mary was very calm, very self-possessed— "for the first time since I've worked for you I entered your room without knocking. I've said I'm sorry. I don't think you're justified in behaving—or looking—like this."

"If I thought you'd come purposely"—what on earth did the woman mean?—"I'd—" Leila Mort made a tremendous effort, and controlled herself, but her lips were trembling. "All right, Wayne. Leave the letters. I shan't want you any more to-day. You'd better go out for a few hours."

"Thank you," said Mary, and she left the room.

She didn't know whether to laugh or cry, so she telephoned Tommy Rumsden. He was in, and his loud, deep voice cheered her, as she hoped it would.

"Hallo, hallo, hallo! I *thought* you'd come. You've managed it, then?"

"I—yes, I can come. But, Tommy—"

"Sweetheart?"

"I'm in a bad mood."

"I'll soon have you out of it. Now look here, it's just after five. Let's take a large car and a long spin—the weather being reasonable—and then get back in time for dinner and a show. Proposal overboard for the day, if you'd prefer it."

"I would prefer it."

"And the agenda?"

"Perfect!"

"Only one thing in this wicked world is perfect," said Tommy grandiosely, "and that's not the agenda, it's the partner to it. All right, darling. I'll meet you at—"

"Piccadilly Circus."

"I don't know that I like the sound of that," said Tommy cheerfully, "but it's all right. Swan and Edgar's?"

"Swan and Edgar's in half an hour."

Tommy said: "Fine," and rang down. Mary Wayne felt more cheerful as she hurried to her room, changed into the nearest thing to an attractive afternoon frock, scowled when she looked at her bun and deliberately undid it, allowing the natural waves of her hair full fling, and slipped into a coat. She looked a little breathless, more than a little attractive, and very lovable. Or so Messrs. Riddle and Holt—who saw her go through the hall—considered.

Wally Davidson—watching for Mrs. Mort and making a note of people who went in or out of the Mort house—duly noted that the girl Tommy Rumsden was crushed over had looked as though she'd won a fortune, and wondered whether Mrs. Mort would go for a spin. He was tired of inaction, but knowing what had happened to Carruthers made it impossible for him to be careless.

The driver of the Rolls had escaped practically unhurt. He claimed that his car went out of control and that he couldn't do anything to help it. As far as Craigie, Davidson, or Superintendent Miller could see, there was nothing else to do but to take the man's story as the true one. None of them believed it; but the driver, who worked for a blameless—or so it was believed—City man, certainly gave them no grounds for suspicion.

So Davidson watched Mary Wayne go for her appointment at Piccadilly.

And Davidson saw the little man—not unlike Gabrell if you thought hard enough—leave a house farther down the road and follow the girl. Wally didn't connect the two events, and certainly made no note about it.

Mary Wayne didn't know she was followed.

It was a fine afternoon; she was feeling exhilarated after her duel with Leila Mort and the prospect of seeing Tommy, and she walked quickly. She didn't realize the man walked just as quickly, and when at last she boarded a bus bound for Piccadilly Circus, she certainly didn't see the little man who jumped on shortly afterwards.

He was a sharp-featured fellow who looked French. He was French, and Bob Kerr would have recognized him as quickly as Toby Arran, for he had been with the Swede in the Hôtel Bristol forty-eight hours before. He also had a sobriquet, which translated meant the Slicer; the Sûreté could have placed him as a particularly murderous specimen of the apache tribe whose sentences had been considerable, but excluded the guillotine or Devil's Island purely because of lack of evidence. The Slicer—or, as he was known at the Grand Palace Hotel, where he was staying, M'sieu Armand Rennu— had one peculiarity.

He always killed with a knife.

He was so expert that he could guarantee to find the heart at a single thrust and to make the kill without a cry escaping from the victim. His speciality was to kill in crowds; everyone could see, and yet no one ever saw. He wore thin rubber-tipped gloves on his hands, for the knife-handle had to carry no finger-prints.

M'sieu Armand Rennu followed Mary Wayne until she alighted from the bus at Piccadilly Circus and then went towards the crowd waiting outside Swan and Edgar's; Rennu knew little about London, but he did know a crowd of people waiting outside that London store could be guaranteed; it was the nightly rendezvous for thousands. Even in broad daylight he could have wished for no better spot.

He drew closer to Mary Wayne, and the knife in his glove was cool against his flesh. He wished he could have smoothed it; he loved cold steel.

Mary looked about her, her cheeks still flushed. She hoped Tommy wouldn't keep her waiting; she felt she couldn't bear to be kept waiting. And then she saw him, standing with his back to the plate-glass window and looking over the heads of the crowd. He caught sight of her at practically the same moment as she saw him, and he took three steps towards her.

M'sieu Rennu took two steps towards her, and slid the knife into his hand. He saw the crowd, but he didn't see Tommy Rumsden particularly. He forced past a stout woman and a weedy man who were embracing, and he was next to the girl.

Tommy Rumsden's hand went out to take her, and the Slicer started to move his hand towards her left side.

It was then that Tommy Rumsden did a strange thing.

He didn't take her outstretched hand; he flattened his palm and pushed hard against her chest. She staggered backwards, and as she went she felt something that seemed very hot jab into her arm. She cried aloud; she staggered and fell, and in a haze she saw Tommy Rumsden, his face fiercer than she had ever seen it before, or imagined it could be, crash his other fist into a little man's face!

It was a blow in a thousand; it took Rennu under the chin and sent him reeling backwards into the embracing couple— the kiss was still lingering, so quickly had this thing happened; and a dozen people, startled by the scream and the girl's cry, saw the knife that dropped from the Frenchman's hand.

And the observant ones saw something else.

They saw something that seemed to bite into the French-man's forehead; saw the spreading red hole—or what looked like a hole—and saw the man collapse. They *knew* the wild-looking man in the colourful clothes hadn't shot him, but they knew he had been shot.

And then the tall form of a policeman shouldered through the crowds, and the law carried on.

"It's all right," Mary said, although her face was very pale. "It's just the thought of it that worries me. Who on earth could have wanted to—to do that?"

"The question," said Tommy, "goes on the next agenda, and we haven't time for it to-day. That doctor made a good job of your arm."

"Ye-es. It'll be a nasty mess afterwards, I'm afraid, but it was inside the arm, so it won't show."

"Oh, these women!" mourned Tommy Rumsden.

"Appearance, appearance, appearance all the time, instead of being thankful they're not dead! Sorry. Call that unsaid."

Mary forced back a tremulous smile, but couldn't keep back tears. Tommy waited until she had tired herself.

Three-quarters of an hour had passed since the 'incident' in Piccadilly. They were sitting in a corner of a café in Wardour Street. Tommy had arranged for the girl to be taken to a doctor near by with a message from him; had told the police what he knew, and had persuaded the policeman to telephone Superintendent Miller, who confirmed that he was working on special business. Rennu being dead, Tommy saw no object in doing anything but returning for the girl.

He didn't doubt that the effort to kill her had been inspired by the same motive as the effort to kill Carruthers on the previous day, and he was worried.

Rennu had been shot—but no one knew who by. Obviously he had had orders to kill the girl, and he'd been watched. Whoever had watched had shot him to make sure he didn't talk. The only thing Tommy was thankful for was that Rennu, not the girl, had taken the bullet through the head. A too peaceful death, Tommy considered, for a man who could use a knife like that. He still felt sticky under the collar when he realized how narrow the escape had been. He'd seen the glint of the knife—purely because he had been glancing down at Mary—in the nick of time.

Well, it was over. Would she have any idea why the attack had been made?

He didn't like to linger over the subject, but he knew she would have to talk, and better to him than Craigie or any of the others. So when he was sure she was composed again, and when she had poured out tea, he smiled at her. Tommy's smile was a thing in a thousand.

"Well, sweetheart? Getting in the bad books of bad men isn't a thing I'd recommend. Any idea why it happened?"

He knew she had, or thought she had, and he felt a tightening excitement inside him. She hesitated for a moment; then:

"It seems absurd," she said, "but—"

"I know a man who was nearly murdered for a postage stamp, and another for half a crown," said Tommy cheerfully, "so the motive needn't be big to be good. Er—you were saying?"

She told him briefly what had happened that afternoon. Mrs. Mort's strange reaction, and the malevolent stare of the man who had been in the salon. Tommy listened quietly; and he knew when that 'at midnight on the twentieth' came that he'd learned something worth learning.

"So you think that's it?"

"I can't think it is; and yet there's nothing else."

"Ever seen the fellow before?"

"Never."

"Not one of Leila's popular fancies, then. What was he like?"

"Well—he was a biggish man. Rather heavily built. His hair was grey, and I'd say he was over fifty."

"Hair long or short?"

"Cut rather short. He was very well dressed."

"I wonder," said Tommy Rumsden, "whether any of the other servants at the house have ever seen him before? He's our man, sweetheart, on your life."

She eyed him quietly for a moment; and then:

"Tommy?"

"H'm-h'm?"

"You seem almost as if you expected something like this. Almost as if you—you've been looking for something."

Mr. Tommy Rumsden, who had congratulated himself only a short while before that he had been putting this across well, felt winded. And then he smiled, and he told a little of the truth. He maintained that his 'fall' was sincere; and she believed him. Somehow she seemed more satisfied now.

"It seemed so mad before," she said, "but if it's something they're planning in a criminal way, I can understand it."

"I'd say it looked criminal," smiled Tommy Rumsden. "Now be a kind soul, drink that tea up, and telephone the house. Your fat and beery butler will probably be the best bet."

Mary smiled at the description of the immaculate Holt, and went with Tommy to a telephone booth at one end of the café. She called the house, and Holt answered.

"Mary Wayne here," she said quickly. "Tell me, Holt—did you see the man who visited Mrs. Mort this afternoon?"

"Which one, miss?"

"The rather big, middle-aged man."

"Oh yes, Miss Wayne, I saw him. I showed him up to her

ladyship's room—begging your pardon—myself. He's often been before, usually to see Mr. Mort."

"Has he?" asked Mary; her excitement increased, and she knew Tommy was dying to get the news. "Who is he?"

"Mr. Fallow, miss—Mr. John Fallow. Lives in Devon, I believe, or somewhere near it. Is there—is there anything *wrong*, Miss Wayne?"

18

NEWS FROM ALL QUARTERS

Gordon Craigie sat opposite Tommy Rumsden and Mary Wayne, and looked as if he didn't believe a word they said. It was not intentional; it was just that the news came as a shock—and Gordon Craigie was rarely shocked.

"You're sure that was the name—Fallow?"

"John Fallow," Mary said. "Holt believed he lived in Devon or somewhere in that direction."

"He does," said Gordon Craigie, and he seemed much older than he had done a few minutes before. "Rumsden, may I use your telephone?"

"Through that door there," said Tommy, pointing to an open door that led from the sitting-room of his studio flat. "You'd rather be on your own?"

"If you've no objection." Craigie smiled, and for the first time Mary Wayne rather liked him. He had been so cold, so distant, so unapproachable, that she hadn't been sure before.

Craigie closed the door behind him. Mary turned to Tommy, who kissed her, as though by habit; and then he apologized, although the colour of her cheeks justified it.

"Who is he?" she asked.

"I offer you romance," mourned Tommy Rumsden, "and you ask about another. His name's Craigie. God alone knows just what he is, but he matters. And he's worried. A friend of mine—you'll have to meet Wally Davidson—worships the ground that man treads on. So, I'm told, do others. But I can't learn, for I've heard that he doesn't use married men, and that cuts me out."

"I'll have to meet your wife," said Mary.

"Now look here..." began Tommy Rumsden, and for a few minutes he didn't care much whether Craigie was there or not. He was playing an important part in this game, was Tommy Rumsden, but he would never have settled down into a regular Department agent.

Craigie, meanwhile, was speaking to a man who was staying temporarily at the Jay Hostelry, Tarrington, Devon. The man was named Beaumant, and he was an agent of Z.

"Yes," Beaumant said. "Fallow left by road about nine o'clock this morning. Dodo Trale followed him. Dodo was going to ring you as soon as he reached London and had breathing-space. Didn't he?"

"He didn't," said Craigie grimly. "You're there by yourself now?"

"Yes."

"I'll send someone else down. Meanwhile ask the local police for some good man. If you see Fallow, hold him. And Ellen Granting. Bring either of them here without losing time. And if anyone who looks at all out of the ordinary calls at The Maples, tackle them too."

"Any special orders?"

"If you're stuck for a question, ask 'em what's going to happen at midnight on the twentieth," said Gordon Craigie, "and watch their reactions."

"Thanks," said Beaumant. "Is that the lot?"

"Yes—but be careful."

Craigie rang down, more worried than ever. He had not seriously suspected John Fallow to have anything to do with this affair, and yet if the man had talked with Leila Mort as this girl said, and the girl had been so close to death so shortly afterwards, it was impossible to read anything else into the affair. Fallow was on the wanted list, and on the short list of suspects.

Craigie was worried about Dodo Trale.

Trale had been with the Department for many years, a man of middle height, sound of wind and limb, blessed with a pair of fists and little imagination. In short, a good general agent. If Dodo had followed Fallow to London, he would have telephoned as soon as Fallow had gone to earth.

He hadn't telephoned, and Fallow was in London. The obvious thing to suspect was that something had happened to Trale, and Craigie was afraid it had.

He telephoned again, this time to the Yard. It happened that Sir William Fellowes, the Chief Commissioner, was in his office. Fellowes and Craigie knew each other well, and were on more amicable terms than plain duty demanded.

"Have a call sent out for John Fallow," Craigie said.

"Ho-ho! He's in it, is he?"

"I'm afraid so. Although Mannopoli definitely tried to kill —damn it!" exclaimed Craigie, who rarely used bad language even in its mildest form, "what does that matter? Fallow was at Mort's place about an hour and a quarter ago, and he's probably still in London. Get him if you can, will you?"

"Yes," said Fellowes. "Anything else breaking?"

"A time and a date."

"What is it?"

"Midnight on the twentieth—the day after to-morrow. But what it is I've no more idea than the man in the moon."

"I think," said Fellowes, "that you're doing well. What about Leila Mort?"

"Davidson's watching her, but I'd like you to supplement it. How many men have you got watching the house?"

"Four."

"Double it, there's a good fellow," and Fellowes promised that he would. Fellowes knew that Craigie was even more worried than he had been before, despite the fact that at last he seemed to have learned something that mattered.

Craigie sat back and stared at the telephone. Midnight on the twentieth something would happen. What would happen?

He hadn't the faintest idea.

He hadn't heard from Kerr since the telephone message when Kerr and Arran had been discovered at the Hôtel Bristol; he'd had no word from any of his agents abroad, although all of them were instructed to look for Julius Mort. From the Continent only silence came, and it was such a drawn-out silence that Craigie was half afraid that his men there had suffered as Carruthers had suffered in Gretley Place, and Dodo Trale somewhere on the road to London.

Well, it couldn't be helped.

Rumsden—a likable fellow—had proved himself to be useful. The girl was all right. They'd got on to Fallow's trail and proved, as conclusively as they could, that Leila Mort was mixed up in this business as well as her husband. If nothing developed in the next twenty-four hours he'd bring Leila in for questioning. And that was as far as he could go at the moment.

He didn't like the Fallow connection; gas wasn't a topic that Craigie liked at all, and gas was certainly in this somewhere.

He couldn't fathom Fallow's connection; he didn't believe the show between Mannopoli and Fallow had been faked. He didn't believe Mannopoli had ever known that letter from Mort had been sent to Craigie.

What did that mean? Were there two sides—Mannopoli's and Fallow's? In opposition?

Craigie didn't know, admitted it, and went into the other room. He had hurried to Rumsden's flat—for he did not propose to interview the woman at the Department office—and the quicker he returned to Whitehall the better. It was quite possible that news would be coming in.

He took his leave of Tommy Rumsden and Mary Wayne, after a couple of sentences congratulating the girl on her escape, and assuring her that any recompense for the damage would be rapidly forthcoming, uttered in such a way as to make her understand why Craigie was popular with men. Tommy saw him to the door of the studio flat; two men— Department men—were on the other side of the road, and no other cars were in sight. Craigie moved off quickly, and Tommy Rumsden, relieved more than he could say that there had not been another dose of trouble, returned to Mary and other things.

The main 'other thing' was that he had a mother who had a house in Hampstead; a large house, with plenty of room. And he had brothers. There was safety in numbers, and she wasn't going back to Gretley Place.

Mary tried to argue, and failed; and in her heart she was immensely relieved. For when she thought of the eyes of John Fallow and the expression of Leila Mort's face she shivered. She knew, now, that she had been given permission to go that evening simply that she should meet her death.

* * *

Robert McMillan Kerr and Tobias Arran struggled to the foot of a mountain road, and sat on a boulder, which was hard enough, but at least a rest for their feet. They looked worse than Tommy Rumsden had ever looked in his life. They were worn out, their arms, legs, backs, eyes, and middles ached as they had never ached before; particularly their middles, for they hadn't eaten for twenty-four hours, and it had been a scratch meal then.

They had had whisky-flasks, and that had saved them. Otherwise, as Toby said gloomily, their bones would have been rotting by now.

"You can thank your stars," said Bob Kerr with his indefatigable cheerfulness, "that it's not winter and there's no snow. These places are impassable, and if you've ever been frozen to death you'll know what I mean."

"Before we get anywhere," Toby said promptly, "we'll probably be frozen a dozen times. Any idea what country we're in?"

"Germany or Poland," said Bob Kerr, and he looked thoughtful. "Unless we're still in Bania."

"You keep talking about Bania," groused Toby.

"I can't imagine anything like this originating in Germany or Poland," Kerr said. "That's the long and short of it. Bania is just the place. No extradition laws, an ideal spot for Mannopoli and Mort to reach if the police of other countries are on their heels."

"You seem to know a lot about it."

"I only wished," said Bob Kerr grimly, "that I could have mentioned the place to Craigie. He'd have had a dozen men in or about it in a couple of days."

"But that house might not be in Bania."

"There's an even chance either way," said Bob Kerr, "but let's forget it. God, I'm hungry."

"Let us," said Toby, with dignity, "forget it. I wonder whether anyone's found the bus?"

Kerr said he didn't know and he didn't care.

They had been forced to land less than an hour after leaving the house on the hills, and they hadn't made a success of it. The miracle was that they were alive at all. They'd landed on the side of a hill, and the tail of the 'plane was still resting against tall pines. Only the shortage of petrol in the tanks had saved them from fire and destruction.

There had been one relief; they were three-quarters of an hour, or a hundred and fifty miles, from the house. By Kerr's reckoning they were somewhere between Leipzig, Dresden and Chemnitz, and as far as he could see they were among the foothills of the Erz mountains. He did not know Saxony well, but he knew it well enough for that.

The prospect wasn't appetizing.

The Erz mountains, winter and summer, were often absolutely empty of people and habitation for stretches of fifty and sixty miles. There might be a few mountain villages, but they hadn't struck one yet. Worse, they hadn't managed to find a road, even an apology for one. For twenty-four hours they had wandered, keeping a straight south-westerly course with the help of the compass Kerr had salvaged from the wreckage of the *Queen;* they had been through mist, rain, blazing sunshine, and dreadful cold. Their clothes were in tatters and their shoes were torn to pieces. And they were still no nearer help, as far as they knew, than they had been when they had first started through the darkness.

Dawn of the second day—the nineteenth of September—was two hours behind them now. There remained a couple of nips apiece in Toby's flask—Kerr's was empty. They had revolvers, and twice they'd shot, unsuccessfully, at birds; they were not sufficiently accomplished woodsmen to get near enough for accuracy without scaring their quarry away.

On the surface they kept cheerful; beneath it each man felt in his own way the tearing anxiety to get news to Craigie. They might have fared better but for the girl.

Ellen Granting had recovered consciousness some twenty minutes after the smash, while Kerr had been carrying her through the darkness. They both admitted that she took the news well, and she did her best to make herself no burden. But on the dawn of the first day she tumbled down a small bank, and her ankle was now so swollen that she couldn't walk. Kerr carried her most of the way, while when the going was smooth the two men made a chair. She made no comment, no complaints, and continued to stick it well.

They'd left her, twenty minutes before, on a couch of bracken where they'd rested the night. Obviously she wouldn't try to get away; the chances of getting lost in the hills were too great. They'd hoped to get within shouting distance of someone human, but the luck wasn't breaking their way.

Kerr toiled back for the girl.

He found her doing her best with powder and puff to restore the ravages of two nights and a day in the wilds; she didn't do too badly, and Kerr smiled in forced admiration. She looked at him coolly enough; her poise was perfect.

"I'm staying here," she said.

"Are you?"

"Yes. I'm not letting you lose your chances of getting away. That's final, Mr. Kerr."

"How well we stick to the proprieties!" smiled Kerr. "I didn't like hitting you once, I shan't like hitting you again, but if you won't be sensible there's no choice. How's the ankle this morning?"

"Hopeless." She seemed sullen now.

"All right. Pick-a-back or cradle?"

For the first time a glimmer of a smile crossed her face, and she shrugged her shoulders.

"Cradle, if it's got to be one or the other. But why don't you go on? You're only taking me into—into something worse than this, if you do find help."

"The issue's too big," said Kerr. "Besides, there's always a chance you might get away without doing anything in the way of a prison sentence. Don't be awkward, my dear. It'll make no difference to what happens, but it'll make things a damned sight more unpleasant."

She smiled again, and for some reason Kerr ran through the few occasions on which he had seen her. At Dummett Street; at the Bristol; and at the house on the hills. He'd asked her once or twice to tell him where the place was; but she'd kept silent. He couldn't prevent himself from liking her; he knew that Toby Arran felt the devil when he allowed himself to think. But—there it was. God knew what would happen when he did get her back to England.

It didn't cross Kerr's mind that he might fail.

He picked her up—she was remarkably light for a woman as tall as she was—and picked his way carefully. Her face was very close to his. Her eyes were wide open, starry, probing. It was almost as if she was trying to read his mind. He didn't speak, and when she broke a ten minutes' silence, he was surprised. She had talked so little.

"Wouldn't you like a rest?"

"We'll reach Toby in another ten minutes."

"Strong as an ox, don't they say?"

"It'll do."

She was silent for a moment, but her eyes were still regarding him, still puzzling. Then:

"It would be very easy," she said, "for me to fall in love with you. If you knew me better you'd realize how remarkable that was."

Kerr chuckled.

"It's remarkable enough, thanks."

"You've no feeling for—women?"

"I've never noticed any in particular."

"You will one day," she said, "and I wish it could be me."

"You know," said Bob Kerr, who knew that it was madness even to let her think he was taking it in any way seriously—God, how difficult it was not to!—"you'll upset me soon, and I'll come a cropper. Another sprained ankle won't help us."

"And you're never serious?"

"That's not true, damn it! I'm usually serious."

"I know," she said, and she laughed; more, she snuggled closer to him and closed her eyes. It was a difficult job indeed for Robert McMillan Kerr not to kiss her, but he managed it. He made himself think of the gun in his ribs, of her laugh when the last interruption had come to the house on the hill, and other things. He remembered Mulling; the man blown into nothing; Gabrell and other things.

And he was remembering some of the other things when the cry rent the silence.

"Hallo, there! *Hallo!*"

Ellen Granting's eyes opened in a flash; Kerr felt his heart thump.

"Toby. Shouting us for a pound."

"He wouldn't shout us like that; he's sighted someone. Oh, if only I could walk!"

Kerr did his best to hurry. Toby was halloing fit to kill, and there was no doubt he'd seen something or someone. Somehow Kerr got down the hillside and sighted his friend; and he laughed. It was the only thing to do.

Toby was standing on the highest boulder he could find, bellowing, waving his arms, occasionally even kicking his legs. He didn't hear the others approach, and when he saw them he glanced just once in their direction and stopped bellowing to snap:

"Over there—two men—shout, Bob! Hallo, there! *Hallo!*"

Kerr joined him.

As he shouted—after putting the girl down—he saw the twisted smile on her face, and he wondered what was passing through her mind. She seemed to realize she was facing something worse than being lost on a German hillside, but that wasn't the moment for going into it. His voice echoed with Arran's, and after five agonizing minutes one of the men looked up.

They were fully a thousand yards away, but voices carried far over the hills, and the sun, behind Toby and Bob Kerr, showed them up clearly against the blue sky. One of the others waved; Toby Arran could have jumped for joy. Kerr picked the girl up—pick-a-back this time because it was more comfortable, and the two parties hurried towards each other.

Just twenty minutes later they met; and Kerr, speaking in a slow but understandable German, made himself clear. He wanted food, drink, a car or a cart, and to know where they were.

The food and the drink, packed in the men's knapsacks, came first, and they fell on it ravenously. Between mouthfuls Kerr learned where they were. The Saxon peasants, good-hearted, slow-witted folk typical of their kind, were slow but sure.

Dresden was thirty miles behind them, Chemnitz ten or fifteen miles ahead. The nearest village where they could get a car was three miles away, but the peasants offered to go and get it. A glance at the wanderers' clothes was enough to tell them how they were placed.

Toby Arran, replete and happy, watched them go and smiled.

Bob Kerr would have liked a sleep above all things, but daren't risk it. And Ellen Granting looked ahead of her, her expression inscrutable and her lips set very firmly, as though she was trying not to be afraid to face what was coming.

"Bob," said Gordon Craigie into the telephone, "I've never been so glad to hear anyone in my life. What news?"

"I'll leave everything but this," said Bob Kerr. "I think the central place is in Bania. I can't make the girl talk, but I'll try on the way over. The gas knocks you off your feet in a flash, but whether it's fatal or not usually, I can't say. Toby had a light dose and was over it in twenty minutes. But I've got a list of names and addresses, clutched in the hands of the man with Mort. I'll read 'em out."

Bob Kerr read them out; he was speaking on the longdistance wire from Dresden, and he was feeling more contented than for a long time past. He finished at last, and added:

"That's a round dozen, Craigie. I'll get over as soon as I can."

"Good man," said Gordon Craigie, and he meant a great deal more than he seemed to.

The twelve names and addresses were of people in different Continental towns. He sent directions to Z agents in those towns, and within twelve hours he was getting news— news from all quarters. And the news astonished Gordon Craigie.

For in most cases the wife of the man named was more important than the man himself. And each woman was, in effect, a counterpart of Mrs. Leila Mort, particularly in the holding of 'private entertainments'!

19

ALL EVIDENCE

B ob Kerr and Toby Arran reached the Whitehall office at half past one on the twentieth of September—ten and a half hours before the thing was to happen. None of them knew what the thing was, but all of them were reasonably sure that it was gigantic, and that its results would be catastrophic unless it was stopped in time. The puzzle was how to stop it; it wasn't easy, as Toby pointed out with his usual gloom, to stop a bull when they didn't know where the bull was, and in any case it might be an elephant.

Davidson was in the office with the others. No one else, although the large and dusty Superintendent Miller was expected at any moment.

"It's a question," Craigie said, looking even whiter about the face than ever, "of getting the evidence together and then trying to use it. But before we go on to that—I learned last night that Dodo Trale, who'd been watching Fallow, was mixed up in another of the 'accidents' that put Carruthers out of action. I've told you of the Frenchman Rennu, and how he went. It's little short of deadly, and I can't think round it."

Kerr, his head as always on one side, rubbed his massive chin. He had managed to get a suit of reach-me-downs in Dresden, and Toby Arran had been as fortunate. They looked respectable if nothing else; but, above all things, they looked tired. There were red rims round Kerr's eyes, and Toby Arran dozed even in the office.

"Directly we've got on to anyone who might have talked," he said, "they've been killed. Mulling—Rennu—and others. Those who haven't been killed have been lucky to get away with it."

Craigie nodded.

"The woman Granting won't talk?"

"She won't say a word," said Kerr, and he looked grim. "I've tried most ways. I can't bring myself to go any farther. She's at Cannon Row now, and Miller and the police are grilling her there, but I doubt whether they'll have any better luck. You've heard nothing from Fallow?"

Craigie shook his head.

"Fallow's disappeared—and Mrs. Mort."

"Couldn't help it," Davidson said sorrowfully.

He felt the disappearance of Mrs. Mort keenly, but, as he said, no blame could be attached to him. He'd watched the house like a lynx; so had three C.I.D. men, all experts at the job. But Mrs. Mort had contrived to get out, obviously dressed as a man. At all events there were no traces of her at the Gretley Place house.

Kerr's first suggestion had been to have the place taken over; Craigie hadn't agreed. The police, it was true, had looked through it, but the development that he had learned from his agents in various countries had made him more careful of Mrs. Mort.

For they knew that there was to be a 'special entertainment' on the evening of the twentieth, lasting until the early hours.

Police occupation of the house would have prevented it. As it was, police and Z agents were concentrated on Gretley Place. Five houses within easy reach were occupied by those agents; cars continually went along Gretley Place, never stopping, but always on the look-out. Others were parked from time to time—as the Daimler that Carruthers and Davidson had used—and chauffeurs were watching. Everyone who went in or out of the Mort ménage was under a barrage of eyes; and Craigie was expecting to get some surprising information between six and seven o'clock that evening—the 'entertainment' started at seven, and most of the guests would be likely to arrive by then.

The information had been obtained from Mary Wayne, who was now with Tommy Rumsden's parents, and chafing a little at being kept in. Craigie—and for that matter Tommy—wouldn't allow her to go out. They were reasonably certain that she had been followed after the knifing attempt, and probably the men who were at the head of this grim game knew she was at Hampstead. But the C.I.D. were concentrated about the house, about Rumsden's flat—everywhere the attack might come.

Craigie and the police were on tenterhooks.

The Home Secretary and the Prime Minister had been informed that something would happen, and probably something grim. They knew Craigie and his men well enough to be sure that he was right, even though they could produce little evidence. But the Government was prepared. Scotland Yard was on the *qui vive*. All reserves were waiting at the various divisional stations and sub-stations—but they had no idea what they were waiting for.

Mannopoli and the others had kept their secret to the last. But—would they succeed?

Could Mannopoli escape from a prison cell, as he seemed confident he could? Would Ellen Granting hold out and refuse her knowledge? She was fighting hard, but once Kerr thought she had been weakening.

He couldn't be sure.

"Well, now," Craigie said, "the evidence. First and most important—there's gas in it."

Kerr nodded. Davidson kept his eyes closed; Toby Arran managed to open his.

"Second," said Craigie, "Fallow has supplied the gas, or the particulars of it; that's reasonably sure. Third—the organization isn't against England—London—alone. There are agents of Mannopoli's—or Mort's—in practically every country, and it's reasonably safe to say the thing will happen simultaneously."

"You've warned the others?" Kerr asked.

"Yes—and I haven't been taken too seriously," said Craigie, with a rueful smile. "I've no evidence—no evidence! I can't even *do* anything at Gretley Place to-night. There'll be a dozen influentials—the type of people we can't touch. If it was an ordinary affair we could have a police raid and risk the consequences. But if we *are* wrong we'd cause so much trouble that the country would be up in arms."

It was then that Kerr had his idea.

"You can't stop bandits breaking in and holding the party up, can you?" He chuckled, for the strength of the thing suddenly appealed to him. "Can you?"

"What's that about bandits?" demanded Wally Davidson, suddenly alert.

"Just how do you mean?" Craigie asked.

"Just like this," said Bob Kerr. "I'm not a policeman, nor's Toby—Rumsden—Wally—a dozen of our men. If we raid the place—fine! If there's real trouble the police can come. Gordon, it's good!"

"No reputations likely to be blemished," murmured Wally, his eyes sparkling, "excepting ours. Mine can stand it. Gordon, it's a winner!"

"I'm inclined to think," said Gordon Craigie very slowly, "that it is. I—"

"Damn that thing!" said Robert McMillan Kerr.

For the telephone was ringing, stridently as usual, and perhaps even more persistently. Craigie, smiling a little at the idea that Kerr had just put across, pushed his chair back and walked to the desk. He lifted the receiver off, and said: "Hallo!" He repeated it, with increasing irritation.

"No one there," he said at last, and replaced the receiver; and as he did so the thing came again, harsh, strident. Craigie's lips tightened and he lifted it quickly.

And there was still no answer.

He put the receiver on the desk thoughtfully. No sound came now. He waited for thirty seconds and tried again; the bell still rang, and the other men were on their feet now, all of them white-faced.

And then the green light on Craigie's mantelpiece glowed —the green light that showed someone was outside, someone who knew where the push was to show the signal—an agent of Z, or else Superintendent Miller. No one else knew it, or ought to know it.

Craigie left the receiver off and stepped towards one of the sliding doors. Kerr, very tense, had his gun in his hand. Arran and Davidson were watching the door, and Craigie pressed a button and jumped to one side.

Nothing happened for a moment; and then Miller fell in. *Fell* in! And close behind him a grotesque-looking man recognizable only by his coat of many colours, for the mask he was wearing hid all the recognizable features of Tommy Rumsden. He pushed Miller clear of the sliding door before it was fully open, and then jumped past him; his voice was distorted but the words were clear enough.

"Shut it, Craigie—shut it quick as hell!"

Craigie pressed the release button; the door banged into position. Miller was lying absolutely still now, Rumsden breathing hard and pointing to his mask. Gordon Craigie was silent for a split second, and then he snapped:

"In that bottom drawer, Kerr!"

Kerr had the drawer open in a trice and pulled a dozen gas-masks out. He tossed one each to the others and then slipped on his own. Not until then did Tommy seem to ease. He dropped into a chair and, his voice still distorted, spoke slowly:

"Blasted streets full of it, Craigie. Dreadful. Car crashes—God, it's beyond words. But everyone's like Miller—*asleep!*"

The four men gathered together in the office of Department Z had seen nothing of the things outside, and, because of the sliding doors and the system of ventilation, the gas had not yet penetrated. How long it would have been before they, like the rest of London, had been asleep, no one knew.

And outside, it was beyond words.

Trafalgar Square, with five hundred cars or buses racing round where the lights showed green, was one of the worst. A thousand people there—it was lunch-time and the streets of London were crowded—saw the things happen and yet hardly realized what it was.

The first driver to succumb to the gas which had been let loose was at the wheel of a small car. He simply dropped across the steering-wheel, and the car turned and smashed into the side of a Daimler running alongside. The big car's driver, the wheel jerked out of his hands, lost control, and he crashed into the Passenger Transport bus immediately in front of him.

And then the chaos started.

Not in one but in a hundred places drivers collapsed across the wheels of their cars, smashing into one another, crushing, killing, maiming. Now and again a high-pitched cry of terror and pain rent the air; but soon they stopped, and no cry came from human mouths.

There was no pain.

The driver of a lorry crashed head-on by a Green Line coach knew nothing of what happened, and would never know a thing again. Car after car piled up against one another. The din of the breaking wood and steel, the flaring of fire as petrol-tanks burst and the flames ignited them, everything merged into one great, thunderous roar.

But few people heard it.

Here and there, from the tops of the big office buildings, men and women rushed to the windows and pulled them open; they stared transfixed for a few seconds at the holocaust below; and then the same insidious gas took them and sent them over. A man leaning out of the tallest building overbalanced and crashed down—

He did not know he was falling; he knew nothing of the pain that should have been his lot as he smashed against the pavement.

He fell across the bodies of two women and a child, lying very still. About him were hundreds—thousands!—of people, who had lost consciousness and dropped down as they walked. The din of the crashing lasted perhaps for five minutes, and then grew less. Soon a deep, near-silence reigned, and the only noise was the roaring of flames where cars had caught fire, and a few engines running although their drivers were useless.

London was asleep.

The Underground was running, unaffected by the dread thing that had come to the Metropolis; but as the passengers and guards reached the surface of the ground they dropped, as though taken in a fit, one after the other. The steps of the subways were crowded with huddled bodies; stations, hotels, shops—everywhere it was the same. People were asleep. *Asleep!*

Men sprawled across counters, over chairs, across tables; men and women slumped half-way down the stairs of their houses, dropped from ladders, everywhere the same. And everywhere the chaos in the streets was appalling. Hardly a roadway was clear for traffic—although there was no traffic to pass. The humming of car engines provided a perpetual hum, never ceasing for a second. Here and there a runaway car, the driver helpless and unconscious at the wheel, raced for a few yards before it crashed into a wall, a house, a window, or another car. And everywhere that hush reigned, pregnant, damnable—London was asleep.

The driver of a London express turned past the points at the first suburb of the Metropolis and dropped across the controls. The firemen fell backwards, and the flames devoured them; the crowded carriages were filling with sleeping people, unconscious people, none of them aware of the horror they would meet; and when they crashed the cataclysm was complete.

Train after train suffered the same fate, one after another as they ran into that dread area.

Not a man above ground was breathing and awake; not a man who was in the open air, or where the gas could reach, withstood it. And slowly it penetrated beneath the ground, and horror was piled on horror until it seemed there could be no end.

And twice, above the low hum of the burning, the running engines and the crashes, there came the distant booming of the bells as two o'clock struck and half past two followed.

And no one heard, no one could hear.

Excepting those who had been prepared or, like Craigie and the men in Department Z, had been warned in the nick of time.

Those who had been prepared waited. There was no hurry even if there were many things to do. For an hour there was not a soul walking or running or moving at all. And then, one after the other, men and women picked their way through the holocaust—masked men, masked women, all of them with a definite objective, all of them stationed so that the objective was easily reached.

The banks were raided first.

The large branches and the small suffered in the same way; treasury notes, silver, and gold—all went. Through the banks the masked men walked, quickly and yet without fear of interruption. Clerks sprawled across the counters or lay huddled behind them; keys were found, vaults opened, and the plunder went on. Banks—safe deposits—private houses—museums. The gold and the silver was collected from them all, and each masked man took his share, each masked man finished when his limit was reached, and hurried—as well as men could hurry—through the dead streets, past the blazing fires and the huddled heaps of bodies, all making towards the one thoroughfare that was still reasonably clear.

The Thames.

At Westminster, Blackfriars, London Bridge—at points a hundred yards away from each other along the reaches of the river the masked men gathered with their loot. Motorlaunches were waiting, soon to be loaded—dozens of them, hundreds of them. One after the other they chugged their way downstream towards the open sea and freedom. The whole incredible fantastic hold-up had succeeded—London had been pillaged while London slept!

And other things happened.

At the hospital where Mannopoli was waiting, complete with guards, three men broke in, past the unconscious nurses, doctors and attendants; past the unconscious detectives and into the room where Mannopoli was lying. Mannopoli too was asleep. They carried him out carefully to the waiting car below, and threaded their way through by-streets to that one remaining highway, the Thames. Mannopoli was gone; Mannopoli had never feared the consequences of his arrest.

At Cannon Row, where Ellen Granting was waiting, knowing this would come, three men walked past the sleeping policemen, took their keys and unlocked the cell door. Ellen Granting was lying on the bench unconscious, or so it seemed. They carried her away towards the river.

One after the other, men were taken, money was taken, gems of untold worth found their way to the river and then towards the river's mouth. The smooth waters of the Thames teemed with launches, while ships had crashed into the banks, water was flooding the streets, small boats had overturned, barges were banging against the piles of the bridges.

Money beyond dreams flowed under London Bridge that day.

And the fire was getting a hold on the city; no one cared. No one could care.

* * *

Augustus Mannopoli and Graff Daakmann stood on the bridge of the pleasure-yacht *Debrees*, three miles outside the Thames estuary. Mannopoli was looking ill but satisfied. Daakmann didn't look ill; he was smiling, and his amber eyes were afire.

"And so we've managed it, Mannopoli, despite them."

"It was lucky," Mannopoli said, "that you decided to bring the time forward, Daakmann. Midnight might have been too late."

Daakmann nodded; and then he laughed.

"If the fools had waited and let us do it, it would have been so much less trouble, eh? At midnight, no one would have known. They forced it on us, Mannopoli—*forced* it on us. How many have died?"

Mannopoli's lips curled.

"How much has come?" he demanded, and he laughed. Alongside, a hundred launches were ready to unload their loot. At the mouths of a hundred other rivers in a hundred ways the same thing was happening. Cities were ravaged, looted, put to flames; men were dying or dead—or asleep. The sleeping-gas...

"Fallow didn't know," Mannopoli said, "what he had given us when he gave us that."

Daakmann's eyes were hard.

"Where is Fallow?"

"I don't know. You've missed him?"

"He hasn't been reported for a week. He's probably still waiting to rake off some of the money for himself. He is very foolish, is Fallow."

"We would have been in a bad way without him," Mannopoli said. "We would still have been asleep, Daakmann. A good chemist can put you to sleep, only a genius can bring you round again. If Fallow comes, you'll be easy with him."

For a moment the eyes of the two men met, and Mannopoli's gaze lasted longer. Daakmann shrugged and looked away.

"Of course, if you wish."

And Mannopoli laughed again.

Bob Kerr, Tommy Rumsden, Wally Davidson, Toby Arran and Gordon Craigie walked into Whitehall and saw the chaos, and felt as they had never felt before. They saw others—masked men and women—moving from this building and that building, all carrying cases. They guessed what was happening. They walked slowly, and with a heaviness of heart greater than anything they had ever experienced before. Five of them—and this. *Five* of them against this. They were helpless. London was being emptied of its price-less things, its gold and silver and its jewels, and they were helpless.

They didn't talk, and it wasn't because the masks stopped them. They couldn't. They walked past the silent Scotland Yard, saw uniformed men outstretched and cars piled up; past Parliament Square, where a car had burned itself out and was still smouldering. They stepped over men and women and children. Papers fluttered in the breeze, released by nerveless hands. People were in the road, on the kerb, on the pavement, and all had that same symptom—the mouth and the nose were puffy, swollen as if by a severe cold.

And they reached Westminster Bridge.

They saw the masked men reaching the launches, loading them, and they realized the cunning of the man who had planned this thing. Craigie's hands were clenched; Davidson, behind his mask, looked devilish; Tommy Rumsden—thinking of Mary and Hampstead—was torn to shreds. Toby Arran was deadly white. And Kerr was staring over the parapet of the bridge—just staring....

And then he swore.

"Craigie—we can stop them!"

Craigie turned; even through the thick glass of the mask his disbelief showed itself.

"Bob—steady. It's done."

"We can stop them—get what they've taken—get them! Listen..."

And Kerr talked, his voice thick from behind his mask, while the others listened, and suddenly found a hope that until a few moments before had seemed quite dead. Kerr was right; they *could* stop Mannopoli.

20
ROUGH HOUSE

K err lost no time in putting the one remaining chance to the test. There was a risk—more than a risk, for the chances against them were ten to one or more. But none of them hesitated. They hurried, doing their best not to let the other masked figures who were walking about the ruins of the dead city like vultures over carrion suspect that they were not members of the same raiding horde. Down the steps to the river past the Houses of Parliament was not a long way, and they reached the landing-stage less than five minutes after Kerr had awakened them to action and the realization that there *was* a chance.

Three boats were just taking off; a fourth, which had been to the *Debrees* and was returning to take a second load of loot, came up as the others moved away.

At the same time a dozen men came down the steps, all of them masked and therefore unrecognizable. They were carrying cases and boxes, and piling them on the landing-stage, ready for the launch's cargo.

"You'll take the launch," Kerr muttered to Arran and Davidson. "We'll handle these fellows. You start."

Tobias Arran didn't argue. He waited until the launch was steady and its crew of four was in the bows; and then he showed his gun.

The surprise of the attack was perfect.

The masked men stopped, and their hands moved towards their pockets. One actually managed to get his gun out, but before he could use it Arran had taken him through the chest, and he toppled over into the turgid Thames, his scream muffled by the mask. The others followed, one after the other, Arran and Davidson firing for the chest, taking no chances.

Kerr was handling the approaching raiders; Craigie and Rumsden were backing him up, and he needed help.

The raiders saw what was happening, and their guns were out in a flash. Yellow flame stabbed a dozen times, and Kerr dropped behind a pile of cases for a moment, his finger on the trigger all the time. For a moment it was massacre! The men were falling one after another, but firing as they went. One leapt forward trying to carry Kerr down with him; Kerr's bullet took him through the head, and the dead body thudded sickeningly into the Department man.

Kerr was out of action for that moment, and had he been alone he must have lost the day. Four of the raiders were left.

And Rumsden grunted as a bullet bit through his thigh.

Craigie, kneeling behind the cases, emptied his gun; two men fell while the others came on, but before they had reached the cases, Kerr had steadied again. It was finished then, and the men splashed over, one after another.

Kerr was racing towards the launch, along the landing. Craigie started after him, saw Rumsden limping and struggling to get along, and stopped.

"Car—carry on," Rumsden gasped. "I—I can't make it."

Craigie didn't speak, but gave the other an arm. Kerr, seeing Arran and Davidson pointing backwards, turned and saw what the trouble was. He knew that Rumsden would be little use on board the launch, and but for one thing he would have recommended the others to leave him.

Other raiders were coming now, and the firing was a fusillade. Two launches in midstream saw what was happening and swung back towards the Department men. If Rumsden was left, he'd be finished.

Even Kerr couldn't face it.

He went back to help Craigie; he didn't know how he reached the men, nor how he managed to get Rumsden back to the launch, but it happened somehow.

Davidson was at the controls of the launch; Rumsden half fell over the side with Craigie, and Kerr jumped aboard; as he did so the engine roared and the launch started on that lone, last hope.

The firing was more intense now; there was only one object in it—to stop the escapers.

From the approaching launches and the banks and the landing-stage the bullets were spitting. A dozen cracked into the woodwork of the launch, yet did no damage. But as they went towards the middle of the stream the others neared it.

They could see the masked faces, the yellow flame and the smoke stabbing from the guns. All of them excepting Davidson were crouched close to the deck, guns in hand. Rumsden was lying full length, but he was active. They waited, while the other two launches sandwiched them.

It was touch and go now.

The fire was withering, but most of the bullets went over their heads; and not until they were within twenty feet of the launches did Kerr give the signal to open fire.

The bullets went out like angry bees. One after another of

the men on the attacking launches dropped down; they weren't, Kerr said afterwards, used to trench warfare. And Davidson opened the throttle of the *Dawn*—their launch—calling for that supreme effort.

He managed it.

They flashed between the attackers with inches to spare, and as they did so the masked men threw caution to the winds and poured lead into the *Dawn*. No one knew who was hurt, badly or otherwise. No one seemed to care. Kerr kept firing, picking off man after man with an unnerving coolness. The river was coloured with red blood as the men dropped from the decks of the launches; one suddenly went out of control and roared towards the south bank.

Kerr heard it crash as the remaining attacker drew nearer— Davidson had to make a detour to avoid a moored craft. Kerr felt something bite into his arm, like a red-hot needle, but hardly thought of it.

There was one man left on the deck of the attacker, and he wasn't left for long.

Rumsden picked him off; and then Craigie stood up, free from the danger of flying bullets for the moment, for they were out of range from the shore, and fired at the man at the engine. He could just see the fellow's back; he saw him crumple up suddenly, and he heard Kerr grunt:

"Good man. They'll send a message, of course, but we'll have the heels of them."

"Keep middle stream," advised Toby Arran, "and we'll see everything that's coming. How far is it up-river, Bob?"

"About nine miles," grunted Kerr. "Damn these blasted masks. Better keep them, I suppose?"

"Safest," Craigie advised and, feeling oddly free in his mind after that terrific bout of gunfire, went to Davidson's side. Kerr and Arran cut a piece out of the thigh of Rumsden's

trousers and stemmed a nasty-looking hole with handker-
chiefs. Behind his mask, Rumsden was grinning.

"You weren't far from perdition, Arran."

Kerr looked at the little man for the first time, seeing the
patch of blood on his head and the wound where the bullet
had scored its path. Arran hadn't noticed it before. Kerr
remembered his arm, to find it was a flesh wound, and not
worrying. Craigie had a bullet-hole through the calf of his leg
and a score across the back of his hand. Davidson was the only
one who had come through unscathed; but all of them realized
they were lucky to be as they were.

They spent little time thinking about it.

The maddest, grimmest chase they had ever led had started
and their mind was on one thing and one thing alone: getting
to Dukes Meadows, Chiswick; Kerr knew the meadow had
been used of late as a temporary landing-field, and he knew
also that a couple of 'planes were stationed there. Once they
could get in the air they were through.

If they could get up.

The launch roared up-stream, with Davidson getting every
ounce he could out of the engine. The others sprawled on the
deck their guns reloaded and ready for action.

None was needed.

They passed a dozen launches, all laden with loot, and on
the way to the *Debrees*, but no one seemed to suspect them.
They could see the chaos on the river-banks and the embank-
ments. Here and there they passed a car which was still
blazing or smouldering; sometimes they passed a heap of
wreckage, a dozen cars and lorries piled one against another.
They did their best not to think of the dreadful carnage, and
they thought only of one thing—getting up, off the earth; and
then...

They daren't think as far as that.

The wake was behind them in a seething white sword, but the curious eyes that might have followed them on a normal day were missing. No one saw them; no one was awake, excepting those few who had work to do for Mannopoli and Daakmann.

After they cleared Hammersmith they saw no more launches, and they realized why.

Mannopoli had concentrated his men where the wealth of the nation was to be found—the City and West End. Now Craigie and the others were clear of it, and hope reared afresh.

Not once had they been followed, and they knew why.

If they couldn't telephone because the exchanges were peopled with sleeping operators, nor could Mannopoli's men. The only means of communication was the Thames, and for some reason which they could not properly understand, they had not been followed from Westminster.

They didn't think much about it, although it worried all of them. There should have been pursuit.

"There isn't any," Kerr said, as the launch swept into view of Dukes Meadows. "Rumsden, you're out of action anyhow; care to try something?"

"Anything once," said Rumsden sepulchrally.

"Take your mask off," said Kerr, "and let's know how things are. I think it will be safe. Forty minutes since the gas was released, and it's heavier than air, take my word for it."

It said a great deal for Tommy Rumsden that he didn't hesitate, and that when he pulled the mask off he was smiling. But there was a tenseness about his smile which was felt by all the others. Only Davidson, still at the controls and sending the *Dawn* like a rocket towards the bank of the river, was free from it.

What would happen now?

How powerful was the gas? Would it still be in the air,

overwhelming them, making their task a hundred times more difficult? Or was it clear?

Bob Kerr, who was an unemotional man at the worst of times, admitted that he prayed to himself that the smile would linger on Rumsden's face, that they would know the air was free.

The seconds dragged by.

Rumsden's grin was as wide as a cat's, and just as set. Craigie, cooler than any of them, was looking at his wrist-watch, and his dry voice broke the silence at last; there was something like a song in it.

"Sixty seconds, and you seem all right."

"I feel fine," admitted Tommy Rumsden; and then he forgot his injured thigh and smote it.

The pain that followed couldn't be hidden even by the artist, although he did his best. Kerr didn't see the incident. He swung round towards the cabin, his eyes gleaming as Davidson looked round, and said:

"What part, old son?"

"The best place for landing, Wally, and for the love of Mike get to it!"

They couldn't see the field from the deck of the launch; it wasn't until Kerr jumped for the bank, scrambled out of six inches of water, and then reached the level of the meadows that they knew what their luck was doing. He bellowed on the instant:

"All clear, Craigie! Two 'planes!"

"One for me, one for you," murmured Wally Davidson. "But what's happening to Rumsden?"

Craigie decided the issue.

"You and Kerr get to the 'planes," he said, "Toby and I will carry Rumsden. Hurry, Bob."

He hardly needed to implore Kerr to hurry, for Kerr was

already twenty yards across the field, towards the nearest 'plane. It was a small passenger biplane; he wouldn't have cared had it been a Moth tied together with string. It was something that would fly, and that was all that mattered.

As he jumped into the cabin, looked at the petrol supply and found it was ample, and began to warm up the engine, his mind was in ferment. There was a chance of putting right some of the things that had gone wrong that dreadful day, and he wouldn't rest until he'd started.

Flight-Commander Knighton of the Dwight Air Force Base was a puzzled man, for he couldn't understand it. "It" covered a multitude of things, for the Commander in this case was in trouble with the telephone cables to London and other large towns. His operator assured him that it was practically impossible to get through any junction, and the Commander was worried because he had a wife whom he'd promised to telephone, and if he didn't...

Several things occurred to him, but he had reached no decision when the first aeroplane droned over the hangars, getting lower every moment. It was followed by a second machine, both small 'planes of the cabin class. The Commander was sufficiently worried by the trouble with the telephones to go out in person to greet the fliers.

He recognized Bob Kerr—most men who had anything to do with the air recognized Kerr—although the other was ragged and bloody, and his voice was like a rasp.

The Commander just didn't believe what he was told, until Craigie came; he also knew Craigie as the Chief of Department Z, and that finished it.

"You—you mean that London—*London's* asleep! I—"

"Knighton," snapped Bob Kerr, "don't stand there shilly-shallying like a nanny-goat. Get every blasted 'plane in the aerodrome manned, and send a 'plane out to every military and civil aerodrome isolated enough to be unaffected by the gas. Everyone, do you get me? And get squadrons concentrated on the mouths of the rivers."

"I—" protested Commander Knighton; but Craigie cut him short.

"This is urgent. Don't waste time."

Knighton realized that when Craigie spoke like that it was time for action and nothing else. To do him justice, Knighton had heard something that nine men out of ten would have called just plain silly; and although he acted he was still dubious.

But the counter-attack—such as it was—was started.

'Plane after 'plane roared skywards from the Dwight aerodrome, and half an hour later the first 'plane dropped on an isolated Air Force base, spreading the story, raising the alarm. Others followed quickly; in the south the alarm came first—the country districts knew nothing of the trouble, except that it was impossible to get in telephone communication with the bigger industrial centres—and hundreds of 'planes began to move. Slowly the news went to the Midlands and the North; slowly the country awakened to the dreadful fact of the sleep that had shattered the big towns.

The Air Force was moving.

The Army was moving.

The Navy was moving.

In isolated cases only; that was the trouble. The big centres had been paralysed; the Kalshott air base was asleep; Southampton and Plymouth were asleep; but the smaller bases were lively enough and active enough. Destroyers and light cruisers, caught while at sea, turned like dragonflies and raced towards the mouths of the rivers; messages went out by radio to all aircraft, messages went to France and Germany, to every country on the Continent. Only one or two responded—the small countries in every case. France was paralysed, Germany was like a dead planet; but America hadn't suffered, and the Near East had escaped.

Over the water, over the sea, through the air and across the land, troops and heavy artillery were rushed, 'planes were flying with only one objective: England. Then the French colonies began to realize what had happened, and the world was awake, suddenly, at its outposts.

But the hub of the West was asleep, and the men who had contrived it there were satisfied.

Graff Daakmann and Augustus Mannopoli, more than contented by their achievements, waited for Ellen Granting to come from London before the *Debrees* moved from the mouth of the Thames to safer waters. Bania had no seaport, but twenty miles north was Dresden, on the Elbe; the bulk of the loot would be sent there, and be transhipped across country to Bania.

Not all of it, by a long way.

For years Mannopoli and Daakmann had been planning this thing; and they had realized that if it was ever discovered that Bania was the culprit, then Bania would be swept out of existence as soon as the other Powers recovered from the shock. Daakmann had hoped it would not be necessary; but he was afraid, now, that it would.

Their preparations had been thorough.

There were a hundred places throughout the world where the gold and jewels would go, where all the negotiable valuables could be stored. And in a hundred places within the next three hours, yachts and launches hove to, messengers were sent ashore to meeting-places—messengers with the one universal token of identity—a red card, diamond-shaped, with a black cross from point to point.

The *Debrees* was one of the larger vessels employed in the ramp, and its hold and storage space were still only half full. Daakmann proposed to wait only until the Granting woman and—if possible—Fallow were aboard. He wasn't nervous; he didn't seriously suspect trouble. But he was half afraid it might come.

It came unexpectedly.

A launch came up, and a man scrambled up the rope ladder to the deck. An officer intercepted him and then hurried forward to Daakmann, his face white.

"What is it?" snarled Daakmann.

"A—a message from Westminster, sir. Someone—someone has broken away. There's been shooting—"

Daakmann laughed; and as Mr. Mort—then in Bania for safe keeping—could have said, it was not a pleasant laugh.

"Some fools think they'll do better if they break away. I expected it. Who's reported?"

"Number 213," said the officer. "He said—he said something about Z—I didn't quite catch—"

He didn't finish.

Mannopoli roared the word, and Daakmann, perhaps for the first time in his life, seemed afraid.

"Kerr!" Mannopoli said, and his face was devilish.

"Department Z," murmured Daakmann, and he brushed his hand across his eyes. "It's—it's nothing, Mannopoli, they can do nothing! But"—he swung on the officer, who, like most people, was afraid of Herr Daakmann—"full steam ahead! Aim for Rabat on the North African coast."

"Very good, sir." The man turned to relay the orders while Mannopoli eyed Graff Daakmann as though he was only now beginning to realize what it meant.

"We'll go at once," Daakmann said with an effort. "Whether the others arrive or not. I— Ah!"

He broke off as another launch arrived; and he saw the woman standing up and reaching for the rope ladder.

Ellen Granting looked pale but as beautiful as ever; she came up easily, and was graceful even as she swayed on the rope. Daakmann and Mannopoli stepped to the side; it was typical that they did not help her to climb the rail, as typical that Daakmann's first words should be:

"Where's Fallow?"

"I don't know," Ellen said. "Why should I?"

"It doesn't matter," snapped Mannopoli. "Let her rest, Daakmann; you can see she's tired."

The girl's eyes were cool, mocking, and somehow disturbing.

"You're very worried, Mannopoli, about me?"

"Don't talk nonsense!" snapped Mannopoli. "I—"

It was then that the girl sneezed.

It was then that she opened her handbag quickly and pushed something to her face; it was then that she looked up, and the others saw the small mask over her mouth and nose, and saw the phial in her hand.

Ellen Granting was threatening them!

21

TRICK-COUNTER-TRICK

In some ways it was absurd.

The woman stood there within two yards of Mannopoli and Daakmann, the mask hiding her loveliness but not the hardness of her eyes. The phial was poised so that any movement from the others would have sent it smashing to the floor, and them to a sleep from which they might never recover.

Ellen Granting's voice came, distorted by the mask but with every word clear enough to be heard.

"I think you're wise." She was mocking and looking at Mannopoli more than at Daakmann. "Fallow has prepared this specially, Mannopoli, with extra strength for emergency." She laughed, and seemed to be at the high peak of nervous tension.

Daakmann gasped:

"Fallow!"

"Fallow," agreed Ellen Granting. "You knew he was working with you at one time, Daakmann; and then it seemed to you that he'd been stricken by his conscience. Is that right?"

"It's true!" snarled Mannopoli, and for the first time the

man's sallow skin paled and there was a hint of fear in his expression. "He was with us and he ratted—"

"I shouldn't talk like that about him," said Ellen Granting.

As she spoke Mannopoli turned his head furtively; the woman's gaze followed his; she saw the officer who had taken instructions a few seconds ago standing near, and she could see the gun in the man's hand.

She laughed almost hysterically.

"Tell him to put it away. To put it away, do you hear?"

She raised the phial as the cry left her lips, and seemed about to hurl it on the deck in front of the two men. Mannopoli hesitated almost as if he was determined to risk what happened; Daakmann didn't. He gestured to the officer arrogantly, as though still in command.

"Stand by, Pierce."

The officer stepped back a few yards, watching that drama of the two men and the woman; and Daakmann said after a deep breath:

"So you had a conscience too, my dear? You were sent to spy on Fallow and he converted you? How admirable that sentiment is, and what a pity Fallow isn't here to enjoy it with you!"

"But he is," said Ellen Granting, and jerked her head towards the launch in which she had arrived. Daakmann started involuntarily; he saw John Fallow, heavily built though he was, climbing up the rope ladder; he saw two other launches filled with men arriving.

The seconds seemed to fly as the raid—the simplest raid conceivable—was conducted. Those members of the crew of the *Debrees* who offered resistance went to sleep, and it was over in five minutes.

The gas spread fear as well as sleep.

Ellen Granting was standing in front of the two men who

made this thing possible; they were rigid; they were convinced that the counter-attack couldn't properly succeed, and they were wondering when Kerr and the others would arrive.

Fallow approached them, smiling behind his mask.

"And so," he said cheerfully, "you didn't get away with it, Mannopoli? In some ways I'm sorry. You've tried so hard."

"*You —!*" swore Mannopoli, and he took half a step forward. As he came John Fallow fired from his pocket, and the bullet took Mannopoli through the chest. Mannopoli coughed and staggered forward, clutching the rail to save himself from falling over the side. Graff Daakmann didn't move; his amber eyes were like a wild beast's, but somehow he controlled himself.

"So you sold us out to the police, Fallow; and you"—he turned to Ellen Granting, and his eyes were vile—"you joined him. You managed to trick me, my dear, but one day…"

"I don't think there's going to be any 'one day' for you," said Ellen Granting calmly. "I very much doubt it, when the police get you. You're responsible for a lot of murders in this country, Daakmann, and when they've searched the house at Bey they won't have much trouble in proving it."

Daakmann didn't speak for a moment; his long hands were clenching and unclenching and the woman could almost imagine the way he was wishing he could fasten them round her throat. She laughed again and slipped off her mask; the sea breeze had blown the gas away now, and she was safe enough.

Daakmann saw her beauty as Kerr and Arran knew it, as many others knew it; and yet he was seeing also a red rage.

"You'll hand us over to the police, will you—"

And Fallow laughed.

"We'll certainly send you ashore, Daakmann. They'll have to have some scapegoat, and you and Mannopoli will do excellently. You see—you've made a mistake. Not perhaps a large one"—John Fallow spread his hands out, palms down-wards—"but important. It isn't conscience that has been worrying me, Daakmann; it's ambition, shall we say? I've never believed you could get away with what you've done. You might be safe for a year, but eventually you'd be brought to book. And I've no desire for that."

Daakmann stared as though he didn't believe what he was hearing. Ellen's smile was as inscrutable as ever.

"You're not—*not* working with the police?"

"My dear man, of course not. We have waited, Ellen and I, until you loaded the yacht; and now the yacht's ours. When the authorities get the other stuff back, they won't worry about the *Debrees*. We'll be safely away, and very comfortably off. You see how easy it was, and how foolish you were with Mannopoli, to think that my conscience was worrying me."

Daakmann drew a deep breath, and seemed to regain his self-control as the real truth flooded through his mind.

"I see. So you and Ellen conspired together. And yet—how did you know when the raid was to start, Fallow? Ellen didn't know of the altered times. The message didn't go out until half an hour before the gas was released. Mort—I've suspected Mort for a long time—is still at Bey. So—"

Fallow laughed—the deep, pleasant laugh of the middle-aged, retired and benevolent country gentleman he was supposed to be.

"So you're puzzled, Daakmann? You forget *Leila* Mort. Your chief London agent, Daakmann. My chief source of information, Daakmann. Just the three of us have worked this thing. Now do you understand?"

The words hummed through the clear air; and then Mannopoli, leaning against the rail and wheezing, with the blood staining his coat, rooted to his pocket for his gun. He didn't get it out. Fallow swung on him mercilessly and fired;

the second bullet went through Mannopoli's heart, and he went overboard without a cry. No one stared as he dropped towards the sea.

And Daakmann was staring like a ghost at Ellen Granting as she laughed and then slipped the mask over her face. Fallow followed suit; Daakmann made a rush towards her, his fists raised, his eyes frenzied; and then the phial of gas burst in his face.

"Excellent work, my dear," said John Fallow, patting Ellen's arm. "Mannopoli's dead; Daakmann's asleep for a long time to come, and when he wakes up he'll be asked to explain some things to the English authorities. And we have enough and more than enough to last us in comfort."

Ellen nodded, and her expression was hidden by her mask.

"Yes—more than enough, John. Get Daakmann away. I heard him mention Rabat; we'll start on the same course."

"It will suit us admirably," said Mr. John Fallow, eying his gun reflectively. "Well, well. To think I actually killed Mannopoli. The first man I've ever killed in my life, and I felt not the slightest compunction. Now"—Fallow drew a deep breath—"it's practically over. We're to pick Leila up off Cape Finisterre—she flew over to France this morning."

Ellen Granting laughed.

"Leila's clever," she said. "And she hates danger, but it doesn't matter. It's the end, John. We've finished; we're through. The biggest robbery in history—"

Fallow eyed her uncertainly.

"You almost sound sorry," he said.

"I am, in a lot of ways, but don't let's stand here talking. We've a lot to do yet. I—"

She stopped.

Fallow stopped at the same time. He saw the three 'planes in the distance, although he could only just hear the hum. They were glistening bright in the afternoon sun; and they were dropping fast, towards the *Debrees. Towards* the yacht!

Fallow was still for ten seconds, and then he bent over the unconscious Daakmann and snatched a pair of binoculars. He stared upwards; he saw the shape of the approaching 'planes, and he knew what they were.

"Someone's got through!" he gasped, and he could hardly get the words out. "They're military 'planes! Oh, my God!"

He left the girl staring upwards, that inscrutable smile on her face, and raced to the bridge. He snapped the orders to the captain—a captain who would obey anyone with that deadly gas under his control, and who cared little whether Daakmann or Fallow gave orders.

"Full speed ahead!" snapped Fallow. "Understand—full speed ahead whatever happens!"

The engines of the *Debrees* were throbbing now and the yacht began to move sluggishly away from England. But compared with the speed of the 'planes above they were crawling, and the flight grew nearer and lower with every second. Nearer—nearer—

The first bomb came ten minutes later, a hundred yards astern. Fallow was staring like a man possessed; Ellen Granting was simply looking behind her, towards the coast.

The second bomb was fifty yards nearer, and the captain gasped:

"We must heave to; we must!"

"Full speed," snapped Fallow. "You can dodge them. They can't be carrying more than a dozen bombs apiece, and you can dodge them! You must, you fool, you must!"

The captain's face was chalk-white; but he tried. The

Debrees began to zig-zag hither and thither; but one after the other the bombs dropped mercilessly from the skies, dark carriers of disaster and death.

Spray shot hundreds of feet into the air, the din of the detonation after detonation was appalling, débris was flying, shrapnel and worse. In a dozen places the sea seemed to be carved in two as the bombs dropped, and the water hissed back again, sending mountainous waves to dash against the *Debrees'* sides.

Would it never end?

Fallow was staring upwards. Ellen Granting was looking at England with that same strange smile on her lips, and in her mind's eye the faces of two men—Bob Kerr and Toby Arran. She could see Toby's puckish smile, and Kerr in the room in Paris when she had tried so hard to win him over, and failed.

She didn't see the thing coming, nor hear the dreadful shouts from the crew. She didn't see the captain fling himself at John Fallow as if to revenge himself on the madman who had caused this thing.

She did hear the explosion.

It caught the *Debrees* in the centre; she heard the tremendous roar, saw the flash of fire, felt the flame singe her hair as the force of the explosion sent her thudding against a cabin. And where that cabin stood there was, next moment, nothing but a gaping hole where the second bomb crashed down. The *Debrees* was already sinking fast, with her stern awash and dipping towards her grave.

22

CLOSE OF PLAY

I t was a month before England was in any sort of order, and the other countries which had suffered from the sleeping-gas were longer in recovering from the worst results of the attack. There was no total of deaths and casualties compiled; Craigie's comment when he was asked about them was that they had been surprisingly few, and it was true.

But they had been more than enough.

Kerr—flying one of the 'planes which had bombed the *Debrees*—learned two hours after the bombing that Ellen Granting and John Fallow had suffered the same fate as Mannopoli and Daakmann. Men in the launches had talked. He couldn't honestly say he was sorry; in fact, he believed it was for the best. Like Toby Arran, he could see pictures of the girl from time to time as though she was still living in his mind's eye.

Toby Arran and Bob Kerr spent a great deal of time with Julius Mort, who was brought back from Bania two days after the outrages, alive but very frightened, and eventually to die from natural causes—his heart gave way when he learned the

266

whole truth. He was at the time the one man of any importance on the other side who was still alive, and Mrs. Mort the only woman. No one ever learned what happened to Mrs. Mort. She had warning of some kind and disappeared. Most people who cared could have disappeared during that month.

But it might have been worse.

The yachts and tramp steamers which had been pressed into service by Mannopoli and Daakmann were rounded up by Naval and Air Force patrols, one after the other, filled with the wealth of the nation, where that wealth was negotiable. Tens of millions of pounds found their way back to the banks and the safe deposits, *objets d'art* to the museums and private houses. Much was lost, but more was recovered.

When his mind had cleared a little, Bob Kerr could see easily enough what had happened.

Mannopoli and Daakmann—a record of whose activities and plans were found at the Banian house—had heard of the sleeping-gas—an invention of Fallow's. They had bought the secret of its manufacture from him, and planned that colossal outrage—a dozen countries and a hundred towns asleep at the same time, while the vaults and banks were pillaged.

With one or two exceptions the headquarters of the organization in each town had been, as at Gretley Place, at the house of a Society woman. After the entertainments the real business had been conducted; the messages were afterwards sent to Daakmann and, in England, to Mannopoli at the 'George,' Michford.

And the card of introduction was always the same—a certain colour which bespoke the country in which the agent was operating, of identical shape and size. Ellen Granting's green card had shown that she was an English agent; Gabrell's dark-green that he was from Portugal. Mannopoli's light-blue that he worked everywhere, as the King Pin of the campaign.

An easy system and one that was reckoned to arouse no suspicion; and would have aroused none but for the affair at The Maples.

Gordon Craigie, his meerschaum busy again, and his face less haggard, was with Bob Kerr and Wally Davidson at the Department called Z in Whitehall a month after the raid and its failure, a month after the desperate rescue effort which had defied all odds and been successful. Toby Arran arrived, breathlessly and pugnacious, five minutes later, and said that Rumsden was downstairs and wouldn't come up.

"He said he couldn't climb," cursed Toby, "but he's as right as rain again, the—"

For once Craigie went downstairs to persuade a man to enter the almost sacrosanct premises of the Department. As he reached the door he saw a cab draw up, and from it stepped Mary Wayne, whose expression when she saw Tommy Rumsden explained many things.

Rumsden waved to her and winked at Craigie.

"I had to wait, old son. Can she be an honorary member, or must I make her hang around?"

"Bring her in," Craigie said; and Mary Wayne wasn't to know that Kerr and the others looked dumbstruck simply because she was the only woman who had ever sat in Craigie's arm-chair or entered that bare office. She never did know. She took what Toby Arran afterwards called an intelligent interest, and, if anything, Tommy Rumsden was less inclined to interrupt, for his eyes were busy.

Craigie hemmed.

"We were going to talk out what there is left," he said, "before I make out my official report, Kerr. Now—you'd better start."

Bob Kerr cocked his head even more on one side, accepted

a cigarette from Wally Davidson, whose languid air had returned again, and started hesitantly.

"I don't know that I can say much," he said. "First and foremost, we can tackle the actual plan of campaign. Mannopoli and Daakmann planned the thing with Fallow's gas. Fallow knew what they were doing. Mannopoli sent Ellen Granting to watch Fallow and make sure he didn't go to the police, and Fallow saw a chance of getting her to join him in a double-cross."

"Call it hi-jacking," implored Tommy cheerfully.

"Call it what you like," said Kerr. "Fallow, who wasn't the man we hoped, worked with Ellen Granting simply to take the *Debrees* after it was filled with money, gold and jewels. He succeeded; he didn't expect us, but we arrived."

Kerr paused, and Toby looked away from him; everyone there knew why. But Kerr went on quickly:

"A lot of these things are guesses; a lot of others are gathered from Julius Mort, who's talked more in the last month than two aviaries filled with parrots. Starting back from the time when you arrived at The Maples, Toby, it runs something like this:

"Mannopoli knew Mort had written to Fallow, suspected Fallow's real game, and yet saw that Fallow had a chance of putting himself in well with Craigie. Fallow did that all right. But at the time Mannopoli thought Ellen Granting was with him; he didn't hit her that night. She just stayed outside the door during the little talk.

"Then after the argument—in which Fallow certainly didn't give himself away—Mannopoli made a fight of it. As Mannopoli went, Fallow hit you over the head, Toby. He didn't want you to break Mannopoli's scheme."

"I'd guessed," groaned Toby Arran, and rubbed his head.

"Fallow and Mannopoli then, were working hard against

each other, yet they couldn't do too much—because Mannopoli might have wanted help with the gas again from Fallow. But he called himself safe while the girl was there, although actually she was telling Fallow every development as she learned of it.

"When Craigie found the green card—"

"*I* found the green card," protested Toby Arran pugnaciously, "and don't let me hear you—"

"Ellen Granting was on the *qui vive*," Kerr went on, steamrolling over Arran's protest. "We discovered pretty well what the cards meant from the books at the 'George,' which Mulling had kept. And here's an interesting point: Mulling and Mort were purely and simply counterfeiters—"

"Eh?" demanded Rumsden. "What's that?"

"Counterfeiters," Kerr went on, unsmiling. "Makers and dealers in dud money at home and abroad. They needed Fallow's help—as Mort thought, knowing nothing then of the gas, or Mannopoli's knowledge of Fallow—for the dyes for the printing. The organization was world-wide, and a tremendous amount of slush was circulated, hence Mort's millions. But the beauty of the scheme to Mannopoli and Daakmann was that if anything was discovered, it would be made to appear like a gigantic scheme for the making of the slush. And it might have done but for the way Mannopoli behaved in Michford. All the same, we needn't dwell on that. Mulling died, the poor devil of a potman went—and other things happened."

"By that time," interjected Craigie, "we knew something was badly wrong, but weren't sure what."

"Exactly." Kerr was always a little pedantic on these occasions. "Bit by bit we got on the scheme. But we were completely fooled by Mrs. Mort. She knew the truth; her husband didn't. She controlled the London operations through her social parties, which were so well patronized that the place was not even suspected for the minor contraventions. But she, probably believing a little with safety was better than a lot with risk, agreed to work with Fallow. She obtained what information Ellen Granting could get, and the three of them were planning to take the money as soon as the affair was blown, leaving Daakmann and Mannopoli to face the music. A good idea, and one that would have succeeded with a bit of luck. And that," added Kerr, "seems something like the lot."

"Oh no, it isn't," interrupted Davidson, suddenly waking up. "What about the wound in the girl's side? What about Gabrell? What about—"

Kerr chuckled.

"Sorry, my son. First—the wound was obviously a branding; Mort says Mrs. Mort had a similar scar on her side, although he didn't know why. Nor do we, excepting that there was a way of making sure deception wasn't practised with the diamond-shaped cards."

"That's the explanation all right," Craigie said, and the others accepted it.

"As for Gabrell…" Kerr shrugged his shoulders. "Mrs. Mort obviously shot him to stop him from talking. The man at the window was all my eye. I half suspected it a couple of days later, but things happened too fast. She shot the policeman in the room too. I fancy," he added, "that Gabrell knew the Portuguese angle very well, and Mrs. Mort cozened him for information.

"While talking of Gabrell, the whole Dummett Street affair looks simple now. First, Mannopoli was afraid the girl would talk when I arrived, and therefore tried to shoot her. She had telephoned Craigie, to try and get several of us there, and I'm inclined to think she wanted an interruption—she guessed a showdown was coming between her and Mannopoli, and it was the only way to avoid it."

"You don't think," Toby said painfully, "she simply lured you to—er—to—er—"

"I prefer not to think that," Kerr said simply. "Anyhow, there must have been trouble in the making there, for the place was cleared of servants. Mannopoli probably planned to have a *tête-à-tête* with Ellen before talking to Gabrell.

"Well—one or two other things. Mulling used two colours of ink, one for his own figures, others for Mannopoli's— which covered some part of the bigger plot, although what it was we'll never know. And," Kerr added, "there really isn't much more this time. Mort was summoned to Paris and then Bania, he says, and had orders to go from place to place, giving instructions for the big blow-up."

"Lie down," murmured Tommy Rumsden, "fits the case better."

"Miss Wayne," implored Kerr in mock exasperation, "marry him quickly or he'll want to come here again. Er— Toby and I were followed to Paris, and others were waiting for us there. We nearly managed to get away with it, but Ellen Granting, playing the double game all the time, told me a story which was probably true, although she had omitted to mention she had already told it to Fallow. When Mort arrived she knocked me out to show Mort and therefore Daakmann how loyal she was. We—luck again—managed to follow Mort. I don't need to bore you with what we found, excepting to say it's obvious Mort or Daakmann busted a phial of sleeping-gas, which explained the ease of our forced entry. And," Kerr added, looking towards Craigie's table, on which reposed glasses, "the rest we know, or we ought to remember. Gordon, I could do with a spot."

He had his spot, and so did the others, with Rumsden

protesting weakly that it ought to be beer. The conversation was general for a while; and then Craigie smiled at the girl.

"And you, Miss Wayne, helped us immensely. You interrupted the conversation between Fallow and Leila Mort. Immediately seeing a way of keeping themselves clear of suspicion with Daakmann, they gave orders for you to be killed. They warned Daakmann—by telephone, I expect—what had happened, and the rest followed naturally. Luckily Rumsden isn't slow to act."

"I'll tell you what," said Wally Davidson before the girl could speak, "how did Leila get out of her house? It beats me. Disguise perhaps, but—"

"Simply disguise," said Gordon Craigie with a smile. "We can't think up anything better, Wally, but don't let it worry you. She telephoned to another house in Gretley Place, of course, where others of Rennu's type were waiting. The house —we know it now—was full of records, and explains why Carruthers—who's better, thank God!—was crashed by that Rolls. But the beauty of the whole thing was that it was easy for anyone to get into Mrs. Mort's house, no matter who they were, without arousing suspicion.

"On the signal for the gas to be released, all Mannopoli's men donned masks, waited to make sure the gas took effect, and then started looting."

Craigie stopped, and was silent for a moment. Then he stood up, and Tommy Rumsden did likewise.

"Well, well, well," boomed that hearty artist, "it's over and done with, and nearly all the mess is cleared up. Most folk owe a lot to you, boys, and I'll even include Mary and me. Do you know," added Tommy Rumsden, lifting Mary from her chair by her elbows and depositing her near the door, "if Mannopoli had pulled it off there wouldn't have been money to buy beer?"

Wally Davidson swallowed hard for Mary's sake; Mary frowned, for there were times when Tommy Rumsden was a fool indeed. Toby grinned. Craigie was expressionless, and Kerr said gently:

"Or a marriage licence, Tommy."

"Do you know," said Tommy Rumsden hugely, "I hadn't thought of that. Don't you get them free during riot and civil war? Mary, say good-bye to the little gentlemen, or they'll throw us out."

He shook hands, after Mary; and although he was still grinning, the others remembered his wounded thigh, and the chances he took with the sleeping-gas, which in so many cases had proved fatal. There was a lot in Tommy Rumsden that didn't meet the eye.

The door closed behind the couple; Davidson yawned; Toby seemed to sink into a dream of what might have been, and Bob Kerr looked half humorously at Craigie.

"Well, that's that," he said. "And although things are quieter, it's just the time for someone else to start trouble. Have you had any reports in lately, Gordon?"

"Yes," said Gordon Craigie slowly. "There's a job in the States, Bob, you'd better look at."

And so it ended and started again, the work of Department Z, with most of the same men to start the game next morning, after the night's close of play.

ABOUT THE AUTHOR

John Creasey, born in 1908, was a paramount English crime and science fiction writer who used myriad pseudonyms for more than six hundred novels. He founded the UK Crime Writers' Association in 1953. In 1962, his book *Gideon's Fire* received the Edgar Award for Best Novel from the Mystery Writers of America. Many of the characters featured in Creasey's titles became popular, including George Gideon of Scotland Yard, who was the basis for a subsequent television series and film. Creasey died in Salisbury, UK, in 1973.

DEPARTMENT Z

FROM OPEN ROAD MEDIA

OPEN ROAD

INTEGRATED MEDIA

Find a full list of our authors and
titles at www.openroadmedia.com

FOLLOW US
@OpenRoadMedia

www.ingramcontent.com/pod-product-compliance
Lightning Source LLC
Chambersburg PA
CBHW020436030726
47495CB00006B/1825